HEART AND HAND

GOLD SKY SERIES

REBEL CARTER

VIOLET GAZE PRESS

Cover Design by Najla Qamber

Edited by Lena Tudor

Published by Violet Gaze Press

20-22 Wenlock Rd

London

www.violetgazepress.com

❀ Created with Vellum

For Erin, Melody, and the Geriatric Friendship Cult. On the bad days you gave me light and inspired me to keep writing, to keep dreaming, and to see that I had all the strength I ever needed right inside of me.

July 4th, 1886

Honest man seeking unorthodox marriage arrangement.

I am in possession of a ranch of considerable size, totaling nearly 1,000 acres spanning Montana and Wyoming territories, and am a man of substantial means and good reputation. Must be resourceful and, above all, an independent woman. Young lady does not need to be proficient in cooking or housekeeping. Town is in need of a teacher, not a cook. Only a highly educated woman with the patience and mental fortitude to run a school-house will be considered.

Further details particular to marriage arrangement will be disclosed in future correspondence. Eager to hear from adventurous, open-minded women who are interested.

Respectfully,
  Forrest Wickes

PS: All wages earned from teaching will belong solely to young lady.

CHAPTER 1

"*H*ave you heard? Julie means to join a veritable rake in matrimony. He intends to lure her to the wilds of the Montana Territory," Julian Baptiste III, gentleman about town and heir to the Baptiste fortune, yelled as he skidded across the polished wood floors of the Baptiste family home.

Julie jerked upright from the letter she had been writing. She barely had time to set her pen down before her twin brother waved a newspaper at her with a swoop of his arm. She frowned, leaping from her chair before he could utter another word.

"What on earth are you talking about?" She clamped a hand over his mouth. "Are you insane? Just bandying about information like that? What if Papa heard you?"

Julian's whiskey-brown eyes widened. He let out a garbled string of speech into Julie's palm, flapping the newspaper at his side.

"What?" Julie shook his face with the hand covering his mouth. "What are you saying?"

Julian rolled his eyes before he reached up and yanked her hand away. "I said, tell me it isn't true, because your reaction makes me wonder what my sensible sister has done."

Julie bit her lip and gave a nervous shrug.

"Define true."

"Oh, God. This is what happens to Vassar girls of a certain age, isn't it? I never would have expected it from you, dear sister."

"You absolute cad."

"Perhaps a cad, but a truthful one. Who would have ever pegged me for the honest twin? That's usually a virtuous woman character trait, which is a you thing."

"How do you know what I've said isn't true?" Julie arched an eyebrow, and enjoyed a fleeting moment of triumph when her brother's mouth dropped open.

"So then you truly are engaged to be married?" he asked, eyes wide in disbelief.

"Well, I…" Julie sighed and tucked her hands behind her back with a grimace. "It's a delicate situation."

Julian pointed a finger at her. "What are you hiding from me? Out with it then."

"It isn't polite to point, Julian," she said primly.

Undeterred, he pointed all of his fingers at her. "Answer. The. Question."

Julie turned away with as much dignity as she could muster. "I guess I should phrase my answer as this: I have accepted Mr. Wickes's proposal of marriage."

Julian gasped. "Who is this man, this Mr. Wickes? He's real? Where did you even meet him? The library? All you do is read."

Julie tittered nervously. "Funny you should say that."

Her brother continued to stare at her like she had gone mad. He blew out a sigh through his nose. "Julie…"

"I haven't met him. I read a...newspaper article."

"Dare I guess this article was featured in a matrimonial publication?"

"Well, yes..."

Julian put his fingers to the bridge of his nose and massaged the tender spot. "You have no reason to marry a stranger. Is the city boring you? Why don't we take a trip to Europe? Perhaps Spain? You adore Spain."

"This isn't about being bored." Julie stopped short and tapped her chin in thought. "However, now that you raise the issue, perhaps it is." She nodded at him, her long curls bouncing. "I think you're right. I was unchallenged here. There really are only so many dresses I can be fitted for, or operas I can attend. I want to do more than that. I want to be challenged by life, Julian."

"No one gets married out of boredom, Julie." Her brother paused and flung his hands out. "I'll admit there are matches made foolishly, but that isn't the type of woman you are. If you're feeling restless, may I suggest taking up a hobby? Needlework, for instance, has been lauded as an exemplary way of keeping young ladies busy."

"I haven't the patience for something so tedious, you know that."

Julian let out a deep sigh, the kind particular to long-aggrieved brothers the world over. "Then learn to gamble, by God. Anything but get married. Is this because you feel a need to nurture something? Shall I get you a kitten? A macaw, perhaps? I hear they have ungodly long lifespans."

"Julian, it's time that I move on. I'm an o—"

"Old? What? You are only 21, which is a perfectly suitable age to be unattached."

Julie crossed her arms. "Old? How do you mean?"

"Wasn't that what you were..." Julian bit his lip and rocked back on his heels. "Umm, about to say?" he finished weakly.

"No," Julie burst out with a glare. "I was saying that I am an out-of-work teacher. I am serving no purpose here in the city."

"Oh." Julian laughed and then nodded along, looking relieved. "Out of work, yes, yes. Not old. Certainly not, my darling baby sister."

"By three minutes."

"And what a world of difference those three minutes have made." Julian winked at her.

It was true that he was the embodiment of an older brother. Protective, teasing, and always, always in command of his surroundings. In that manner, Julian was very like their father, while Julie took after their mother. She made careful decisions, observed rather than participated, and preferred the fantasy of books over the crowded ballrooms and salons of the New York's haut monde.

No matter how Julie tried there always seemed to be a disconnect between herself and her peers. By all rights, she should be, as her brother was, secure in fortune, looks, and charisma. But for Julie, her place within the Four Hundred was a different experience. She wasn't the simpering debutante or heiress society expected her to be. And though it would have made her life simpler, Julie wouldn't change for anything.

Her father, Jean Baptiste, who had fought for the Union in the War between the States, had met her mother,

Manon Greene, on a dusty road somewhere between Richmond and Atlanta. Manon was a stunning woman, the product of French Creole and enslaved parentage. Jean and Manon had been married by the company chaplain, and her mother had remained by her father's side every moment until the war had blessedly ended.

Julie and Julian had been born a mere five months later.

Since childhood, the Baptiste twins' place in New York had been comfortable and secure with only moments of what her father referred to as "that ugliness" laying itself bare. Julian navigated their social sphere with the adeptness of a crown prince, but Julie drew into herself, her dark eyes observing from her place on the sidelines. In another world she could have been the debutante society expected, but that was a world in which her heritage didn't cause her to exist at the frayed edges of blue blood lineage, where she didn't stand with one foot in high society and the other planted on the red dirt of a Georgia road.

By all accounts, Julie and Julian were happy, well-respected, and considered the cream of society by the social pages. It was hard for them not to be with their striking looks: all tawny skin, dark eyes, high cheekbones, and curly dark hair. The considerable Baptiste family fortune, link to the Spanish throne, and vast land holdings all helped.

Or vexed, really. It depended on which Baptiste twin you asked, considering how hard Julie had tried to remain a wallflower through her formative years. It was all in vain, for she was a beauty, and there was no corner dark enough, no potted ficus tall enough, no dress hideous enough to hide her from the city's eligible bachelors.

She had enrolled at Vassar College and reveled in the refuge it provided her. But all good things come to an end and now, at 21, Julie was once again forced to participate in society's most elite gatherings. And thus Julie had pitifully examined her future: a future full of days spent with men and women she couldn't connect with, all the while feeling inadequate in her social failings.

Unless she was married.

Then she couldn't possibly be expected to attend every ball and opera, now could she? At the thought she had sat up so suddenly in the carriage that her mother had offered her a snifter of brandy to calm her nerves, but Julie had declined, her mind already putting together a plan to catch a husband.

But not any husband. He had to be a man who valued intelligence, freedom, and resourcefulness. A man who wished his wife to be independent. A man wholly uninterested in her family's money or status.

But where could she find a man such as that? Julie hated having to utilize the one venue society expected her to cheerfully pursue, but what she hated even more was trotting out, powdered and primped, in front of the same men she had known since diapers.

How to secure an introduction to a man without the social pages splashing it across the headlines was another matter. Stumped by the problem of meeting her future-egalitarian-kind-educated-perhaps-also-mildly-attractive-husband, she found salvation when she lucked upon the *Heart and Hand Matrimonial Times*.

She had almost discarded it as the maid's afternoon reading, but a cursory glance of the newspaper had her reconsidering. Here was a veritable feast of men in search of wives. And so Julie had sat down and poured over the paper, and every subsequent issue she could get her hands on. And then she had found Mr. Forrest Wickes's advert. It seemed nearly perfect in every way.

Julie had written Mr. Wickes as soon as she was able and had waited anxiously for his first response. Thankfully, it had come far faster than she had expected. The two had fallen into a comfortable pattern of letter-writing.

It was in those letter exchanges that the unthinkable happened. Against her better judgment she fell head-over-petticoats for Forrest Wickes.

When he had proposed marriage to her after their sixth month of correspondence, she hadn't been able to get her answer in the post fast enough. The ink had still been damp when she rushed her letter to the post only an hour after she had read Forrest's succinct but heartful entry to her.

I have fallen completely and wholly under your spell. If you find it agreeable, I ask for your hand in marriage.

Four months had passed since then, and now Julian's innate ability to disrupt any and all of her careful plans had surfaced, just when she had begun finalizing plans for her move to Gold Sky, a small town in the Montana Territory.

To be fair, she had wondered when this moment would occur.

"How did you find out?" Julie asked, putting her hands on her hips.

"This," Julian said, holding up the newspaper he had entered the parlor with. "It's plastered from here to Gramercy Park."

Julie balked but said nothing, snatching the paper from

her brother. She almost fainted when she read the headline.

Heiress succumbs to desperation! Joins the mail-order craze!

"Who intercepted my letters to Forrest? And I am not *desperate*," Julie screeched. Immediately she made a mental note to begin an investigation to find the culprit and, upon succeeding, to exact a fitting retribution. Though she wasn't sure what that would entail, she was certain there was a book or handy manual she could reference. "Of all the foul-mouthed things to call a lady! Desperate!"

Julian steepled his fingers and considered her. "Are you...particularly sure on that assessment?"

Julie glared at her brother and strode toward the fire. "Quite," she said, throwing the newspaper into the flames with more force than necessary. "I just...well, I'm not desperate. I'm in love."

"What?"

"When I looked to the *Heart and Hand* publication, I was looking for a way to be free, nothing more. I didn't intend to fall in love, but it seems fate had different plans."

"You're a few heads removed from the Spanish throne. How much more free should you like to be, Julie Anne?"

"I'm not like you, Julian." Julie sighed and ran her hands over her skirts with a frown. "I am not made for the Four Hundred. You are and you do it so well, but me..." She wrung her hands. "I tried, but I was never more happy than at Vassar in pursuit of my studies. I thought that if I found a man who would be content to allow me to do as I liked, then I could be happy."

"Oh, Julie." Julian sighed, but his sister held up a hand and continued on.

"That was when I found a matrimonial times, you see? I found the most sensible one... Forrest, er, Mr. Wickes."

8

Julie blushed and then swallowed at saying his name out loud. "I only meant to see if he was as agreeable as his advert made him out to be, and he was."

"And then you fell in love with him."

"Yes," Julie said, lifting her eyes to her meet his gaze, "I did."

"And you mean to marry this man? Where are you even going? The newspaper said Wyoming, but that can't be right. Please, tell me that isn't right."

"No, not Wyoming."

Julian let out a relieved sigh. "Thank God."

"I'm going to the Montana Territory."

Julian let out a strangled cry. "That's very nearly as bad. It's absolutely primitive. Are sure I can't talk you into a summer in Paris? Madrid?"

Julie smiled at her brother. "No. No Paris."

"But—"

"I'm marrying him. He will make me happy."

At that, Julian paused and gave his sister an assessing look. It was one that they had often shared over the years. Julie knew it was particular to them, because for all their differences they were as close as siblings could be. She met his gaze with as unwavering a look as she could manage, knowing that her brother would see the truth of her affections for Mr. Wickes there.

After another moment of silence, Julian let out a groan.

"You do love him."

"Of course. Why on earth would I be marrying him if I did not? I will admit that I am," she said, waving a hand, "behaving out of character." Julian snorted at that but she continued with a glare. "But this is, *he* is, what I want."

"I've often heard Vassar girls are pernicious at best but

9

now I believe it," Julian said, but he smiled at her. Julie's lips quirked up and she laughed.

"Are they now?"

"Yes, but they are also blessed with true and stalwart brothers who care deeply for their well-being."

"I have heard that." Julie reached out, taking her brother's hand in her hers.

He squeezed hers. "Mother and father will try to stop you."

"I know."

Julian sighed at her and touched her cheek. "I will help you carry out your foolhardy plan, of course."

"I expected nothing less," Julie replied and hugged her brother.

"When do you leave?" he asked, resting his chin against the top of her head.

"Three months." She tucked her cheek against his, breathing in his familiar scent.

Julian sighed, his breath warm against her forehead. "You are a truly perfect example of a Vassar girl."

"Thank you, brother."

"You're welcome, sister."

That night, with Julian at her side, Julie braved the task of informing her parents of her decision to marry and move west. She wasn't sure what she had expected, but it wasn't the calm reception her parents had given her. Her family wasn't prone to angry outbursts, but she was sure they would have much to talk about over breakfast the next morning, once the revelation had sunk in. They loved her and she them, and hopefully that love would sway their opinion when they came to the same conclusion Julian had about her affection for Mr. Wickes.

They better than any could understand the pull of love

and how powerfully it could motivate a person in the pursuit of a happier tomorrow. And with her parents' all-encompassing love as an example, there was not an event short of divine intervention that could dissuade her from taking her place in history as the Baptiste family's first ever mail-order bride.

CHAPTER 2

*T*hree months later—July 17th, 1886

Julie blew out a quick breath, her eyes on the wild and ever-changing landscape outside her window. The gentle swaying of the locomotive forced her to brace a hand against the wall of her compartment. She squeezed her eyes shut before looking at the worn newspaper clipping clutched in her free hand: Mr. Wickes's advert from the *Heart & Hand Matrimonial Times*.

Funny to think how such a small bit of ink and paper had spurred her toward the Montana Territory, a destination practically on the edge of the known world when compared to New York City's familiar streets.

Turning away from the window, Julie folded the clipping along the well-worn lines of the creases she had made nearly a hundred times before, and tucked it into her reticule. A perpetual romantic with her head forever lost in her books, Julie had saved the clipping for luck. It wouldn't do to lose it.

She needed the assurance of good luck now more than

ever, because in a few moments' time she would finally be face-to-face with Forrest Wickes, her betrothed.

Forrest Wickes was about to assume a real and tangible form. He would no longer be relegated to the scribblings of cherished letters. He would be her husband.

"Husband," Julie said, testing the word out, careful to keep her voice low lest the nosy elderly passengers in the next compartment conclude she had finally succumbed to the madness the society pages had diagnosed her with.

Her departure had been an absolute circus. New Yorkers of all walks of life, employ, and station eagerly speculated as to why the Baptiste heiress had chosen to trade a life of luxury and comfort for the frontier. Naturally, madness seemed the most logical reason. Julie had arranged the details for her trip west, and the Baptiste family had done their best to keep her departure date a secret. However, the crowd of reporters and onlookers greeting the Baptiste family upon their arrival at the train depot demonstrated whoever continued to expose Julie's intentions had, once again, been just a step ahead.

She wished unholy terror and ill-fitting shoes upon them for their meddling, and mornings full of cold oatmeal, and evenings spent with wet socks. Maybe even the curse of perpetually cold soup.

Yes, especially that.

Publicly observed goodbye or not, Julie had tearfully hugged her family goodbye, with kisses for her mother, hugs for Julian, and adamant promises to telegraph the moment she set foot in Gold Sky to her father, who pressed a small Swiss Holbein dagger into her hand, whispering, "This belonged to your great-great-great grandmother. She used it to fend off untoward advances. Use it similarly should the need arise with your new husband."

Julie had tucked the dagger into her carpetbag, an item purchased solely for the journey, though she was very nearly certain she would have no need to take up the dagger in defense. Mr. Wickes didn't seem the type of man to force a woman to do anything beyond her wishes, and he had met every requirement on Julie's list for her future egalitarian-kind-educated-perhaps-also-mildly-attractive husband.

Though it was one thing to present oneself on paper and another to have it match reality. Julie understood her father's gift and his instructions to use it. After all, there was no shortage of cautionary tales detailing the unfortunate circumstances of young brides, especially those in possession of means, who had fallen prey to men of ill repute.

Despite the risk, Julie trusted her gut feeling about Forrest Wickes. And in her mind, he was every bit the warm, kind, and intelligent man she had fallen in love with over the course of their correspondence. Besides, Julie was willing to assume the risk of being a mail-order bride, a disparaging title she had decided to wear with pride and honor, rather than resign herself to the available suitors she had known her entire life.

Julie's time at Vassar had more than adequately equipped her with the skills necessary to educate young minds. All the long nights studying to obtain her certificate had been infinitely more rewarding than worrying about keeping the attention of a fickle beau. Her future husband giving her an avenue to utilize her training was a wedding gift Julie considered to be more valuable than all the European honeymoons or hand-cut crystal glassware the society pages would expect her to receive. Julie could only imagine their ridicule at her excitement over the simple teaching position, and for not the first time she was happy she had boarded the train a month ago.

A light rap on her compartment door caused Julie to jerk in surprise. Her reticule and her carpet bag tumbled to the floor.

"My apologies, Miss Baptiste. I didn't mean to startle you," the conductor said with a grimace. He rushed forward to lift her things from the floor, and handed her reticule back to her with a sheepish smile as he stepped back toward the compartment door. "I wanted to be certain you were ready to step off here at Butte City. You are our only guest with it as a final destination."

"The only?" Julie raised an eyebrow. She followed behind the conductor, who gave her a quick nod of his head as he carried her bag.

"Oh, yes," he said, throwing open the train car's heavy door. "I must say that you, Miss Baptiste, have been the talk among the staff. A young lady such as yourself, coming all this way on her lonesome." The conductor hopped onto the platform and turned back to her, extending a hand. "I understand there has been a fair amount written about it in New York City. Are you certain that your people will meet you here?"

Julie frowned at the conductor's words. Even all this way from New York and she was still plagued by gossip. She took the conductor's hand as he guided her over the gap between train and platform.

"I'm quite sure I'll be met by my…" She paused and dipped her head. "People."

The conductor grinned at her. "You'll have to get used to talking like simple folk out here, Miss Baptiste. No other gently bred ladies such as yourself are this far from New York."

"I'm not that gently bred," she said, doing her best not to sound as exasperated as she felt, and gave her fashionable bonnet a tug. Suddenly the seemingly innocent and understated straw bonnet, with its single ribbon of green silk velvet and spray of sunny yellow blossoms, seemed far too fine for the platform she stood on in the middle of nowhere. Said platform was little more than a work of elevated cement and wood planks, with rickety-looking stairs leading down to a rocky dirt road disappearing off into what looked to be Butte City, if the word city were being used creatively.

The barely leveled road, covered in a smattering of gravel and rock, was slightly concerning, but the small collection of ramshackle clapboard and brick buildings made her curious to know if the founders of the settlement had ever gazed upon a city in their lives. The platform was empty save for the crew member unloading her two trunks from the storage car, and Julie swallowed hard at Forrest Wickes's absence.

The conductor gave her a kindly smile. "Oh, you are where it counts, Miss Baptiste. I hope you don't take this the wrong way, but this is no place for a young lady like you. Not on your own, anyhow."

A sudden holler pierced the air in perfect timing to the conductor's words, and Julie jumped in alarm. Her gloved fingers once again tightened on her reticule. If Mr. Wickes did not make his entrance soon, she was going to have to make use of the smelling salts in her bag to keep her wits about her. The society papers expected her to return New York within a month of arriving in the Montana Territory, and Julie had no intention of proving them right. With or without Forrest Wickes at her side, she was absolutely not returning home.

"No offense taken." Julie inclined her head to the man, though her eyes once again swept hopefully across the platform. A gunshot cracked from the collection of buildings, and this time Julie's gloved hand flew out to grab onto the conductor, whom she stepped behind for shelter. A tense moment passed in which her resolve wavered, but it didn't break as she forced herself to step away from the man.

She would sort out her next move with a clear head. She would not rush back onto the safety of the train, not even when there was a veritable gun duel—fight—no, battle—happening within earshot. At least she had the Holbein dagger in her reticule.

The thought cheered her, though she was sure there was some disparaging adage concerning daggers and guns capable of destroying the confidence the weight of the weapon in her reticule lent her.

"Ah, there, there, Miss Baptiste." The conductor made as soothing a voice as he could manage, though Julie didn't miss the wry grin he gave her. "That's probably just the saloon down the road. Nothing to worry about this far away."

"That all of it?" the crew member asked, nodding at her two trunks, which looked forlorn on the empty platform.

She frowned at the luggage. This was absolutely not the romantic scene she had played out countless times in her daydreams. This was what she got for reading penny novels. The fanciful things were capable of rotting a woman's brain when it came to men, and Julie vowed to end her habit.

"Yes, sir. Thank you for your help," Julie answered the man with a grateful smile. He looked startled at her genuine expression, but recovered a moment later by pulling off his work cap and returning her smile with one of his own.

"Of course, ma'am," he said before giving the conductor a curious look. "We're not leavin' her here, are we?"

"It is her intended destination," the conductor sighed, looking as if he didn't care for it one bit.

"It's too dangerous." The crew member frowned, taking a step forward, his cap still in his hand. "She needs an escort. A woman like her has no business traveling alone in the first place."

Julie's cheeks flushed and she lifted her head at the statement. "I am perfectly capable, but I thank you for your concern all the same, sirs." She threw her shoulders back with as much dignity as she could and marched over to her trunks. At the center of the platform stood a small bench, and she intended to drag her luggage there and at least have a seat while she planned her next move. She had just taken her first few steps with the trunk in tow when the crew member rushed up beside her.

"I'm sorry to have given you offense, ma'am. I meant none." He stood tentatively beside her before clearing his throat. "May I?" he asked, gesturing at the trunk Julie had dragged behind her.

Julie considered telling the crew member that she was more than able to handle her own belongings, but she let out a sigh and gave him a quick nod. He was only trying to be chivalrous, after all. It wouldn't do to take her own poor mood at her lonely reception out on the man. "Yes, please."

"I hope you'll accept my apology," he said, taking her trunk and moving it toward the small bench with ease. He had just set the trunk down when Julie registered the neighing of a horse and the rattle of wagon wheels behind them. But it would be rude to turn away from a gentleman when he was making amends, so Julie kept her focus on the crew member.

"Of course I accept, and I offer my sincerest apologies as well. A month on a train has me more than a little out of sorts." She offered him a smile.

He tucked his cap into the front of the coveralls he wore. "I'll just get your other trunk, ma'am."

"Thank you, sir," Julie called after him.

"Now, Miss Baptiste, I'll arrange for an escort to come and fetch you so that we might leave." The conductor glanced down at the pocket watch he wore and shook his head. "I'd prefer to stay until your people arrive but I'm on a very tight schedule." His eyes moved to the train where curious passengers either regarded her through the glass of the compartment windows, or, in a brash move, hung out from the windows with open interest.

"You aren't leaving that girl here, are you?" an old woman called out to them from an open window. "She's naught but a child."

"I told you that was the Baptiste heiress," another voice crowed.

Julie blushed. "I understand, sir. I do not wish to be any trouble."

"I'll stay with her," the crew member who had just deposited her trunk by her feet said. "Catch the next train back, easy."

"Very admirable, John." The conductor looked impressed. Julie felt piqued once more and she opened her mouth to express as much.

"That won't be necessary."

Julie froze. The words she had just been about to speak had come from thin air. She turned her head to see a man striding across the platform toward them with a pained expression on his face. "Miss Baptiste, my sincere apologies," he said, blue eyes fixed on her.

"Mr. Wickes?" Julie asked, her voice catching in her throat when he gave her a nod.

In all her love-addled daydreaming she had never dared to picture the man standing strong and sure in front of her. He more than fulfilled her request of mildly attractive.

Forrest Wickes was powerfully built, standing at 6'2 with skin tanned from hours in the sun, fine muscles, and a pair of broad shoulders visible even under the flannel of his work shirt. The abashed figure standing in front Julie was all man. No trace of boyishness in his face, unlike the suitors who had tried their hand at courting her in New York.

He yanked off the brown wide-brimmed hat he wore with a jerk of his hands, revealing hair that looked like spun gold. Julie wondered if it was as soft as it looked and her cheeks flamed at the thought. Swoon-worthy, indeed. An aquiline nose, chiseled jaw, and lips that could lead a woman astray rounded out the picture of Mr. Wickes, but it was the pair of blue eyes looking at her in apology that had Julie fighting the urge to pull out her smelling salts then and there. She was struck dumb at the sight of the man and could only stand in silence as he apologized to her.

"I meant to be here when you arrived but there was an incident, ah, just—" He jerked a thumb over his shoulder in the direction of town. I, we, had to intervene. I apologize for not meeting you."

Julie bit her lip. "W-was it the gunshots?" she asked with wide eyes.

He cleared his throat. "Yes, ma'am."

"Oh my," Julie breathed, her hand going to her throat.

"But don't trouble yourself over it. It's being seen to by, ah, my partner." He held out his hands in a placating gesture before looking at the crew member and conductor as if he had just noticed them for the first time. "I thank you for bringing my fianceé safely to her destination."

"Fianceé?" the crew member squeaked. Julie scowled at the man but said nothing as Forrest nodded.

"Since the New Year," he said, and Julie warmed at the note of pride she heard in his voice. He turned to her with a tender smile. "After all the letters it's awfully nice to meet you finally, Miss Baptiste."

Julie's early assertion that she wouldn't need the Holbein dagger against Forrest Wickes's advances was heartily confirmed by that single, achingly sweet smile.

"You're a mail-order bride?" the crew member gasped, interrupting Julie's thoughts. The man had put together the pieces of the puzzle surrounding Julie's solo journey, which only exposed him as a man who didn't read. That fact alone would be enough to lower her opinion of him but the look he gave her now, a stare equal parts horrified and pitying, reduced her assertion of him to a negative summation.

Julie gave a nod of her head and did her best to look unaffected at his comment. "I am, sir."

The crew member spluttered in shock. Julie cast him an annoyed look and toyed with the idea of offering him her vial of smelling salts. It looked like he would need it before long if this conversation went on.

Thankfully, the conductor seemed unruffled and tipped his hat to Mr. Wickes. "Glad you came along to collect her, then. I'll rest easier about the young lady knowing a man of the law is with her from here on out."

Mr. Wickes's shoulders squared, causing the sheriff's badge pinned to his leather vest to gleam in the sunlight. "Nice of you to say, sir."

He put his hands on his hips, the movement drawing Julie's eye to the revolver that lay snug there. She'd never seen a gun up close. Not even an hour into her new life on the frontier and things were already looking up in the ways of adventure and intrigue, far from her days spent hiding from suitors and avoiding social galas.

"Gentlemen." Mr. Wickes put his hat back on his head with a nod at them before turning to regard Julie almost shyly. "Miss Baptiste?" he asked in a softer voice and held out his arm to her.

"Call me Julie, please," she replied, tucking a gloved hand into the crook of his arm.

"Only if you call me, Forrest, ma'am—ah, Julie."

"Certainly, Forrest." Julie's cheeks burned hot from noticing how solid Forrest's arm felt under her hand. Thankfully, she managed to keep her voice even in reply. She followed him across the platform, mind racing for her next words when Forrest spoke.

"I'm sorry I was late," Forrest sighed, clamouring down the stairs and turning to help her. "Never fails that we go somewhere early and end up having to settle the people down around here."

Julie nodded, though she was more focused on how Forrest's large hands felt on her waist as he bypassed the shaky set of stairs to set her on the ground beside him. She had little time to marvel at how deftly he had handled her when the sudden sound of a horse's hooves made her turn to see a man approaching them on the back of a beautiful chestnut mare.

Stern gray eyes regarded her coolly from beneath the brim of a sweat-stained hat. He had, she saw, one hand resting on a shotgun at his side, and she wondered if it had been the gun she'd heard fired only minutes before. She couldn't help but notice that while Forrest had done his best to clean up, his blond hair neatly combed, clothes freshly laundered and pressed, boots and badge shined within an inch of their life, this man had done anything but. In fact, it appeared to Julie that he had barely deigned to wash the sleep from his face before making his way to the train station.

"Will." Forrest nodded at the man. "Everything settled in town?"

"If by sorted y'mean did I throw him in a jail cell? Then yes." Will gave him a cheeky grin, leaning back in his saddle with a flick of his reins. "It's all sorted and just in time, I see."

Forrest blew out an irritated sigh. "Get Miss, ah, Julie's things from the platform while I get her settled in the wagon."

"Already calling her Julie, then?" Will hopped off his horse and gave Forrest an appraising look. "I'm impressed."

"Knock it off," Forrest said with a pinched look on his face. Julie swallowed hard, unconsciously stepping closer to Forrest, when Will walked past her without so much as a glance. Forrest leaned close to her with a weak smile. "M'sorry about him. He's in fine form today."

"I see," Julie murmured, her eyes following Will's

athletic form as he ambled up the stairs and toward her trunks.

"He'll warm up in no time, ma'am, I—" Forrest blew out a sigh. "I mean, Julie."

She gave him a smile. "I'm sure he will, Forrest."

"The wagon is just this way." Forrest led her toward a sturdy-looking wagon. It wasn't the prettiest thing she'd ever seen but it did have a cover over it for protection from the sun, and she was absolutely positive that it was built to last. She was touched when she saw the pillows that had been tossed onto one side of the wagon bench, a sure attempt at comfort by the men for her sake.

"Thank you," she murmured when Forrest picked her up and placed her in the wagon with ease. It was like she weighed nothing to him, and it made her feel small, dainty even. A feeling that had long eluded her in New York where the debutantes seemed to shrink a bit more every year. Julie did her best not to notice how Forrest's biceps flexed beneath the starched material of his flannel, and instead trained her eyes on the platform where Will made quick work of bringing her trunks to the wagon.

"This all you bring?" he asked after he'd brought both trunks down to the wagon.

"Yes," Julie replied and bit her lip when Will gave her a grunt and tossed one of her trunks roughly into the back of the wagon. A warning look from Forrest caused Will to place the second with more care.

"I, well, we got these for you," Forrest said, holding out a bouquet. It was mostly wilted from the heat but still lovely. A bunch of wildflowers, daisies, marigolds, and violets made up the cheery offering.

"These are lovely, Forrest." Julie brought the blooms

up to her nose and gave them a happy sniff. "I love them. Thank you."

Forrest beamed at her then, his face breaking into a wide smile that made him look infinitely younger than his 34 years of age.

"M'glad you like them. There's fields of them where we're going," he said, giving the reins a snap and starting the wagon off down the road Julie had eyed suspiciously upon her arrival. "I-I'll make sure to get you fresh ones every day."

"Really?" Julie looked up in surprise. His cheeks were dusted with pink but he kept his blue eyes on the road ahead of them.

"'Course, if it makes you smile like that," he said, his voice soft.

"I'd like that very much," Julie murmured, tucking the flowers next to her.

Forrest said nothing but Julie didn't miss the smile on his face. It was nice, sitting like this next to him as they drove along in their wagon. She glanced about and was relieved when they passed through Butte City with no incident.

It wasn't long before they drove through the open country of Montana. It was all so beautiful, with its lush prairie grass, endless blue sky, mountains rising like jagged teeth in the distance, and splashes of colorful wild-flowers, that Julie wasn't sure which way to look first.

"How long is the ride to Gold Sky?" she asked, attempting to break the silence that had fallen between them. She wanted to ask Forrest a million questions but she also didn't know where to begin, and on top of that she'd never been alone with a more handsome man.

In fact, she couldn't think of a time when she had ever been completely alone with a man.

Ever.

Never mind the fact that Forrest was going to be her husband in the near future.

"It's an hour's drive away," he replied, giving her a sidelong look. "I know it's not what you're used to but I know you'll settle in. The town is grateful to have a teacher like you coming to manage the school."

Julie dipped her head but her lips pursed at Forrest's words. She didn't want to simply be seen as a teacher to this man. She wanted to be more, infinitely more, than a resource to the community.

"I'm honored to have a teaching job so soon after graduating." She glanced over Will, who rode alongside the wagon. His gray eyes moved constantly, scanning the horizon, whether for pleasure or if he was looking for hostile parties she wasn't sure. He held himself like a tightly-wound harp string ready to snap at the first pluck. Clearing her throat delicately, Julie folded her hands in her lap and decided to push ahead to the question that had been hanging over her head during her month-long journey.

"The wedding," she began, instantly attracting the attention of both men, "when will it take place?"

Forrest and Will exchanged a look over the top of her head before Forrest spoke. "We were thinking it would be best to, ah, have it as soon as we returned to Gold Sky."

"Oh." Julie blinked at the new information. She hadn't anticipated such a quick turnaround upon her arrival, though she supposed she should have considered it at some point on her train ride to Montana. But then again, there had been so much time to read on the train, and with a seemingly endless supply of solitude to indulge herself Julie hadn't thought of much other than what book to begin next.

Will said nothing but fiddled nervously with his hat, or with what Julie imagined to be nervousness. Perhaps it was agitation, given his quietness.

"That seems efficient," she said finally, once she had processed the new timeline.

"You don't—" Will said, his voice coming out gruffly and suddenly, "don't have to do this." He looked at her then, his gray eyes intense and focused. Julie felt her heart clench. It was like Will saw straight into her deepest parts.

"I know," Julie said, eyes still locked with Will's gaze.

"Y'sure about that?" Will leaned to the side of his saddle, closer to where she sat on the wagon bench. He looked away to the horizon with a frown. "You're young, pretty, smart. Don't have to be stuck with us. Not proper."

"I wouldn't say that I will be stuck with you," Julie returned. "Nor would I judge so quickly what is and is not proper."

Forrest gave her a thin smile. "He's right. You change your mind and the teaching job is still yours. The town is set for you to begin in a week's time, and there's a little house in the town for the teacher. You'd be safe."

Julie frowned. "Are the pair of you trying to get rid of me now? After all this time? All th-those letters?" She wrung her hands together, her mind already leaping to what the society pages would proclaim at her being rejected as a mail-order bride. The fallout would be horrendous.

If she wasn't wanted then she would become a dagger-wielding outlaw of some kind with a penchant for literature. Better a life of crime than to suffer the slander and pity of the Four Hundred.

Forrest sat up straight when he heard her frustrated tone. "Now, Julie, we weren't—"

"Because I'll have you know that I very much have made up my mind to be married, gentlemen." Julie crossed her arms over her chest in defiance, though it was hard for her to stay sitting upright given the swaying nature of the wagon, and she almost cursed when she fell sideways, prompting a quick hand from Will to catch her before she tumbled headfirst out of the wagon.

If she had to turn to a life of crime, it was absolutely going to have to be carried out by train. Wagons be damned.

Will let out an exasperated grunt. "Life won't be easy with us."

"Yes, I know this. Forrest was perfectly clear in the year of letters we exchanged." She gave Forrest a meaningful look that had the big man blushing.

"So I was." He glanced over at Will and added, "So we were."

Julie raised an eyebrow in surprise. "You wrote me?" she asked, looking at Will, who leaned back in his saddle looking like he wished to be anywhere but there.

"Sure did," he answered, but said no more.

"You never...I mean, I didn't know it wasn't *you*." She gave Forrest a look of reproach, but he only shrugged.

"Made sense for you two to talk beforehand if you were serious about having the both of us."

"Well, I suppose so," Julie sighed. She leaned back against the pillows and bit her lip at the thought that she had written to Will but never known it. Just one more item for consideration on the learning curve. Why it surprised her, she didn't know. Perhaps it was because until she had made up her mind to answer Forrest's advert, to fall in love with him as she had, she had never done one thing out of line with what society and her family expected of her.

Her cheeks burned when she thought of how her mother would faint if she knew what her only daughter had agreed to nearly a year ago. If polite New York society thought it already had the juiciest drama from her little adventure, it would fly into an absolute tizzy over what Julie had truly decided to do. Though the spy who had told the pages about her plan to go west had ruined her efforts at secrecy, they hadn't discovered the whole of it. If they had, Julie wouldn't have just made the society pages, she would have sustained them for months, possibly even years.

And she might still if her secret ever came to light, which was that she, heiress of the esteemed Baptiste family, hadn't simply agreed to be a bride for the sake of a teaching position and the chance of adventure on the frontier to one man.

She'd agreed to do it with two.

CHAPTER 3

$\mathcal{A}$ cheery sun overhead complete with a gentle breeze worked wonders for Julie's frazzled nerves at meeting her husbands-to-be. Enjoying the coolness of the breeze on her skin, Julie felt glad for the change of pace from her grueling train ride west, a journey in which she had begun to run troublingly low on novels to read.

Blessedly, the ride to Gold Sky passed peacefully enough for the triad with a companionable silence settling among them, or as companionable as humanly possible. Julie glanced at Will out of the corner of her eye, seeing him glare at the horizon. He'd fallen silent after Forrest had disclosed the wedding plans, and as much as Julie wanted to ask him about himself she dared not.

There was something almost angry about his silence, and the glower on his face inclined her to avoid the man's grey eyes.

That didn't mean she didn't want to look at Will, or Forrest, for that matter. Both men were veritable specimens of manliness, and she wanted to peruse them like a new novel. And that meant Julie played a dangerous game of sneaking glances at both men from the corners of her eyes while ostensibly examining the contents of her reticule, or straightening her bonnet. She engaged in another rousing round of bonnet straightening, eyes drinking in Will's profile, when Forrest's hand lightly touched hers, startling her.

Forrest gave her a small smile. "Give him time."

Putting on as brave a face as possible, Julie returned his smile. She could give the man time; she had, after all, read the entirety of Tolstoy's *War and Peace*. If anyone understood the virtue of patience, it was her.

Sneaking another look at Will, she bit back a sigh at his profile, which made her think of the figures she had come across in her Greek classics studies. All sharp planes and smooth skin, save for the dark stubble covering his jaw. When he removed his hat to wipe at the sweat on his forehead, she saw that his hair was longer than Forrest's, which he had pulled back in a low knot. Julie bit her lip when she realized Will's handsome features were screwed up in consternation. It was quite easy to see that he was annoyed, but bothered as he was, he was still beautiful.

How utterly unfair.

Julie sighed and looked away, swaying along with the wagon as it dipped low into the dirt road. Even though he wasn't warm and welcoming like Forrest, she still wondered if Will would ever concede to let her run fingers through his chestnut hair. There was something about the man that urged her to touch him, to smooth her hands over his tense forehead and muscled shoulders, to try and coax him to relax, even a little, from the rigid form he displayed sitting astride a horse.

It was only when Gold Sky came into sight that Will relaxed.

"Goin' ahead," he called over to them before he spurred his horse forward with a snap of his heel. Dust kicked and pebbles flew up as he shot off at nearly a gallop. He leaned low over the horse's neck, one hand holding onto the hat at his head. Almost instantly the lines of his body loosened.

Julie smiled when she heard an excited whoop escape his mouth as he raced toward town. He was carefree and Julie was glad to see it.

"He's happy about this. Honest," Forrest said as they watched Will disappear into the city limits of Gold Sky.

Julie sighed. "I don't know if that's true…but maybe in time," she told him.

Forrest's hand found hers again, and this time he intertwined their fingers, the thin material of her gloves the only thing separating their flesh. She froze, eyes riveted to his hand covering hers.

A touch like this wasn't allowed, not for young ladies, and certainly not when unaccompanied.

Her brain demanded her to pull away, but Julie quieted it. This was not New York City where the watchful eyes of society dogged her every step.

This was the frontier.

The only thing between Julie accepting and taking comfort in Forrest's touch was her own reservation. This was a particularly bothersome realization, as she was set to marry Forrest that very day. If there was any hope of her enjoying her time as a frontierswoman, Julie needed to get out of her own way.

"Meant what we said, Julie." Forrest's voice pulled her back to the here-and-now with a jolt. He glanced at her and swallowed hard. "The job is yours if you decide we aren't, ah, well, if we don't all suit."

"I think we all suit just fine," Julie said mulishly. She had no intention of going back to New York. And at the moment, she was contemplating the speediest manner of divesting herself of all she had learned at Lady Pim's Fine Etiquette and Finishing for Young Ladies. If only she could steal back those countless hours of being conditioned. What a waste of reading time it had proven to be.

Forrest smiled at her and ran his thumb along the back of her gloved knuckles. "Teacher like you is just the thing this town needs."

Julie's shoulders slumped. Those touches, which had seemed tender, bordering on scintillating, now only seemed friendly.

Perfunctory, even.

"Right, of course. The town requires a teacher," she said. She withdrew her hand from Forrest's and folded both hands in her lap.

Forrest bit his lip, sensing that he had said the wrong thing. "I-I mean to say that, well," he said so quickly his words came out in a jumble, but Julie looked up at him with a slight smile.

"I understand," she said softly. "It's all right, Forrest."

He frowned. "What do you mean?"

Julie gestured between them with a flick of her hand. "I think I understand what this is."

"Which is?" Forrest raised an eyebrow.

"Gold Sky needed a teacher and you two need someone to keep you out of trouble."

"Is that so?"

"Seems like it."

"So, by your calculations, you're going to be teachin' and babysittin'?"

"Appears that way," Julie replied, but she paused with a frown. "I'll do my best to learn to cook, though I will remind you that you both specified it was not a necessary skill."

Forrest let out a snort. "Then we'll hire a cook."

"We will?" Julie blinked in surprise.

"'Course we will, if you'd like. Aim to keep my wife happy."

"But I th—"

"Thought what? We just wanted a woman, and any would do?" Forrest asked, shifting in his seat next to her. "Had over a hundred women reply to us, Julie."

"What?" Julie breathed in shock. A wagon wheel hit a hole and jostled her almost in tandem with her gasp of surprise. Forrest reached out a steadying hand to keep her upright and squeezed her arm, fingers warm through the material of her sleeve.

"Picked you for a reason," he told her reassuringly, though Julie was far too distracted by the large hand on her arm. It was difficult to keep on task but she managed.

"And that was?" she persisted.

"First off, you wanted the both of us, didn't even make you bat an eyelash." Forrest grinned at her, finally pulling his hand off her, though he seemed reluctant to do so. "Anyone that knows us knows we'd never make it separate. Not after the war."

"Yes, that." Julie blushed, looking down at her cream traveling gloves.

"Uh huh. That," Forrest echoed her with a chuckle. "Second, you are a smart woman, one I can see us spending nights enjoying conversation with. You're capable of critical thinking and that makes you a real partner for us. A woman who can share her outlook on life, someone we can build a life and have children with."

Julie's breath caught in her throat. "Children? You want that?"

Forrest leveled her with a steady gaze. "Not just me. We want that."

"Will?" Julie's voice was barely above a whisper but she knew Forrest read her surprise.

"With you."

Julie swallowed hard. "With me."

"I was, ah, trying to pay you a compliment." Forrest sighed and rubbed a hand along his jaw with a chagrined look on his face. "Not easy becoming a teacher, and thought you'd, well, thought you'd like that I paid mind to the effort you put into your education."

Julie blushed at Forrest's clumsy apology. "I am. Thank you."

She gave a little sigh and looked off at the beautiful scenery stretching out in every direction from them: mountains, blue sky, all color and manner of flowers she could ever want. It was painfully beautiful, just like the man next to her.

But this wasn't one of her stories she could step into and see the plot so clearly, with the next word or emotion already planned for her by a writer. It was a daunting task being alone with her fiancé unchaperoned, as was evident by the mess she has made so far.

"I'm just tense, I think. The train ride was quite long. Do you know what happens to the body when it exists on a sustained vibration level akin to the train and those godforsaken train tracks?" She knew she was babbling, but it couldn't be helped.

When Forrest declined to answer her, Julie was relieved. He gave her a kind look and patted her hand while he flicked the reins with his other. "Will isn't helping," Forrest muttered with a dark look.

"He'll come around...just like you said." Julie gave him a slight smile and reached out to lay her hand on top of his. "I think, well, from your letters—" She paused, and pushing away all thoughts of sustained vibrations and their effects on the human physique, met his clear blue eyes and said, "That we could be happy."

"All three of us. Whether William admits it now or not," he said, gazing at her then with an expression that could only be described as tender, "we agreed that you are the woman for us. This I swear to you."

Julie's breath caught in her throat and for a moment it was difficult to focus on anything but the man next to her. Perhaps she hadn't wasted what little free time she'd been afforded at Vassar with her novels after all. Every daydream or hopeful romantic fantasy her literary hobby had ever entertained her with now seemed adequate preparation for the sweet words falling from Forrest's mouth. Her countless years reading women's novels were, in that moment, the only training keeping her from swooning into Forrest's arms.

Lady Pim's Fine Etiquette and Finishing for Young Ladies, indeed.

"I'll do my best not to disappoint."

"Sweetheart, that's somethin' you couldn't do, even if you tried."

"Maybe wait until I try cooking and then we'll see what tune you sing," she told him.

Forrest barked out a laugh. "Fair enough." He sobered up after another moment of laughter and asked, "Do you have your things for the wedding? We planned on taking you ahead to the boarding house so that you could get ready in peace."

"Not, ah, at the ranch?"

"Oh, no, that's about another half hour ride out from town. But don't worry, the schoolhouse is between town and home. You can walk if you like, only take you twenty or so minutes to get there."

"That sounds lovely," Julie replied with a genuine smile at Forrest, though her thoughts had skipped ahead to what lay after the wedding ceremony and reception. Her mind had, belatedly, caught up to her present situation and before long visions of nights alone with the two men —nights that would lead to the children and the family Forrest spoke of—danced in Julie's mind.

Children didn't magically appear beneath Christmas trees or by way of a stork. They needed making.

God, what had she gotten herself into? And what did it say about her as a well-bred lady of society that she was not only willing, but eager, for the chance to do whatever it was that she had agreed to with them? After-dinner sherry had nothing on the feeling the men inspired in her. Mercifully their arrival in Gold Sky curtailed her thoughts. It was the perfect remedy for a head full of soul-searching questions.

"So this is Gold Sky," Julie said in an attempt to rein in her rapidly wandering ideas. She was pleased to see that there was a dress shop, mercantile, post office, saloon, bank, and even a small selection of restaurants. She turned in her seat and craned her neck, trying to get a look inside the saloon, which took up a formidable slice of real estate.

"Home sweet home. I'll take you across the way to the

boarding house that Miss Hill runs. She'll have a room for you to get ready in."

Julie nodded, suddenly feeling shy. The people who had been bustling through the streets only moments before had all stopped to regard them. There was no mistaking their interest, not that any of them tried to hide it.

"It's a lovely little town," she observed, taking in the town square.

"It is," Forrest told her. "People are like family here."

"That sounds nice," Julie replied, thinking back to New York and her family. She wondered how Julian was getting on, if he was staying out of trouble and if their father had finally made good to send him to Canada. It was odd being on her own as she was now, a state she had not quite gotten used to even after a month of traveling.

"Miss your family?" Forrest gave her a knowing look.

"You're very observant."

"I know you're close to them. Makes sense you would miss them."

"Is there anywhere I can send a telegram?"

Forrest nodded as they pulled up in front of the boarding house. "Certainly. Will and I have free reign of one in the sheriff's station. I'll take you tomorrow and we'll send them whatever you like."

"Thank you."

Forrest smiled at her with a gentle look in his eyes. It was as dangerous a weapon as had ever been formed, and Julie made a mental note to guard herself against it in the future.

"Anything for you."

Forrest hopped out of the wagon before she could respond and then handed her down with the same ease as he had before. Tucking her close to him, he walked her up to the front door of the two-story boarding house. It looked out of place with its elegant wrap-around porch and massive bay windows. A beat passed before the door flew open and a woman with dancing blue eyes greeted them.

"You're here," the woman exclaimed with a warm smile. She reached out and gave Forrest a squeeze before stepping forward and sweeping Julie into a tight hug.

"I'm so excited to meet you, Julie Anne!" The woman drew back and regarded her with a raised eyebrow. "Or is it just Julie? Or would you prefer to go by Mrs. Wickes, or are you going to double bar the name? I happen to think that Wickes-Barnes has a lovely ring to it."

Julie was speechless at the tiny woman's energy. Well, that and her casual mention of a double last name.

"I, ah, just Julie is fine," she said. She turned to give Forrest a sidelong look in confusion. "Do people—" She stopped speaking and cleared her throat, hoping that he would infer her unasked question.

"Do people know you're marrying the set?" the woman asked with a cheery laugh.

Julie blushed scarlet. Forrest let out a groan. "Miss Hill, has anyone ever made you aware that you have a blunt way to your manners?"

Miss Hill rolled her eyes.

"Yes. Everyone in this town, and I don't particularly care. Didn't we all come west to be who we truly are? Spent enough time biting my tongue back in Philadelphia, and I have no intention of spending one more second doing so." She turned back to Julie and winked. "Don't worry, you'll find that the people of Gold Sky are accepting of just about anything. That's what family does and we are tickled that someone is taking on the pair of them. The entire town has been excited since we heard you were coming out to join them. Bless the Lord above for you, Julie. You're a godsend."

"Thank you." Julie inclined her head to Miss Hill. The other woman's ready acceptance of their intended marriage arrangement lifted a good amount of worry from her shoulders. If the citizens of Gold Sky were as accepting as Miss Hill then there was no reason why she couldn't settle into a life resembling normal.

Now all that was left was how to manage to reconcile the particulars of her marriage with her family. She didn't even want to begin to think of how she was going to keep the information from the papers. That would be a circus of the highest magnitude.

"Think nothing of it and call me Alice."

"Of course, Alice."

Alice beamed and led Julie into the boarding house after her. "Come on now, I've got a bath all drawn and ready for you. Do you have your wedding dress with you?"

Julie pointed a finger behind her. "It's back in my trunks. The red one."

"Forrest, you heard your intended. Bring the red trunk in after us. Last door on the left," Alice called over her shoulder to a chagrined-looking Forrest. Julie barely had time to give him a small shrug before Alice hurried her along the hallway toward the aforementioned room. "Now, we have three hours before your wedding is set to start. I'll press and freshen up your dress, and if we get you right in the tub it should be just enough time to get all that pretty hair of yours dry. I bet you'd love a soak after that train ride."

"A soak sounds heavenly," Julie moaned. "I'm surprised I don't smell more than I do. I think my dress can manage to stand on its own from the amount of sweat that I've put into it over the course of today alone."

Alice tsked and tutted with a shake of her head. "That train ride is from the devil. Believed I would lose my mind before we got here." She opened the door to a beautifully appointed and comfortable bedroom with a sweep of her hand. "I hope you'll be able to relax before the wedding. Will made sure to come ahead and get it all ready for you. Wanted it just right, but you know how that one is." Alice grinned at her while Julie glanced at her in confusion.

"I don't reall—" she began, ready to tell Alice that she hadn't gotten off on the best foot with William just yet, but the sound of footsteps interrupted her.

"Speak of the devil," Alice chirped.

Julie turned to see William striding into the room carrying her red trunk. She hadn't realized that he had made his way to the boarding house when he had gone ahead of them earlier.

The thought that he had come here to make arrangements for her comfort touched her heart. Maybe Forrest was right, and all William needed was time.

"Where y'want this?" he asked, eyes moving over her coolly before he focused on Alice.

"Set it right where you are and then I want you out of here," Alice said, making a shooing motion at him. "I've got to get your bride ready for her walk down the aisle."

Will made a grunting sound that Julie assumed was an affirmative, and set her trunk down. He turned on his heel and left the room without another word.

"Don't worry about him," Alice remarked, taking in the

41

look of disappointment on Julie's face. "He'll come around. He just likes to act like he's a prickly pear."

"I don't imagine he's pretending," Julie huffed.

Alice laughed outright at Julie's frank remark. "I like you."

Julie smiled and opened her trunk. "Thank you, and I like you too." Alice hummed in approval and moved closer to watch Julie pull out a carefully wrapped parcel. "My mother helped me pick all the fabric and trimmings for this dress. She was absolutely insistent that it be classic," she said with a smile at the memory of her mother bickering with her over her dress. "It's a little like she's here today because of it."

Alice nodded. "It's always nice to have a mother's touch on a wedding." Her eyes widened when she took in the dress Julie pulled free of the heavy brown wrapping paper. "Oh, it's sensational."

"It is, isn't it?" Julie agreed and ran her hands over the cream silk satin material of the dress. It was fitted to hug her form just so. The skirt fell gracefully to her feet with layers of cream Chantilly lace embroidered with orange blossoms for a touch of color, and the bustle of the dress was a masterpiece of more Chantilly lace and sumptuous silk. A pair of lace gloves and white kid leather ankle boots complete with pearl fasteners rounded out the picture. Julie smiled, remembering the afternoons spent shopping and planning with her mother for this very day.

"You're going to be a vision," Alice whispered with a sniffle. "This town will have never seen a more beautiful or elegant bride."

"Oh, thank you, Alice. That's lovely of you to say."

Alice yanked her close into a hug. "You're going to take

their breath away. You're going to take the whole town's breath away when you walk down the aisle to those two."

Julie pulled back in shock. "What do you mean, the whole town?"

"Did they not tell you?" Alice asked.

"Tell me what?"

"They invited the entire town to the wedding."

Julie's mouth dropped open in defiance of every last finishing school rule of etiquette she had learned from Lady Pim.

"What?" she gasped.

Alice winced. "The entire town i—"

"I know, I know, " Julie whispered, her fingers going to her temples, "but why?"

"Gold Sky is accepting, but putting a human touch to the situation never hurt anyone that might be on the fence," Alice explained, gathering Julie's wedding dress up against her.

"So it's to...sway those undecided citizens? The wedding, I mean?"

"A beautiful bride and a sweet wedding are sure to soften even the skeptics."

Julie slumped down onto the bed. She had thought it would be a small affair, a quick ceremony, perhaps, before she was free to learn more about her husbands in peace. But she did have to admit, it was a shrewd move by the men to plan a town-wide celebration for their wedding. It would be difficult for anyone who attended the wedding as their guest to openly hold ill will against them.

At least publicly.

"Prudent of them," she said, giving voice to her thoughts.

"You'll meet everyone in town and it'll be the merriest

occasion we've had since the barn raising last spring." Alice gave her an excited smile. She held up the wedding dress and nodded at the tub of steaming water in the center of the room. "Now get in that tub and scrub every inch of yourself. You have a town to impress."

Julie acquiesced and after Alice left her, she made short work of sinking into the hot water. Being on the train for so long had been hard on her. She wasn't accustomed to swaying constantly, nor was it comfortable to be in a near state of vibration for every hour of the day. She hadn't realized that her body had been in a constant state of numbness until it hit the water.

"God bless bathtubs," she hummed, slipping lower in the steamy tub. But now wasn't the time for relaxing, at least not completely, so she sat up and went to work washing her hair.

In no time at all she was out of the tub and feeling more like her old self. She worked at drying her thick hair and settled on plaiting it down her back. It would curl naturally, but the long braid would work to control the curls. Once that was done she turned her attention back to the room, taking it in for the first time. Bright sunlight poured in through the open window, a gentle breeze wafted in, and she sighed, stretching her arms up over her head.

She had begun to debate if she had enough time for a short nap when she saw the tray of food and drink sitting on the bedside table. The tray held an assortment of finger sandwiches, fresh fruit, cold water, juice, and even a slice of chocolate cake. A single white rose lay across the tray, and she hesitated before reaching for it.

Had Will put this here when he had ridden ahead? She sniffed at the bloom and decided that she preferred her fantasy world where he had. It made the fact that their wedding was a town-wide production more bearable.

A soft knock at her door pulled her from her thoughts and a second later Alice popped her head into the room.

"All clean? I've got your dress sorted. Shall we get to work on your hair and makeup? I cut fresh flowers for your hair." Alice held up a few pink blooms. "These would look so beautiful in those dark curls of yours."

"That's so thoughtful. Thank you, Alice."

Alice bustled over and smiled at her. "That's what friends are for."

Julie grinned at the statement. It cheered her to have someone calling her friend so soon upon her arrival, and she was happy to listen to Alice chatter on about the people she would meet that day. Before long and with a head full of information on townspeople she had yet to meet, Julie stepped into her wedding dress, Alice's capable hands ensuring that she looked every bit the radiant bride her mother had dreamed of.

Alice had just finished placing a final blossom in her hair, which had been formed into a crown of braids and curls atop her head, when there was a quick knock at the door.

"Who is it?" Alice called, still focused on making Julie's hair just so.

"Peter," a voice answered. "I've been sent to fetch the bride."

Alice rolled her eyes. "A bride is not fetched, young man."

An almost tortured groan came from the other side of the door. "Ma…"

Alice winked at Julie. "My son will take you to the chapel. I'll be along shortly."

Julie nodded, following the woman to the door where a boy of fifteen stood, looking impatient, at least until he saw Julie.

"Goodness," he breathed, eyes widening.

"Isn't she breathtaking?" Alice hummed in approval. Peter wordlessly nodded and stumbled back when Julie took a step toward him.

"Stop gawking and take Julie to the chapel. And wipe that look off your face while you're at it. I don't need Will teaching you a lesson for staring at his woman like that."

Peter blushed a deep scarlet. "Ma, I, well…" He sighed and then nodded quickly. "This way, Miss Julie."

"Thank you, Peter." Julie smiled as brightly as she could and followed him out of the boarding house.

"It's just on the other side of the square," Peter said.

They weren't the only ones on their way to the church and before long a crowd shadowed the pair as they walked along.

"It seems we are very popular," Julie joked with a nod toward the crowd behind them.

"Not we, Miss Julie." Peter shook his head. "You. They've never seen a lady like you before."

"Oh." Julie frowned but resolved to keep her spine straight. She was used catching eyes often in New York, but that was where everyone knew her and her family. Her parentage was often the topic of hushed whispers.

She bit her lip at the thought of experiencing more of the same in Gold Sky.

"It's just—" Peter swallowed hard and looked around. "I don't want to offend the sheriffs, but you're very, well, you're the prettiest woman in town."

"Oh." Julie smiled and looked down at her feet at the unexpected compliment. "Thank you, Peter."

"Mr. Barnes and Mr. Wickes are very lucky," Peter added, tucking his hands into his pockets. "But don't tell them I said that," he said with a furtive look around.

"I promise to keep it between us. Our secret." Julie winked at him, causing Peter to blush once more. When they arrived at the chapel, a pretty little white building with a shining bell in its steeple, Julie felt like she couldn't breathe.

The moment she had anticipated since Forrest had proposed marriage to her months before was finally here.

Peter rushed up the stairs ahead of her and opened the door. Julie forced away the images of a romantic and intimate wedding from her daydreams. There was no music or fanfare of any kind, but none of that mattered, because the wedding was one of her own choosing. Julie stepped into the chapel with what seemed like the entire town only a step behind.

She froze just inside the doors of the chapel. Two handsome figures at the back of the church drew her eye, one with hair like burnished gold and the other with chestnut brown. The men were dressed simply but nicely with Will having changed into a freshly pressed suit alongside Forrest. Will's hair was also washed and neatly pulled back, and Julie saw that she was right. He was handsome when he wasn't glaring, though the intensity of his gaze on her was something very similar to a glare, save for the fire it ignited in Julie's belly.

Desire, she thought, registering Will's heated look. And Forrest looked at her in the same manner, his summer sky eyes shifting to something deeper. She swallowed hard, catching sight of the pastor standing between them.

Peter hung back, slipping into a pew by the back door

47

while she continued toward Forrest and Will on numb feet. She was aware of the chapel filling behind her, of the low murmur of voices and footsteps filling the space, but she didn't dare look away from her men.

"Pleased to meet you, Pastor," Julie greeted when she stepped closer to them. The pastor gestured for her to stand in front of him, between the two grooms.

"Looks like we have a full house," he said, eyes sweeping over the rows of full pews behind her. Julie cautioned a look at the packed chapel and swallowed hard. Her nervousness must have shown because Forrest took her hand and at a sharp nod from him, so did William.

"Hi," Julie whispered to them finally, unsure of what else to say.

Forrest broke into a smile. "Hello, sweetheart."

Will cleared his throat. "Julie."

"No need to worry," Forrest told her with another easy smile. "Just getting married."

"Oh, is that all?" Julie asked, earning her a smirk from Will.

The pastor opened his Bible with a grin. "I'll just get us started then, shall I?" Julie gave him a slight nod and tightened her grip on the hands that held hers. It was a bit easier to contain her nervousness while the pastor addressed the crowd with the two men on either side of her. Though if Julie were honest, the ceremony passed her by in a blur and she only managed to refocus when her turn came to slip a gold band on each of the men's fingers with a soft but sure "I do."

She was surprised when Forrest and Will produced their own rings, one for each of her hands, both of them distinct in their own way. Forrest's was a classic choice of white gold with scrolling filigree and a carat diamond at its center. William's was smaller though no less special, a rose gold band with three little emeralds along the center.

"I now pronounce you wife and husbands. May you cherish one another for all for your days."

There was only one matter of business left and it had Julie blushing. The kiss to seal it all up with a pretty bow. She wasn't sure what she expected, perhaps a chaste peck, which Will provided easily enough, moving forward to kiss her quickly and far more gently than she had suspected.

What she hadn't anticipated was the passion of Forrest's embrace, and she nearly fainted from the force of his lips against hers, but she recovered quickly and opened her mouth to him so that he could deepen their kiss. His arms were tight around her, hands holding her firmly so that he was able to dip her without incident in front of the cheering and whooping crowd.

A second later, Forrest set her on her feet with a wink and a wave to the crowd. Julie struggled to not sag forward in a swoon, and Forrest's arm proved to be the only thing holding her up. Thankfully, Alice was there to press a vial of smelling salts into her hand.

Thank God she had brought them after all.

CHAPTER 4

"*M*rs. Wickes-Barnes?"

Julie sipped her champagne and swayed along to the band playing beneath the darkening sky. A makeshift dance floor had been put together for reception festivities, and she smiled, taking in the scene that seemed to encompass the entirety of Gold Sky's population. Unaware of the woman at her elbow, Julie took another sip of her drink, about to step forward for her own turn on the dance floor when a delicate cough caught her attention.

"Ahem." A woman cleared her throat and stepped in front of Julie with an apologetic look on her face. "Mrs. Wickes-Barnes? Er, Barnes-Wickes?" The woman appeared to be in her mid-forties, with auburn hair and too sharp eyes that put Julie on guard. There was something in the other woman's stare that resembled the always assessing and calculating look of the Four Hundred.

Julie took a hesitant step back from her and wished Forrest, or even Will, would materialize at her side. It dawned on Julie, after another moment of staring silently at the woman, that she had been addressing her. She cleared her throat and forced herself to smile.

"I apologize. I'm not quite used to the name or being called a missus just yet."

"No troubles. I can see how it could be a mite overwhelming." The woman extended her hand to Julie. "I am Mrs. O'Hare, by the way, wife of the Mayor. I thought this was the perfect opportunity to introduce myself to you, but I should have anticipated you might be a tad shocked from this whirlwind. Stepping off a train and finding yourself married to our two lawmen can be nothing but intimidating for a gently bred woman such as yourself. I hear you are to be our new school teacher?"

"I am." Julie cheered at the mention of her work as a teacher. She had studied for years to be ready for her own classroom, after all. "And I am quite eager to get to work with the children."

"What a relief to hear. Our last school teacher absconded in the middle of the night. Too hard on the poor dear, you see." Mrs. O'Hare gave a little sigh before pinning Julie with a sharp look fit for New York's finest ballrooms. "A refined lady such as you might find that it will be too much work. Your life was quite comfortable in New York, wasn't it?" She arched an eyebrow at Julie, who reluctantly nodded at the question.

"I thought so." Mrs. O'Hare sighed in an almost resigned manner. "It would be such a shame for you to travel all this way only to fail at the post."

Julie held back a frown. Mrs. O'Hare's glittering eyes and tone indicated it would not be a shame.

"I promise you, Mrs. O'Hare, I am made of sterner stuff than that," Julie replied, doing her best to keep her tone cordial. She decided that she didn't like Mrs. O'Hare one bit, but the occasion offered her little recourse. It was her wedding, and Julie didn't suppose such an event allowed for the bride to be unfriendly. On account of that, she worked to keep a happy face on despite Mrs. O'Hare's less than pleasant demeanor. In a week's time, she would take pleasure in proving the woman wrong on her assessment of Julie's ability to teach.

She returned her attention to the beautiful outdoor reception the town had put together for her, for the three of them. All of the restaurants had put forward their best food and there was no shortage of delectable bites spread over several tables. The saloon had brought out a nice selection of spirits for the townsfolk, and her cake was an amazing collection of pies and other sweet treats the church's women had baked. Lanterns and pretty flower and ribbon garlands swung in the light spring breeze from the trees overhead.

The night was charming in its simplicity, and Julie had been charmed by the kindness and welcoming nature of the citizens of Gold Sky. At least until Mrs. O'Hare had introduced herself.

"I hope that you are." She smiled at Julie, but the gesture was far too calculating to be genuine. "Lord knows you'll need to be practically iron-forged if you expect to last a month with your, ah," Mrs. O'Hare gave a little laugh, "husbands."

Gold Sky's first disapproving guest had Julie nearly rolling her eyes at the woman's attempt to make her feel awkward. She had been a debutante of the Four Hundred and a colored woman in command of respect and position in high society, where women who looked like her were only seen fit to cook and clean. Never mind the fact she had been at the focus of the society pages for months. And lastly, but most importantly, she was a *Baptiste*.

There was nothing she couldn't endure.

If Mrs. O'Hare wanted to make her feel small or embarrassed, the woman would have to get creative.

"Blessedly, the Lord has seen fit to equip each and every one of us for the journey ahead," Julie countered with a tip of her champagne flute. She cleared her throat and took a step away from the other woman. "If you'll excuse me, Mrs. O'Hare. I need to refresh my drink, but it was so good to meet you."

"Certainly. Eat, drink, and be merry, of course," Mrs. O'Hare called after her with a barely concealed smirk.

Julie gave the woman a small wave goodbye but kept her feet moving until she stood in front of the makeshift bar set up for the reception. She didn't usually indulge in more than a single glass at an event, but tonight called for multiple glasses. More glasses than she presently had hands for, if she hoped to calm her nerves at what would follow the dancing and music of the reception.

"Mrs. Barnes-Wickes!" the barkeep greeted her with a grin. He reached for her glass with a knowing smile. "A refresher?"

"Please." Julie smiled at him, thankful for a kind face after her encounter with Mrs. O'Hare. She leaned forward on the bar with a little sigh and wondered who else among the guests held the same opinion as Mrs. O'Hare.

"Name's Rhodes, ma'am," he said, placing the champagne flute back in her hand. "I must say that that I can't tell you how happy I am, how happy my whole family is, that a woman like you will be teaching in the school."

Julie paused, surprised at his comment, but she inclined her head. "Thank you, Rhodes."

Rhodes leaned toward her, elbows on the bar top. "They say your mama was," he said, and paused, looking away before his eyes darted back to meet hers, "well, that your parents met in the War." He drummed his fingers on the bar, eyes intent on Julie's face, while the meaning of his words hung in the air.

She cocked her head to the side and looked at him with new eyes. "She was," Julie said, answering Rhodes's unanswered question.

"Same as my ma."

"Really?"

"Well, she didn't marry a fancy Union soldier from a high society family, but close enough." He smiled and shrugged. "Makes me feel proud to have you teaching my girls all the way out here."

Julie smiled. "I'll do my very best by them, sir."

"Oh, don't go calling me sir. Belle of the ball does no such thing on her wedding night." He tossed a towel over his shoulder with a wink at her. He lowered his voice to a conspiratorial whisper. "And ignore Mrs. O'Hare. She's mean as a snake, always has been and always will be."

Julie snorted, taking a sip of her champagne. "I came to that very conclusion, but thank you for the warning. I'll heed it."

Rhodes chuckled at her and moved to take another guest's drink. A guest whom Julie hadn't been introduced to yet. The realization that she was well and properly alone struck her. She was unable to recognize anyone at the reception—well, save her husbands.

Where had the men disappeared to?

It didn't take her long before Forrest's large form caught her attention. He was on the dance floor and, curious about her new husband's dance skills, she made it to the edge of the crowd to see him spinning a woman with a practiced hand. Julie sipped at her champagne and forced down the spike of jealousy stirring in her at the sight of Forrest dancing with another woman.

It was a celebration, which called for dancing. A dance meant nothing, not when he'd married her only an hour before.

Although...what kind of reception had the groom dancing with anyone but the bride?

Julie almost groaned at herself the moment she entertained the thought. She was not the type of woman who was prone to jealousy. She was level-headed, not one to fly into dramatics, but here she was nursing a glass of champagne while she contemplated how strong a force it would take to send the woman in Forrest's arms off the dance floor. Who was she turning into

Perhaps it was the drink, not that it mattered. She had no intention of putting a pause on her imbibing, at least not until she was calmer. A sip later, Julie's cheeks had warmed pleasantly enough and she was eyeing the bar when Forrest appeared in front of her.

He gave her a deep bow. "May I have the pleasure of this dance, wife?" he asked, extending a hand toward her.

Julie blushed when she saw the townsfolk all around them watching with interest. She almost bolted from her new husband, but the scrutiny of so many Gold Sky citizens forced her to stand her ground. If she couldn't manage a single dance with Forrest, how was she going to survive more intimate quarters? Steeling herself, Julie closed her eyes and tossed back the remainder of her champagne with a long swallow.

"Let's, husband," she answered feeling bolder from the champagne in her belly, and slipped her hand into

Forrest's. She turned and handed her empty glass off to the first person who offered to take it with a murmur of thanks.

Forrest laughed as he led her onto the dance floor. Julie frowned and gave him a pointed look. "What's so funny?" she asked with an indignant sniff.

"I don't think I've seen anyone drink that fast since the war."

"A little liquid courage never hurt anyone," Julie replied with a smile.

"And why, little wife, would you need liquid courage to dance with one of your husbands?" he asked, leading her through the familiar steps of the waltz.

Julie laughed at the question. "For the reason that I have two husbands. I feel that one would be intimidating enough, but two?" She shook her head and blew out a long sigh that had Forrest chuckling. "I don't know how I'll survive it."

Forrest leaned close, lips grazing her ear. "Don't worry, darling. We'll be gentle." He gave her a squeeze that promised more and raised her temperature to downright feverish.

She swallowed hard but said nothing, her mind already skipping ahead to what Forrest's words meant for her as a new bride. Daring to glance up at him, she saw he regarded her with the same intensity as when she had first entered the chapel. His eyes skirted along the low neckline of her dress as they continued to dance. At the song's end Forrest pulled her close to him.

"I think it's almost time we retire for the night."

"Oh," Julie breathed. Her hands were still in his and he raised her hand to his lips, pressing a kiss there.

"One more dance is in order. It would be a shame for

more people not to see what a beautiful little bird you are in this dress."

Julie blushed at his praise. "You like the dress?"

Forrest nodded. "Very much, Julie. But you would be beautiful even without it."

"Thank you," Julie replied, feeling suddenly shy despite Forrest's scintillating promise to be gentle with her—well, that he and Will would be. She turned her flushed face away, lest her imagination serve to scandalize her in the middle of the dance floor any further, when she noticed Will walking onto the dance floor. A pretty blonde woman in a richly appointed dress was on his arm, and Julie bit her lip in annoyance at the still too sharp teeth of a certain green-eyed monster trying to claw its way out of her.

God, she was going to exhaust herself if she kept this behavior up! Perhaps the two glasses of champagne hadn't been the best of her ideas.

Forrest noticed her frown and tugged her closer to him. "No frowns tonight."

Julie gave him an embarrassed look at his keen observation. "I..." She looked back toward where Will guided his partner through the dance, a happy grin on his lips. That single smile stung far more than she wanted to let on. Though it was their shared wedding day, Will hadn't looked at Julie with half as much mirth in his eyes.

"Who is she?" Julie finally settled on asking.

Forrest shrugged. "Rosemary Stanton," he said, as if that explained anything. Julie arched an eyebrow at him for further explanation.

"She does a little of this, and a little of that. Writes for the newspaper," Forrest continued on.

Julie would have said more but when her eyes unexpectedly locked with Will's she abruptly turned her eyes back to Forrest. If he noticed, he said nothing, a mercy Julie was thankful for. They remained in comfortable silence until the band neared the end of their set, and he leaned close to whisper in her ear, "It's time to go home, darlin'."

"Really?" Julie asked in surprise. She scanned the still lively crowd with a frown. The citizens of Gold Sky didn't show any signs of winding down the celebration. "It's still early yet, Forrest. Wouldn't it be improper to leave before we see to the reception's end? Why we still ha—"

"I think they'll excuse a hasty departure on our wedding night."

Julie licked her lips. "Right."

Once the band finished playing Forrest wasted no time in slipping his hand in hers and leading them off the dance floor. She almost pulled back when she saw he made his way to where Will stood with Rosemary. The way the two were positioned, their bodies just a tad too close, heads bent in conversation, had Julie feeling like they were about to ruin an intimate moment, but Forrest paid it no mind and continued forward.

"Goodnight, Rosemary. Thank you for the dance." Will gave a slight nod of his head to the blonde.

Rosemary winked and reached a hand out to squeeze his arm. "Of course, what kind of lady wouldn't dance with you?"

Julie bristled. Though Rosemary had her back to her, the comment seemed directed at her and her first instinct was to fire off a sharp remark. Inhaling, Julie worked to calm herself. There was no sense in feeding any rumors with erratic behavior. She was just sensitive today from all of the excitement of the wedding. And the excruciating exercise of vibration torture via completing a month-long train ride. Then there was her uncustomary alcoholic consumption. Not to mention, there was the matter of her wedding night to attend to—a wedding night that featured two husbands.

Yes, staying silent until she was more in control of herself was the best course of action.

Will shrugged. "I can count a few who might make a run for it."

"Well, I'm not one of them," Rosemary said, taking a step far too close to Will for Julie's liking. She stiffened at the sight of it and Forrest cleared his throat, announcing their arrival to the couple.

Rosemary sprang back from Will and gave Julie a contrite look. "Mrs. Wickes-Barnes, so good to meet you. Finally."

Julie hummed a greeting to the woman but the champagne she'd drunk sang through her veins. Gossip or not, she suddenly didn't care too much about being polite to the blonde woman. She was lucky Julie was even choosing to keep her mouth shut. Julie leaned against Forrest's side and the man caught her with a chuckle.

"Rosemary," Forrest greeted her and then looked to Will. "I think it's time we took her home."

"We don't have to," Julie said, forcing herself to stand taller. "If you'd like to stay, that is," she added, looking at Will, trying to gauge his response. She didn't miss how Rosemary also looked to him for his reaction.

Why did the woman care so much about what Will thought? Why had he deigned to dance with Rosemary when he hadn't so much as touched Julie after their wedding kiss?

"Been waitin' on you to call it," Will replied gruffly.

And though his features no longer looked relaxed, or even held a hint of the smile he'd given Rosemary, he stepped close to Julie and slipped an arm around her waist. "Goodnight, Rosemary. Thank you for coming." He turned to Julie. "Come on, I'll put you in the wagon while Forrest makes our goodbyes," he said.

Julie nodded with a yawn, a glow of pleasure warming her better than the champagne had at the pinched look their sudden departure put on Rosemary's face.

"Goodnight!" she called with a cheery wave on her way to the wagon with Will. She snuck a look at him and wondered why he was the one putting her in the wagon and not Forrest. Before long, they were in front of their wagon and Will lifted her to her seat.

"God, woman, where are you in all this lace?" he huffed, making sure to get the entirety of her train safely up on the bench next to her.

"It's the height of fashion," she informed him primly.

Will snorted, still shoving swaths of silk satin up next to her. "Seems like a waste."

Julie stiffened at his casual comment and looked down at her hands, even though she knew he couldn't see the hurt in her eyes, not with the near darkness they were in, relieved only by the bright light of the moon.

Noticing that she'd gone still, Will sighed. "I didn't mean—Julie, you looked beautiful today."

"Thank you," she said, her voice small. She kept her eyes on her lap and, working to keep her voice even, began to ask about Forrest when Will spoke.

"Darlin'," he tried, one of his hands coming to rest over both of hers, which were clasped in her lap. "I'm sorry. Sometimes I speak before I think. Y-you were the most beautiful thing I've ever seen in my life today." He picked up a fistful of her skirt and gave it a gentle shake. "This wasn't a waste. Not an inch of it." His voice was low and husky. She could hear his sincerity, and she swallowed hard at the raw emotion she heard.

"Will," she whispered, touched at his words. She opened her mouth to say more but Will surprised her when he surged forward and caught her lips in a kiss. For a moment, Julie didn't move, far too stunned by the kiss to think, but then, under his adept and coaxing lips, she relaxed. A little moan caught in her throat, her mouth finally parting under Will's ministrations.

Their kiss deepened, his hands tightening on her as he explored her mouth. When Julie reached out to run her fingers through his hair, he pulled back to swing himself up beside her on the wooden bench of the wagon. He pulled her into his lap with eager hands and kissed her again once she was settled against this chest. The kisses were a soothing balm to the early sting of his dance with Rosemary, and were a step in the right direction at looking past his inattention.

"So sweet," he whispered against her lips. The soft tone in his voice prompted Julie to whimper and wiggle in his lap in search of more contact. She could feel the firm planes of his body despite the layers of lace and silk between them. Her corset, already a troublesome garment, was suddenly more constraining than normal and she cursed the item's designer. Her fingers slid down to brush against the buttons of Will's shirt, which prompted her to decide she also hated buttons. Damn the little monsters for keeping her husband's skin from her touch during their little rendezvous.

When Will's fingertips brushed the top of her neckline she squirmed. All of this was new and heady to her, the passionate kisses, the heated touches and breathy gasps. She was frantic to feel his calloused fingers on her body in far more intimate places. Her friends at finishing school and again at Vassar had told her numerous stories about their stolen moments and trysts with their beaus, but until this moment Julie had never been in such a scandalous or compromising position in her life.

Yet, how compromising was her perch in Will's lap when they had married not an hour before? Wasn't this how they were intended to enjoy the other's body? After his perceived coldness during the reception, Julie found the closeness soothed her nerves. She wondered suddenly if that was Will's intention, but Julie barely had time to consider the fleeting thought before a sudden cough broke the frenzied embrace the pair had been locked in.

Will lifted his head up with deliberate slowness. "Forrest," he grunted out, sounding annoyed, though his hands were still gentle on Julie's sides.

"Should have known I would come back to this," Forrest's voice floated to them from the dark. Julie pushed at her hair, which had started to come loose from the pins Alice had used to secure her curls.

"I-I," she stammered, already pushing herself off of Will's lap, "I'm sorry. I didn't mean to—"

"What? Didn't mean to enjoy a moment with your husband?" Forrest asked, swinging himself up on the bench next to them. Now that he was closer to her, Julie could see his features in the moonlight. And there wasn't one thing about him that didn't scream arousal. He bit his lip before darting forward to press a kiss to her lips. "Nothing wrong with what you were doing, Julie."

She gave him a quick nod, breathless at being kissed by not one but two men in the span of as many minutes.

Before tonight her romantic history had consisted of nothing more than a few rides in a caleche to park outings and socials. There had been a picnic here and there but always with a chaperone, never alone, and not once had Julie allowed any of the gentlemen to take liberties. So small was their social circle that Julie knew better than to fall for the fanciful words men spewed in order for a few moments of pleasure. She almost laughed at the thought, because before now, there had hardly been a handful of words spoken between them other than 'I do.'

Though Julie supposed in the grand scheme of things, those two simple words were the ones that mattered the most.

Julie bit her lip with a smile. "I'm beginning to see that," she said quietly. Will relaxed where he'd been sitting stiffly next to her and touched her cheek.

"Been trying not to touch you all night, Jules," he said, fingertips just grazing her skin. "Didn't mean to lose control like that. I'm sorry."

"Don't apologize. I quite liked it," Julie told him. At her reply, Forest husked out a laugh while Will made a noise Julie couldn't quite interpret.

Forrest made short work of untying the reins of the horses, and as he worked he said, "Let's get her home before you both drive me to undo all the good work our little reception did. Plenty of time to get acquainted at home."

"All right. I'll go ahead. Get the fires lit," Will replied, already moving from the bench, but a gentle touch from Julie stopped him. She leaned close to him and caught his face between her hands.

"I liked it when you called me Jules," she said. Then before he could say anything she kissed him, slow and clumsy from her lack of experience, but Will didn't seem to mind it and returned her kiss. When they parted Forrest groaned, hands tight on the reins of the horses.

"Going to be the death of me, the pair of you," he muttered.

"Don't act like you won't love every second of it," Will shot back before he jumped from the wagon and disappeared into the darkness. Forrest made a sound in his throat in answer, but worked on getting the wagon ready for their journey home.

Julie blushed, settling back into her seat. She knew that her marriage was unconventional. That more than a fair share of her acquaintances in New York wouldn't understand, that most likely her family wouldn't understand why she had chosen to do it.

But in that moment, she found she didn't care. The dynamic that had begun to form between them felt right. And that was only after a few hours of knowing each other. What would her feelings be toward them in a few days? What about in a few weeks, or even a few years?

Forrest's arm settling over her shoulders and pulling her close to him drew her from her thoughts, and she gratefully leaned against his muscular frame for the ride home. The gentle rocking of the wagon had begun to lull her into a doze when she spotted bright lights ahead of them in the darkness.

"Is that the ranch?" she asked, sitting up.

"Sure is. I see Will wanted to impress you," Forrest replied with a laugh. "Thing is never that lit up all at once."

"It's beautiful," Julie breathed. As they approached she saw that Will had made sure every window was blazing with light. The house was two stories and massive, judging from the number of windows that shone in the darkness. When the wagon pulled up she could make out the dim shapes of several buildings in the distance. Most likely a barn and storehouses, but her attention went to the main house's wrap-around porch. The grand windows that lined the sitting area and dining room were stunning, and she adored the porch swing that moved in the night breeze.

"I love it," Julie exclaimed, practically clapping her hands. Forrest looked pleased at her words and gave her a proud look.

"Wanted our wife—well, you," he said, "to be comfortable. There's plenty of room for children, too."

"How many bedrooms is plenty of room?" Julie asked when he handed her down from the wagon.

"Six."

Julie laughed nervously. "Six?"

Forrest shrugged. "Best to plan for all sorts of things. Never know when we'll need the rooms. There's a sitting room, formal parlor, dining room, library, nice big kitchen, and a wine cellar." He opened the front door, a massive mahogany door inset with colored glass that reminded her of the way sunlight shone when it hit cut glass just so.

"This is beautiful." Julie paused and touched her fingers to pieces of turquoise and purple glass. "Where did you get it from?"

"I made it," Forrest replied, holding the door open.

Julie gaped. "You made this?"

"I did. For you," Forrest added, making Julie blush.

"It's lovely," Julie told him. She stepped into the house and was greeted with a beautiful foyer. There were two doorways off the side of it that led to a dining room and sitting room, respectively. The walls were covered in gorgeous cream wallpaper and the dark wood floors shone with a high polish that even her mother would envy.

"I can give you a tour now, or we can wait, if you like."

Julie considered Forrest's words carefully before she answered. "A tour tomorrow morning would be lovely."

"Are you sure?" he asked her, blue eyes dark.

Julie understood the unspoken meaning in his question and nodded, moving toward the staircase in front of her. "The bedroom is, ah, upstairs?"

"It is." Forrest was beside her instantly, a gentle hand on the small of her back. He cleared his throat as they slowly walked up the stairs. "Would you like your own room tonight? We have one made up for you... or would you like to go ours?"

The prospect of spending a night with both men had her short of breath, but there was never a better time than the present to face down one's fears, so she gave him a nervous smile.

"I would very much like to spend the night in our bedroom." She paused and glanced down the hallway from where they were now standing at the top of the stairs. How exactly were the sleeping arrangements expected to work out? Would they share a bed? Or perhaps they had more than one bed? More than one room? Did they mean to alternate with the days of the week?

It was enough to make her head spin. Why hadn't she given a single thought to the logistical side of her marriage when she had so blithely said yes months ago?!

"When you say ours, what do you mean?" she asked

hesitantly, giving voice to the questions swirling through her mind.

Forrest paused a beat before he answered her. "I mean ours, as in all three of us."

A relieved sigh escaped her lips and she pressed a hand to her chest. "Oh thank heavens." His answer was by far the simplest for Julie to deal with.

Forrest raised an eyebrow. "Thank heavens? We were worried we might offend you with that little piece of information."

"Why?"

"Not something a young lady like you is accustomed to."

Julie shrugged, following him down the hallway, plush maroon carpeting beneath their feet muffling their steps. "I'm not the usual young lady."

"So I'm finding," Forrest told her. He opened a door at the end of the hallway and ushered her into a spacious room with high ceilings, crown molding, and expansive windows along one side of the room for plenty of light. A fireplace crackled at one end of the room, giving the space a cozy feel. Julie instantly loved the room, but what caught her attention the most was the massive bed opposite the fireplace. It was unlike any bed she had seen before. The frame was an elegant four-poster affair with lovely scrolling woodwork covering nearly every inch of it.

She would have to examine it the next day to take in the particulars of the work, but right now her focus was on the bed itself. A cream down-filled comforter covered a mattress that had to be of custom dimensions, and an untold amount of pillows rested at the head of it. Julie grinned, remembering the pillows on the wagon bench.

The thought of Will and Forrest practically hoarding the town's supply of pillows in anticipation of her arrival made her giggle.

"What's got you so tickled?" Will's voice came from behind her. Julie whirled around to see him entering the room, his gray eyes softer now than they had been all day, and they rendered her speechless.

"I—well, pillows," she spluttered, flinging a hand at the excess of down feathers on the bed.

He nodded at her and closed the door with a soft click behind him. "Forrest was worried you wouldn't be comfortable without 'em."

"I see." Julie clasped her hands in front of her, unsure of what to do. Her nervous gaze bounced between the two men and she looked down at her feet, unsure of what to do next. "Ah, what—what do we do now?"

Both men spoke at once, their words tumbling over one another.

"Whatever you like," Will said.

"You tell us," Forrest told her.

Julie smiled at their effort to put her at ease. From their honest and open faces she could tell they meant every word. "I think..." She bit her lip and raised her eyes to meet theirs, the champagne still lending her courage. "I'm sorry," she sighed, causing both men to stand up straighter, their mouths opening, she knew, to give her more reassuring platitudes, but she held up a hand.

Both men fell silent at the gesture and Julie found she liked having husbands who listened.

"I meant to say that I know I want to have a proper wedding night, not, I think. Never offer a half-truth of an answer when a firm response is the best response," Julie said, rattling off a lesson from Lady Pim by heart. She almost groaned aloud at herself but both men gave her approving nods.

"Tell us when to stop, little bird," Forrest said, moving toward her. Will licked his lips but said nothing. Julie could see they held themselves back and she squared her shoulders, resolving to dissuade her husbands from treating her with kid gloves. The marriage was her choice and her request for a wedding night was her decision.

Julie wanted every second of this night, and she intended to experience it to the fullest.

Clearing her throat, she gave her husbands a smile she hoped was sultry. She'd never tried her hand at seduction, and she found herself woefully unprepared.

First thing first, she was going to have to adjust her reading to adequately encompass how a woman was meant to employ her wiles in the pursuit of sexual satisfaction. By the heated look in her husbands' eyes, Julie estimated the attempt a success. There was a small stirring of power at being able to elicit such a response from the two men, and the boon spurred her forward with newfound confidence.

Julie discarded her gloves, a move that neither men missed, their eyes tracking the movement as she let the scraps of fabric fall to the floor. Slowly and with an exaggerated sway in her hips, Julie walked forward until she stood inches in front of them. She turned her back to her husbands and then with a final fortifying breath, looked over her shoulder at her husbands.

"I'll need help getting out of my things, please."

CHAPTER 5

*J*ulie's soft request turned the room into a flurry of activity as the men sprang into action. She blinked, finding herself swept up against Forrest before he placed her on the bed. Will shoved a veritable mountain of pillows onto the floor. Forrest knelt in front of her, already pushing her skirts up to begin working on unfastening her boots. Will cracked his knuckles and gazed at her still pinned-up curls as if they were a complicated piece of machinery. She stifled a laugh when he reached forward and eased the first pin out. The release of pressure against her scalp earned him an appreciative sigh, which made both men freeze.

Forrest's hand on her ankle tightened as he slipped the first boot from her foot. "Tonight is gonna be full of pretty sounds like that."

Julie opened her eyes, which had drifted shut at the gentle touch of Will's hands in her hair. "What?" she asked, opening her eyes to see him looking up at her.

Forrest took off her other boot and set them both aside.

His hands were warm as he touched her ankles, fingertips dragging up her stockinged legs. The touch made Julie shiver, a reaction that had him smiling up at her.

"That little sigh you just made," he said, hands already up by her knees, arms fully under the material of her skirt, "was like music to me."

"Us," Will interjected, pulling out another pin. He ran his fingers through the lock of hair that it had released and pulled the few remaining pins out. The flowers that had been in her hair fell around her shoulders. "That sigh was like music to us."

Forrest gave the other man a pleased look. "I like the sound of that. Us."

Julie leaned back on her hands, trying to keep her bearings, but it was proving difficult with Forrest on his knees and looking at her like she was a goddess come to life. Then there was Will, so attentive to her, his fingers combing through her hair, lifting a bloom to her nose for her to sniff, and pressing feather light kisses up the side of her neck.

If she wasn't careful she'd come undone before they even got her shift off of her.

Nothing in all of her novel reading had prepared her for this. Those more erotic moments of romances always seemed to cut out just before the scene got interesting. Lady Pim was an absolute waste on the matter. As such, Julie was in uncharted waters.

"Tonight is going to be all about you, Jules," Will told her, already working on the buttons at the back of her dress.

"I think that would be fine," Julie replied, her breath starting to come faster now that Forrest's head had vanished beneath her skirts. She felt his lips against her knee while his hands stroked her thighs.

"Just fine?" Will leaned over her shoulder to look at her, smirking. Julie almost rolled her eyes at him—almost, because Forrest's tongue joined his lips against her skin. She gasped, her back arching at the unexpected touch, and Will ran his hands down her sides. "Easy. Relax," he whispered to her in a tone that she was very nearly sure he could have used on a spooked horse. She might have been indignant at the realization, if his tone hadn't been so effective.

He eased her dress further down and she knew he'd unbuttoned it fully. "Let her up, Forrest."

A muffled groan sounded before Forrest emerged from beneath her skirts. His hair was rumpled and his eyes shone brightly in the soft lighting of the room. The sight was enough to make Julie whimper. She'd never imagined that such a simple sight could ignite a fire in her, but here she was, desperate to touch and be touched.

Forrest grinned at the sound and leaned forward, one hand on either side of her on the bed. "My little wife is such a proper lady," he murmured before he kissed her, all pretense of civility stripped from the embrace, and Julie found herself yielding to Forrest's hungry mouth.

Will worked her dress down her arms while Forrest kissed her. The blond pulled her up against him to help Will work her dress free. Julie tried to help with her bustle ties but Will nudged her hands away with a chuckle near her ear.

"Know my way around a lady's underthings, Jules."

She flushed at his words but nodded. Forrest gave her a wicked grin before slanting his mouth against hers once again. He licked against the seam of her lips, asking for entrance, and Julie was only too happy to oblige. She felt Will loosening her corset strings with more than nimble fingers. The thought of how many women he would have to undress to achieve the familiarity his hands currently displayed stirred an uncomfortable and unwelcome feeling in the pit of her stomach. How many before Forrest had learned to kiss and tease as he had?

The torturing thoughts lasted for only a second until Forrest's hand cupped her breast and Julie wrestled her mind free. This was not the time for irrational jealousy. Not when there was irrational, and infinitely more pleasing, lust to indulge.

She was reaping the benefits of their skilled hands and mouths. It wasn't fair, nor was it in step with her upbringing and education to succumb to jealous thoughts for actions taken before either man had known her. Julie startled when she realized her corset had been removed and she was now down to her shift and drawers. She blamed her overactive mind with its slew of chattering thoughts for catching her unaware of both men's efforts to disrobe her.

"Most beautiful woman I've ever seen," Forrest moaned against her neck. He pulled back to look at her with unblinking blue eyes. "Lay back, darlin'. Wanna see you all laid out."

Not trusting herself to speak, Julie didn't say a word, but went pliant in the men's hands as they guided her back onto the mattress between them. She looked up at them as she settled on her back and took in a deep breath when she mulled over the fact that these men were now her husbands. The thought filled her with excitement, lust, butterflies or whatever she supposed made her stomach flutter. It was a heady sensation and she wondered if she would ever be used to it.

"You're both still dressed," she said, surprising herself.

"Because tonight is about you," Will replied with a pointed look.

"I still want to see you," Julie shot back, her hips wiggling beneath Forrest's determined hands. He drew down her drawers, not the least bit concerned with the glaring match Julie and Will had engaged in.

"Jules, this ain't about that," Will told her, crossing his arms.

Forrest pressed a kiss against her now naked thigh, his eyes darting between Julie and Will. He reached for her shift and hummed in approval when Julie let him pull it off her. She was far too focused on arguing with Will to notice, which suited his plans just fine.

Julie lifted her arms to help Forrest slip off her shift. "Isn't about what?" When Will didn't answer she sighed and sat up. "Isn't about what, Will? I thought you said tonight was about me? About what I wanted?"

Will didn't answer her but made a low groan in his throat. "You work fast," he said, casting a sidelong look at Forrest, who smirked from his perch on the side of the bed.

Julie stifled a gasp and blushed when she realized the men stared at her now naked body, and she crossed her arms over her chest and drew her legs up to achieve a modicum of modesty. She had never been anywhere near naked in the company of a man, much less two, and two who were fully clothed at that.

"Seemed the best use of time while you two bickered," Forrest muttered, standing from the bed and shedding his suit jacket. He nodded at Will. "Get undressed."

74

Will glared at Forrest, who had started undoing his tie. "Tonight is about her."

"And can't you see this is trying for her?" Forrest tossed his tie on top of his jacket, already working on unbuttoning his dress shirt. "Poor little bird is intimidated. Besides, we said whatever she wanted us to do, we would do, and right now that means getting undressed."

Will scoffed. "She isn't intimidated—" He broke off when he caught sight of Julie edging up a corner of the comforter to cover herself. "Damn it."

"Language," Forrest admonished. Will glared at him but said nothing as he got up and joined Forrest in undressing. Within minutes both men were as naked as she was and Julie felt a little less nervous about her current state of nakedness.

"Better?" Forrest asked her. Julie gave him a quick nod and let him pull the comforter from her hand. "Never have seen a more beautiful sight in my life," he said, sliding up onto the mattress next to her. His blue eyes moved over her body almost feverishly. He looked at her like she was the ending and beginning of everything that mattered, and Julie ducked her head from the attention.

"Thank you," she whispered, eyes on the soft sheets next to her. Forrest's gentle fingers on her chin tilted her head back to look at him.

"Thank you, little bird. You don't know what an honor you did the both of us today. Made us the happiest men in the territory." He held a hand out to Will, drawing him close to them. Julie's breath caught in her throat when she felt Will press up against her other side, his hand linked with Forrest's.

"Best day of my life," Will murmured. He pressed his lips against her shoulder while lowering his and Forrest's clasped hands to her hip. Their fingers flexed against her bare skin, causing her to let out a whimper. What she wanted, she didn't know. Her mind was racing now, heartbeat too fast for her liking, and she squirmed between the men.

"Shh, shh." Forrest nuzzled against Julie's collarbone. He licked his way up to her lips again. "All we are going to do is make sure you feel as lovely as you look."

Julie nodded, laying back down under the hands of her husbands, who were pushing her back against the bed. "I —all right." She sighed at herself, wishing for the moment of bravery she'd had before to resurface. She wanted this, but it was hard to express it to her husbands.

Will shot her a raking look while he settled himself between her legs. Julie nearly came undone at the sight of the man, hair hanging to his broad shoulders, poised between her legs and looking at her as if she were a feast. Forrest pressed himself up against her with a hand lazily running up and down her side, his big warm hands pausing to pet or pinch her in his course along her flesh. Julie's fingers gripped at the sheets underneath her while she tried to manage her body's response to both men's naked bodies.

She had, like her classmates and girlhood friends, talked in secret about what men's bodies looked like. She had enthusiastically studied the human figure in her art classes, with particular attention to the male models, and she had on occasion participated in a round of reverent staring while watching the men of the nearby university playing rugby.

However, she had not anticipated what it would be like to be confronted so directly by so much maleness. There was nowhere for her to look, move, or simply exist without the men dominating the experience. Both were virile, handsome, and in possession of bodies honed by physical labor and long hours in the saddle.

And then there was the matter of their manhood, which in her non-existent experience seemed above average, at least according to what Sally Porter and Jessica Ramsey had told her in secret about their rendezvous with their beaus. Long, thick, and at attention... Julie felt a thrill, wondering what it would be like to have them inside of her.

Would they make love to her one after another? Would there ever be a time that they would both want her at the same time? She bit her lip at the thoughts, which were far racier than she had ever entertained before tonight.

What was happening to her and her overly anxious mind?

"I feel wanton," Julie confessed, her eyes squeezing shut when Will hooked his hands under her thighs and pulled her body toward his. She let out a pained groan when she felt the ghost of his warm breath over her the tops of her thighs.

"Not wanton if it's your husband," Forrest told her matter-of-factly. He kissed her shoulder and smiled at her when she slowly opened her eyes to meet his gaze. "Let us make you feel good, little bird."

Julie nodded. "I want you to," she whispered. "I want you. Please."

Will let out a hum of satisfaction, pressing kisses gently against her skin. He had kissed a course across her left thigh toward that pulsing place at the apex. His tongue joined his lips and it was all Julie could do not to sob from frustration. She needed more of him; she needed friction, pressure, all of it. She wiggled, trying to get her hips where she needed, but his hands came up to hold her down firmly by her hip bones.

"Patience," Will rumbled against her, his breath hot against her core.

"Oh God," she moaned, eyes squeezing shut once again when she felt the first brush of Will's lips. "Will!" She let out a short cry of pleasure.

Will's hands tightened on her, but he said nothing. His mouth kissed and tongue licked at her, devouring her in a way that she hadn't known possible. Julie's panting moans filled the room as Forrest spoke sweet nothings into her ear. She practically sobbed when Will's tongue and lips closed around that bud of pleasure. His fingers joined in his ministrations, a finger slipping inside of her, making her squirm.

"So pretty like this," Forrest whispered. He kissed her neck gently and ran his fingers through her curly hair. Julie turned her face into his shoulder, his body her anchor. His presence grounded her while her body climbed higher and higher to a place that she hadn't known existed until now.

"Will!" she cried out, fingers clutching at the sheets beneath her. Forrest reached down and moved one of her hands into Will's hair. Under the gentle guidance of Forrest she gave over to the side of her that wanted and needed more from this man. Her fingers tangled in his hair as she rode a wave of ecstasy so intense that at its zenith she was left screaming Will's name until her cries turned hoarse.

"Will, Will, Will," Julie sobbed, her back still arched off the bed, the heels of her feet digging into his back from where he had thrown her legs over his shoulders.

"Oh, I-I, oh, please." Julie knew that wasn't making any

sense, but she didn't have it in her to care. Nor did she have it in her to fight the tears that spilled down her cheeks. If this was what a wedding night was like, then she finally understood why so many of her friends rushed toward marriage with all the force of cannon fire.

It was exquisite.

"Oh, sweetheart," Forrest sighed, his hands coming to her shoulders. He pushed down, fingers gently squeezing and rubbing into her shoulders. The calming action helped bring Julie back to herself, though she still gasped for breath when she did.

Julie looked down up at Will, who was on his knees, still between her legs. He had a hand on either side of her and was leaning over her with a concerned look on his face.

"Are you all right?" he asked. She couldn't help the laughter that bubbled up and escaped from her at his question.

"I feel like I just experienced what all the spiritualists say happen when they make contact with a spirit," she croaked. Forrest tossed back his head and laughed.

Will cracked a smile at her. He reached down and touched her cheek gently. "You were beautiful."

"So were you," Julie replied, earning her another laugh and tender look from Will. Taking a shaky breath, Julie pushed herself up and reached for Will. She might be inexperienced in the ways of sex between man and wife, or in this case, men and their wife, but she knew that men had needs.

Her mother had made sure she understood exactly what she had agreed to when she had accepted Forrest's proposal. Of course, her mother hadn't quite told her how enjoyable the experience of fulfilling her wifely duties could be, and if she could even give Will and Forrest half of what she had been gifted, she was eager to do so. Leaning close to him, she reached for that hard length of flesh standing at full attention, but Will shook his head with a grunt and drew away from her touch.

"Can I hold you?" Forrest asked her, kissing her cheek when she frowned at Forrest.

Julie sighed and made to reach for Will again. "But I jus—"

"Tonight was about your pleasure," Will said, cutting her off. He settled down next to her on the bed. "Let Forrest hold you."

Julie nodded and leaned back into Forrest's arms. He tucked her back snugly up against his chest. "Get some rest, little bird."

She wanted to protest that she wasn't tired but couldn't manage to get the words out as a wave of exhaustion overtook her. It seemed her trip and the day's whirlwind of activities had caught up to her. The aftershocks of her orgasm, mingled with the champagne she had drunk at the reception, ensured that Julie relaxed into Forrest's embrace with a sigh.

Will made sure to stoke the fire before he climbed up into the bed beside her, drawing the comforter over the three of them. Julie gave a sleepy smile when Will slipped an arm over her body as well, his shoulder sliding beneath her cheek.

It was cozy between her men. Their bodies were far warmer than hers, and she didn't see being cold in her future so long as they were in her bed. Forrest kissed her temple before he closed his eyes, and Will surprised her when he leaned close to her ear and whispered so softly that she almost thought she imagined it.

"Already love you."

Julie started at that, her brow furrowing as she searched for the right words. She wanted to tell him that she was happy, that she felt the same for him and Forrest, but her sleep-addled brain made it difficult.

"I—" she murmured sleepily but Will ran his hand and gently up her side and tucked the comforter around her chin.

"Shh, sleep, Jules."

With a tired sigh, Julie nodded and buried her nose against Will's collarbone. Sleep finally swept over her. Never in her wildest dreams had she anticipated being sandwiched between two men on her wedding night, but she wouldn't trade this for the world.

This felt right.

CHAPTER 6

*W*hen Julie awoke, it was to an empty bed. She sat up and frowned at her unfamiliar surroundings. The once cozy and thoughtful room wasn't quite as intimate as Julie remembered when she had fallen asleep between her husbands the night before. She bit her lip, wondering where they had gone so early, or perhaps not so early.

The sunlight streamed into the room, making Julie wonder exactly how late she had slept in. She had always been an early riser, but the previous day and night had more than worn her out.

Padding to the window, Julie winced, seeing where the sun was in the sky. It was high, not quite noon but very nearly.

Good Lord.

No wonder they had left her sleeping, she thought. It was only logical that her husbands, the only lawmen for miles, needed to attend to their civic duties in Gold Sky while she continued to sleep. They had done her a kindness by letting her rest, she told herself, trying not to feel stung at waking alone.

Glancing around the room, she was grateful to see that her trunks had been brought up to the bedroom and now rested at the foot of the bed. She paused, seeing that her wedding dress and undergarments had been folded and put in the chair by the window. The attention they had paid to her things dulled the ache of waking on her own. But no matter how she tried to tell herself it was all right, there was a sharpness in her chest.

Yes, as a girl, she had read romance novels by the bookcase, and yes, that had created a rather picturesque idea of the intimacies of marriage. But that had been when she was a mere girl, enthralled by the romance story of her parents' love.

She was a woman now, and this was...well, this was what she supposed everyday life was like. Yet for all that, and all the unknowns of what this morning would bring, Julie had never dreamed it would bring an otherwise empty bed.

"You must get a hold of yourself," Julie whispered. There was a reason her husbands were absent. She knew it. There was no sense in turning to dramatics.

At least not yet, anyhow.

Julie dressed and opted for a simple plait for her curly hair, which was still a bit wild from the previous night's festivities. At the thought of what had happened in the bedroom, she blushed. The memory warmed her from the inside out, which at least served to push back the chill left by her husbands' absence.

Once she was dressed and presentable, Julie made her way out of the bedroom and set off for the stairs. She was grateful when she found them without any problem, but she hesitated, looking back at an open door she had passed.

She stepped closer to the open doorway and peeked in to see the bones of the library Forrest had told her about. Five empty bookcases sat in a group by the door, but not much else save for a writing desk, which puzzled her.

If her husbands were in possession of the land and wealth they spoke of, why was the house, beautiful as it was, so empty?

Further exploration revealed several other bedrooms, all of which were empty save for a bed or table here and there.

Feeling much like the heroine of *La Belle et Bete*, she hesitated, unsure if she should keep looking. Thankfully, the faint smell of cooking caught her attention and she abandoned her route for the kitchen. She wasn't alone in the house, and there was food to be had. She could continue her wanderings after breakfast.

When Julie hit the bottom of the stairs, she heard the bang of a skillet against a stove, accompanied by a muffled curse. Letting her nose lead her, she wandered through a formal dining room and pushed open the door to the kitchen. The sight that greeted her made her clap a hand to her mouth to stifle a laugh.

The kitchen looked like the scene of a small war. It was, in a word, chaos. Numerous bowls and utensils lay scattered along nearly every available surface. A smashed egg smeared the side of one cupboard, a real feat, and a fine sprinkling of flour covered the table at the center of the room. The flour tracked along the soapstone counters that butted up to the large iron stove Forrest currently hunched over.

How the flour had managed to cover everything, Julie

didn't know. The only clean items were an almost ready silver tray that held a pitcher of orange juice, silverware, and an empty plate. She grinned, watching Forrest angle the skillet in his hand as he worked on whatever was meant to fill said empty plate. Julie cleared her throat, causing Forrest to jump.

"Julie!" He looked surprised to see her and gave her a sheepish smile. "You weren't supposed to be up yet." His blond hair was anything but neat and looked like he had been running his hands through it.

"I'm not? It looks to be past ten," Julie replied, walking into the kitchen to survey the other bits and bobs scattered around Forrest.

"Just after," Forrest replied, finally turning toward the plate with the skillet. He held a spatula in the other hand, and Julie watched as he slid his creation onto the plate.

"Crepes?" she asked with an excited smile.

"You said they were your favorite." Forrest dropped the pan onto the stove with a grimace. "I just didn't anticipate the things being so finicky. Planned on surprising you with breakfast in bed."

"Forrest, that's so thoughtful." Julie reached out and put a hand over his. Her heart soared. She had known there was a reason, and here it was: a surprise breakfast.

He grinned at her as he spooned chocolate onto the crepes. "Would have been if I hadn't burned over a dozen before now." Forrest nodded at a pile of his morning's trials and tribulations, making her giggle. He pointed to a seat. "Sit down, and I'll bring this over to you."

Julie slipped into her seat without a word. She was happy to know that she hadn't been forgotten, at least by Forrest.

"Where's Will?" she asked after a moment.

"Had to go into town to make sure no one burned it down last night."

Julie laughed at the thought, but Forrest only gave her a dispassionate look and continued to slice fruit.

"Oh, my word. You're serious!"

"As the day is long. The people of Gold Sky are good folk, but that doesn't mean they can't be rough around the edges when they're excited, and last night we put on a big celebration for the lot of them." Forrest placed the tray in front of her. At the center of it was a plate with a crepe stuffed with chocolate, strawberries, bananas, and a sprinkling of sugar over the top.

"I hope everyone was able to contain themselves."

Forrest took the seat across from her. "I haven't gotten word back from him, so I'm assuming they did."

Julie picked up her silverware and gave the breakfast in front of her an appreciative hum. "Thank you for this," she said, reaching over and squeezing Forrest's hand. "I can't believe you remembered me writing you how much I love crepes."

"Remember just about everything you ever sent us," Forrest told her with a shy smile. He ran his thumb along the back of her hand. "Got your handwriting memorized. I could pick it out anywhere."

Julie felt a warm pleasure sweep through her that was as strong as anything she had drunk the night before.

"I remember everything you sent as well. However, I fear I'm not as familiar with your handwriting as you are with mine," she frowned, chewing.

"How do you mean?"

"You said Will had been writing me along with you. I never noticed the change in penmanship or tone, and ah, now I'm not sure who wrote what." Julie bit her lip and cautioned a look at Forrest, who nodded, considering her words as he leaned back in his chair.

"I can help you figure that out if you like."

In the time that Julie had written to the men, she had somehow never separated them from one another. Even after understanding the particulars of the proposed marriage arrangement, the two men had always felt like one to her. Forrest's offer to help was tempting, but it felt like cheating. Like she would be giving up on the hard work of getting to know her husbands as they were and in their own time.

Besides, there was no time quite like marriage to get to know her husbands, right? Julie cut into her crepe, her eyes fixed on her plate, smiling.

"Might be fun to guess on my own," Julie said, taking a bite.

"Plenty of time to figure it out." Forrest reached over to touch her hand once more. "I'm sorry you woke up alone. I wanted to have this done as a surprise for you."

Julie swallowed and gave him a nod. "It's all right. I understand."

"No, it's not all right. Your first night with us...like that." Forrest shook his head. "One of us should have been there with you. Meant for it to be me, but you've witnessed my prowess in the kitchen. I'm just glad I didn't burn the house down around you, little bird."

Julie smiled at the nickname. "I'll hold you to that, sir." She gestured with her fork and at her rapidly disappearing breakfast. "Though if you continue to cook me breakfast like this, then I might just be persuaded to forgive a great deal."

Forrest laughed, and the two settled into companionable conversation while Julie continued to eat her breakfast, a delicious offering from a first-time crepe chef. Forrest looked pleased when she finished her meal in record time.

"Would you like to send the telegram you mentioned yesterday?" Forrest asked while they worked together to put the kitchen back in order.

"That would be lovely. I know my family is anxious for word and I haven't been able to send anything decent in nearly two weeks. My father is probably driving my brother and mother insane with worry at this point."

Forrest nodded and held an arm out to her. "We can do that, and after I'll take you around town for a proper tour."

Julie took his arm and followed him toward the front door, but she paused in the foyer, having caught sight of the sparsely decorated parlor and sitting room. The rooms held nothing more than the bare essentials, and she bit her lip at the recurring theme.

Unable to keep her curiosity in check for a moment longer, she turned and said, "Forrest, I meant to ask you about something I noticed this morning."

"What's that?" Forrest closed the front door behind them and led her toward the waiting wagon. She only spoke once she was seated on the bench.

"Well, the house is lovely, but it's just that it's..." Julie bit her lip and stared off into the distance, feeling awkward about asking after the furniture and furnishings. She didn't want to appear as if all she cared for were material items but she was curious as to why the house was minimalist at best. Not at all what a new bride expected to be presented with.

"The house is a bit Spartan in comforts..." She let her

voice trail off and looked toward Forrest to gauge his reaction.

"Ah, that." Forrest nodded, easing the wagon into motion. "We wanted to wait for you to arrive so you could have your say in how the house and furnishings were arranged."

Julie blinked at Forrest's answer. "Really?"

He nodded, eyes on the road in front of them as he urged the horses on. "If I learned anything from my Pa it was that a happy wife meant a happy life. Felt like you would be more particular about how things in the house looked, so we only got what we needed until you arrived. If you want, I'll take you by the mercantile to pick out whatever you like. We also have a few craftsmen in town if you'd like something more custom."

"You're offering to take me shopping today?" Julie asked in shock. Her father and brother had never hidden their distaste for shopping. They much preferred for others to do their shopping for them.

Forrest leaned back on the wagon bench with a chagrined smile. "I suppose I am. Is that something you would like to do today?"

"As a Baptiste, I think I should tell you that shopping is in my blood," Julie told him with a lofty smile.

"Then I look forward to seeing you exercise your skill."

Julie laughed, and it seemed her good cheer was more than suited to the task of squashing her earlier trepidation at waking alone in bed. Not even the direst of situations, Julie decided, would be capable of wiping the smile from her face as she sat next to her husband under the warm morning Montana sun.

∽

IT TOOK NO MORE THAN TWO STEPS INTO THE SHERIFF'S station for Julie to realize that she had been terribly wrong about her earlier assessment at having obtained unpenetrable happiness and mirth. And the reason for such a realization stemmed from three happenings.

First, the enticing smell of bacon and coffee. Second, the grating sound of Rosemary Stanton's laughter peeling through the air like a bell. And finally, the fact that Will laughed right along with her.

Separate, the three small occurrences were innocent and commonplace, but together they formed a trifecta worthy of making Julie see red. Instantly the good feeling and joy she had felt with Forrest on their morning ride into town disappeared.

"Will." Forrest nodded at the other man and then gave Rosemary a perfunctory nod. "Rosemary." His hand dropped to the small of Julie's back as he guided her into the room.

If not for that steadying hand, Julie might have stepped back out of the station at the image of her new husband enjoying a cozy breakfast with another woman. Too bad her other husband didn't waste a moment to shut the door behind her, heading off her exit.

She arched an eyebrow, wondering if he had sensed her discomfort and done it on purpose, but Forrest only met her look with as guileless a gaze as she had ever seen, so she turned away from him with a swish of her skirts.

She had received enough instruction from Lady Pim on how to act aloof and unaffected, and the lessons were, in Julie's estimation, her most prized bits of knowledge.

Chin up. Eyes cool. Breathing even.

A hint of a smile.

With a straight back and steady step, Julie ventured further into the office, but her seemingly unconcerned eyes swept over the breakfast setup, and it was all she could do not let her discomfort show on her face.

Thank the God above for Lady Pim and her Tsarina-like demand for debutante perfection. Julie was secure in the knowledge that her face revealed none of the turmoil she felt at seeing Will and Rosemary sitting at a table so small it looked meant for one, with their breakfast plates pushed right up next to each other...just like their knees were.

But there was no hiding her displeasure when she had noticed the single rose that lay across one corner of the tiny table.

It seemed Will had a thing for roses and women. How lucky for her *and* Rosemary, she thought.

Julie took in a fortifying breath before she turned back to the couple and inclined her head in greeting, saying nothing. Tucking her hands behind her back, she followed a step behind Forrest, who had sat down in front of the telegraph machine.

"Do you know what you'd like to send them?" he asked her.

"No...well, not completely." She removed her gloves and gestured toward the empty desk to the left of the room. "May I have a few minutes to get my message together? It won't be but a moment."

"Of course, little bird." Forrest hopped to his feet as she took a seat at the desk. She gave him a grateful smile when he set a pad of paper and pencil in front of her.

Julie thanked him and picked up her pencil, all the while careful to keep her eyes away from the couple still eating their cozy breakfast together. If she let her gaze linger on them for too long, she would lose hold of the jealousy sitting in her stomach. She had never felt this possessive of anyone, but she supposed it was a natural enough reaction upon seeing one's new husband enjoying what looked to be an intimate occasion with another woman.

Julie had just pressed her pencil to paper when Rosemary spoke.

"A telegram? What might the emergency be?"

"No emergency. Just sending word to Julie's family back east," Forrest answered from where he stood fixing coffee at the station's stove.

Rosemary made a sound that bordered on disbelief. "A telegram all for that?" she asked.

Julie put her pencil down and looked up with a sigh. She suddenly wished that she hadn't been so eager to send the telegram first thing. "They haven't heard from me in over two weeks," she explained.

"Two weeks is hardly anything to quibble about." Rosemary took a prim sip from her cup and gave Julie a smile that didn't quite reach her pale blue eyes. "You'll learn that living out here on the frontier, but then again I shouldn't be surprised with a city girl like you wanting things quick, fast, and in a hurry." She laughed at her little joke and it was all Julie could do to not throw her pencil at her.

Instead, Julie gave as charming a smile as she could manage. "If you say so," she replied. She had learned long ago that the most effective way to best a catty woman was to simply agree. It left them nowhere to go without fully exposing the meanness of their words.

She felt a flash of triumph when she noticed Rosemary's mouth press into a thin line. Julie wanted to look at Will to see what his reaction was to her seeing him having breakfast with Rosemary, but she avoided looking at him for fear of giving herself away.

Already the words she had thought she'd heard him mumble to her the night before seemed to be slipping away from her in the bright sunlight of the day.

Put simply, it hurt. Badly.

Turning her eyes back to the page in front of her, she focused on steadying her breath. She had only written down the first few words of her missive to her parents when Rosemary interrupted her with a little laugh.

"I hope I haven't put you out this morning, Julie Anne."

Julie's eyes snapped up to the other woman. "Whatever do you mean?" she asked.

Forrest ambled over then with a cup of hot coffee in each hand, watching the women interact with interest.

Rosemary gestured at the small breakfast set up in front of her and Will. "Well, with breakfast, dear."

"Why would that put me out?" Julie wondered, taking the cup of coffee from Forrest with a murmur of thanks.

"Oh, Julie Anne." Rosemary gave her a knowing smile. "Your William was surely missed this morning."

Julie's hands froze where she had been raising the cup to her lips. "Please, call me Mrs. Wickes-Barnes. I haven't been called Julie Anne since I was a girl," she said, fixing Rosemary with a frosty look that bordered on a glare.

Forrest's eyes shot to Will's, but the other man didn't react to the change in their wife's tone. Forrest, on the other hand, did his best to edge out from in between the women, his perch on the desk no longer deemed suitable or safe.

"Of course." Rosemary had enough grace to blush at Julie's response.

"As for missing my husband, well, I understand that my husband has duties to perform." She looked at him then, seeing that he regarded her with the same cool and guarded look that he had used on her the previous day. "Honeymoon or not."

"I just couldn't help myself, you see." Rosemary grinned, already brushing past Julie's earlier rebuff. "I saw poor William sitting here with a breakfast of dry toast and barely tolerable coffee, and I had to act!"

Julie swallowed past the lump in her throat and inclined her head in thanks. "And I thank you for seeing to my husband's comfort."

"What kind of woman would I be if I hadn't?" Rosemary wondered aloud with a little titter of laughter.

Julie dropped her eyes to the depths of her coffee cup and took a hasty sip to avoid telling Rosemary what kind of woman Julie thought her to be. The slight against her was unmistakable, and it set Julie's teeth to grinding, but she smiled prettily enough at the other woman, with barely a twitch of her fingers to betray her anger.

"What are you doing today?" Will said suddenly. His voice was a merciful distraction to Julie in the tension-filled room, which she longed to kick Rosemary out of.

If only this were one of her well-worn paperbacks. A sensible course of action would be so clear to her against the woman encroaching on her place at Will's side. But alas, this was not the stuff of pen and fantasy, but real life, and real life did not always allow for the handy dispatching of forward women.

"Shopping," Forrest answered, leaning against the desk.

Rosemary made another one of her little disbelieving sounds. "New Yorkers simply must shop, even on the frontier, hmm?" she purred to Will, as if the pair of them were sharing an inside joke at Julie's expense.

Julie's cheeks flamed from embarrassment, and she looked down at the paper in front of her as if it were the most important thing in her world. Discovering her husband gone and having breakfast with another woman was one thing, but she would not be the butt of a joke.

The quicker she finished composing her message, the quicker she could escape Rosemary's presence without saying or doing something she would regret immensely. Hastily, she began to scribble out a simple note addressing her safety and promising to write them all.

"Make sure to take her by the carpenter. I went in last week and had them work up a few designs she might like," Will told Forrest, ignoring Rosemary's cutting remark. Julie's eyes darted up to him to see that he had leaned back in his chair, his eyes on her though he spoke to Forrest.

"Designs?" Julie asked raising a questioning eyebrow.

Will nodded, crossing his arms. "Cradles."

Rosemary's fork hit her plate in an undignified clatter. "What?"

Julie didn't have time to think of the other woman's shock as she dealt with her own. She nearly spit out the sip of coffee she had just taken. Forrest took her coffee cup from her hand while she coughed in the most undignified manner possible.

"What?" she asked in an echo of Rosemary's question.

"Stark's good with his hands but even he needs time to make us something special," Will replied, looking between the women with barely a reaction. "He's booked out for months and won't be able to start on it for a while yet, but deciding on a design is a good idea."

"It's already on our list of places to go," Forrest said, sipping his own coffee. "Made sure Stark had a couple rockers ready for you to choose from."

"I—ah, I..." Julie swallowed thickly. Now she only had eyes for her husbands who were regarding her with interest. "Of course," she finally said.

"Expect we'll have a whole new house by the time we're done with today." Forrest smiled at the others in the room before he pointed at the message she had somehow managed to finish. "Should I send that?"

"Of course, thank you." Julie held the paper out to Forrest, still in shock from Will's statement.

From how quiet Rosemary had grown, it was safe to say that she wasn't the only one who needed a moment to come to terms with Will's cradles.

The blonde woman dabbed at her lips with her napkin before she stood up in a rustle of skirts. "I should be off. I'm needed at the newspaper for a meeting."

Will nodded at her, standing to see her to the door. "Thank you for breakfast, Rosemary."

"Certainly, William. I look forward to our next." The woman put her hand on his arm before she turned to Julie, who had pinned her with an unwavering gaze. "Have fun with shopping," Rosemary said to her.

"I will. Good to see you again so soon," Julie lied through her teeth with a fake smile. Thankfully, the other woman only lingered for another moment before she left, and Julie let the smile slip from her face.

Julie relaxed once the door closed. She was glad the other woman was gone. There was something about her and the way she looked at Will that Julie didn't trust. She glanced at Will to see him regarding her from the door.

Looking away from him, she cleared her throat and sipped at the coffee Forrest had brought her.

"There, message all sent." Forrest smiled at her. "Where would you like to go first?"

"The carpenters would be nice." Her curiosity had gotten the better of her, and she wanted to see the designs he had put together for her consideration.

Forrest stood with a nod. "Good choice. We can have a nice tour since it's on the other side of town."

"That sounds lovely." Julie beamed at Forrest.

Even with her back turned, the weight of Will's gaze had her feeling uneasy, and she shifted on her feet with a little sigh. "Is there something I should know?" she ventured.

Will raised an eyebrow. "Such as?"

Julie shrugged, slipping her gloves back on. "It just...seemed like you had something you wanted to say?"

"No, nothing I've got to say." He turned then, grabbing his jacket from the hook beside the door. "I should be going. I promised I'd swing by the Chapman homestead and check on things while Clint is on the road."

"We'll see you at dinner then, I expect?" Forrest asked.

"Might come in late."

Will shrugged his jacket on, turning his eyes to Julie. "Anything you want me to bring back with me?"

She shook her head. "Just you."

"Good choice." Forrest came to stand beside her with a smile. He crossed his arms over his chest and nodded at Will. "Heard the road out that way washed out, so don't do anything stupid."

Will tipped his hat but said nothing and opened the door with a yank. He paused in the doorway, looking over his shoulder at Julie.

"Get anything you like today. Don't listen to any of them if they make a fuss, and if someone doesn't help you, tell Forrest. Understand?"

Julie bit her lip but gave a quick nod. "Yes."

"Good." Then Will was out the door and on his way before she could get in another word. Julie was still staring after Will when Forrest stepped in close to her and offered his arm. The transition between the men was seamless. They were flawless in their ability to switch places in Julie's world.

It was uncanny, really, her husbands' balance of dark and light, of sweet and...well, what was slightly sweet but not entirely enjoyable? Bittersweet?

And how did Rosemary manage to pull more sweet out of her husband than she?

Perhaps because you've known him for all of a day, a voice whispered to her. Julie bit back a frown. Yes, that. How could she forget it?

"If we don't get to Stark's within the hour we'll have a wait ahead of us to see him," Forrest said, pulling her away from her spontaneous brooding.

It wouldn't do to wallow in a sour mood over her bittersweet marital status. Julie took Forrest's arm. She had a house to outfit and comforts to bring to her husbands, and that was precisely what she aimed to do

THE AFTERNOON PASSED IN A WHIRLWIND OF NEW acquaintances and purchases. Before long, Julie was delighted that she could find her way around with relative ease, and she could even locate the small but finely appointed and well maintained white clapboard school.

She had met several of her soon-to-be students and their families. Each one was excited to have her for a teacher, and she found that she was quite eager for the next week, when she would begin.

Julie and Forrest had managed to make the necessary arrangements, so now a cherry dining table and matching eight-chair set sat in the formal dining room. A plush settee, a pair of end tables with matching lamps, and a trio of rocking chairs from Stark's Carpentry now occupied the space in front of the parlor's fireplace.

There were also plans for the working of a beautiful cradle made from mahogany.

She grinned, thinking of the lively carpenter who had seemed to get on Forrest's last nerve, and relished that he could do so. The moment she had set foot in Stark's workspace the man had made it his personal mission to compliment her at every turn and give her as many flirty smiles as possible. Julie had laughed it all off, sensing the man wasn't serious, but Forrest had seemed ready to put him through his workbench.

After their visit to the carpenter, whom Julie promised to visit frequently, much to Forrest's frustration, they had stopped by the mercantile to put in an order for new linens, curtains, and an assortment of household items.

The woman at the front counter had been over the moon at their business. "This is the largest order of the year! Delighted to make your acquaintance, Mrs. Wickes-Barnes." Julie had smiled and added on a few more luxuries like bath salts and a pound of honey candies at that.

Another visit to the bank to set up Julie's personal bank account and a later stop to the grocer for dinner that night had all but exhausted her. At least, until Julie happened by the bookstore. The mere thought of all those gloriously bound books, their pages rich with beautifully composed stories, caused her to hesitate by the storefront for a moment before she moved to continue on, but her observant husband had allowed no such thing.

"You love novels. And we," he had said with a grin as he began to usher her toward the shop door, "are going to buy every last thing that catches your interest."

It had taken little more convincing, and he marched her inside with strict orders that she purchase whatever she liked. Julie had to give credit to her husband, who hadn't so much as faltered in his patience beside her while she piled his arms with books and dragged him through the shop.

It had been a marvelous ending to her first proper day in Gold Sky.

Now she stood in the middle of the kitchen, a newly purchased apron made from a pretty pattern and sturdy fabric tied around her waist. Julie took a step closer to the counter and considered the chicken she was supposed to prepare for dinner that night. Potatoes boiled away on the stove, she had what she hoped would be edible enough cornbread in the oven, and now the last culinary challenge that remained to her was the chicken.

It was a daunting task considering she wasn't completely certain what to do with it. Why hadn't she paid closer attention when she'd been sent to learn on Saturday mornings with their kindly cook?

"Need help?" Forrest asked. He had been watching her stare at the chicken for some time now, and now he moved to push away from the doorway he had been leaning against to enter the kitchen.

Julie tilted her chin up in defiance.

"No, I can manage it." She sidled toward *The Lady's*

Cooking Compendium, one of her many new hardback purchases made that afternoon, and tried to peek at the book's section on poultry.

Forrest laughed, but when Julie arched an eyebrow he held up his hands. "I'm sure you're going to make a delicious chicken."

She flipped through the book with a sigh. "If I can find the right page."

"Oh, just throw it in the oven."

"It's not that easy, Forrest," she said now that she had found the right page.

Forrest hitched a hip against the counter and leaned close to the page. "Then what does *The Lady's Cooking Compendium* have to say on the matter? And how can I be of help?"

"Garlic cloves and lemon. Lots of lemon." Julie grinned, watching him spring into action.

It was nice making dinner with Forrest. She wasn't used to thinking of him as her husband, but she was trying to, and Forrest seemed determined to help her along with his light touches, stolen kisses, and sweet smiles. The couple continued to prepare the chicken, which before long took its place in the oven next to the cornbread.

Once they were done, she leaned against the counter and returned his warm smile with a shy one of her own. As much as she enjoyed her time with Forrest, there was a matter that hadn't left her thoughts, not even through all the excitement of the day.

In fact, it had seemed to loom larger over her, especially when her movements in town took her past the newspaper office where she had seen Rosemary through the window.

"Forrest?"

He looked up from where he washed his hands in the sink. "What is it, little bird?"

"Do they have breakfast often?"

Forrest lowered his eyes to his hands with a frown. There was no need then to clarify who 'they' was. He understood her, which she found provided both a measure of relief and of distress.

"Sometimes. He's got a soft spot for her. Not sure why."

Julie froze, her hands tightening in the folds of her new apron. "Rosemary?"

"She's got a way with him."

"But not with you," Julie observed, taking in the pinched expression on Forrest's handsome face.

"Rosemary's always been...forward. Very transparent in what she wants," he said after a second of deliberation. "But don't pay her any mind."

Julie crossed her arms over her chest. "You expect me not to worry about a woman that's so forward? A woman who was having breakfast with my husband just this morning? Unchaperoned, at that!"

He wiped his hands and came to stand beside her. "You're jealous, little bird, aren't you?" he asked, his voice low and gentle and full of understanding.

Julie blew out an annoyed breath and yanked her apron off with a snap of her hands. She hated that she was so easy for Forrest to read. How infuriating it was when she wasn't even able to tell the men apart in their writings to her!

"I'm not jealous," she insisted.

"There's no reason to care what Rosemary Stanton does or says, or how many breakfasts she brings Will. Do you hear me?" Forrest tipped her chin up to look down at her. "You're our wife, and that's that."

"Is it?" Julie whispered, wondering why she let Rosemary get under her skin like this. If it had been only catty or disparaging remarks from the other woman, it would be a situation Julie understood. One she was a master at. She was no stranger to churlish behavior from her time as a debutante in New York's social scene, but the blonde's obvious interest in Will made her feel unnerved and defensive.

"I'm not even sure what I know about either of you," she said, voice tight as she referenced the morning revelation regarding their letters. "Will knows far more about Rosemary than he does me. How can our letters be enough?"

Forrest shook his head, his summer sky blue eyes clouded in confusion. "We promised in front of God and this entire town that we would never forsake you. Not for anyone. Not ever," he said, as if it were that simple.

But if there was anything Julie had learned as an avid reader, there was nothing simple when it came to matters of the heart. An uttered promise in front of a chapel full of strangers wouldn't mean much if Will realized Rosemary was the woman he preferred as a wife. Julie looked away at that thought; she couldn't meet Forrest's earnest gaze.

"Will seems to like her very much."

"They're friendly, is all."

"He isn't friendly with me."

"That's not true." Forrest sighed. He touched her face with gentle fingers. "He's head-over-heels for you. Already."

She shook her head. "He barely looked at me today."

103

"That's just his way. He cares for you, Julie."

"If he's so *'friendly'* with Rosemary, then why didn't you both just marry her?" Julie wondered aloud, giving voice to the thought that had sprung to mind when she had seen Will laughing with the other woman. There didn't seem to be a shortage of warmth or smiles.

How was it that she wasn't able to elicit that type of response from her own husband?

"Like I said, he's friendly with her. I'm not. We don't suit," Forrest replied, looking uncomfortable. The confirmation that Rosemary had been in the running as a wife for the men hurt more than Julie realized it would. She closed her eyes briefly as she mulled over the new piece of information. Rosemary's behavior toward Will, and herself, suddenly made more sense in light of it.

How had they approached the topic with the woman? How had they handled the fallout after not selecting her? How much longer would Rosemary's evident affection for Will persist?

"What are you thinking, little bird?" Forrest's question made Julie open her eyes, and she frantically tried to order the chaotic mess of thoughts swirling in her mind. After a moment she finally spoke.

"So you both... you had considered marrying her."

Forrest shrugged. "She's a widow and of the right age. Not many available women in Gold Sky," he said, his tone matter-of-fact.

"Why didn't you suit?" Julie pressed. "They seem to get on very well."

"Not the woman for me."

"So you were the one that didn't suit her? She was accepting of the arrangement? I mean..." Julie hesitated then, as she stumbled over her words. How was it Rosemary and Forrest hadn't suited? The blonde was everything she supposed a man with the marrying inclination should desire, and yet they hadn't suited?

"Rosemary knew that a marriage included the both of you and was amenable to it?"

Forrest rocked back on his heels. "Yes, she was... amenable to it."

"Oh." Julie looked away.

The niggling feeling that she had pushed down when she had seen the couple dance the night before, the way Rosemary had looked at Will, and the companionable way they had shared breakfast that morning all suddenly made sense. Will and Rosemary had suited just fine. It had been Forrest who hadn't meshed with the couple for a triad marriage. And that had her feeling uneasy about where Will's true affections lay despite Forrest's assurances.

"Let's talk about something else, little bird."

Julie nodded, knowing that Forrest was doing his best to take her mind off of the train of thought that had taken off with her little discovery that Rosemary had been their first choice.

Their. First. Choice.

Julie Anne Baptiste had never been second in anything. Funny that it should happen with such a permanent arrangement as marriage.

Clearing her throat, she tried to put a smile on her face, but she found that it was no use. She pushed away from the counter and attempted to run through a list of things she could do to keep her hands busy now that dinner had been prepared. She could settle into their bedroom more than she had with her hasty unpacking of her trunks that afternoon when they had returned home.

Anything but dwell on her place as Will's second choice as a wife.

"I'll just be upstairs," she said, already starting for the stairs.

"Julie, look at me," Forrest called to her, a pained note to his ordinarily warm voice. Julie didn't have to turn around to know that her husband was upset. Reluctantly, Julie raised her eyes to his. She saw that he was upset. In fact, he looked nearly as unsettled as she felt.

"I don't want you making too much of this."

"I'm not," she said quietly.

"You are. I can see it."

"You don't know me that well, Forrest."

He smirked. "I know you well enough. Tell me that I'm not right about what's running through that pretty head of yours."

She looked away at that with a frown but said nothing in rebuttal. Damn him and his ability to read her.

Forrest sighed. "She was not our first choice. Never was, little bird."

"But she and Will get on."

He shrugged. "Don't mean she was the woman we wanted."

Julie arched an eyebrow. "Because she isn't a teacher?"

Forrest scrubbed a hand over his face. "That isn't why we chose you. We fell in love with you. The both of us, Julie. Your letters made us do that. Every last one of them put you in our heart. Now, I know Will can be short, but he cares for you. There's a lot that's happened to him that makes it hard for him to show that side of himself to new people."

"Not Rosemary," she said with a barely concealed pout.

"No, not Rosemary." Forrest came up to stand beside

her. He slipped his arms around her in a hug. "But that doesn't mean what you think it does. They've always been close."

"Why is hard for him to show his feelings?" Julie asked, choosing to focus on something else other than how much she disliked Rosemary's relationship with Will.

"The war," Forrest replied without hesitation. "I wrote to you about it briefly."

"You served when you were just 13." Julie looked up at him. "So young."

Forrest shrugged. "Not so young in the grand scheme of things." He cleared his throat and led her over to the small table she had taken her breakfast at that morning. "I didn't share too much because I didn't want you to get the wrong idea about Will or me. About who we are now. But that doesn't mean things weren't hard. We lived in Kentucky, as you well know, and it saw a lot of the bad days of the war with them passing through us like paper every few weeks." He looked down at his hands, his knuckles white from how tightly he clenched his fists.

Julie put her hand on his and gave them a gentle squeeze. At her touch, Forrest forced himself to take a breath and slowly uncurled his fingers.

"Will and I joined young to send wages back to our families. You have to understand there was nothing to eat, nothing at all. And when there was, you couldn't afford the prices from the gougers. We had to do something to keep our families fed."

"You lied about your ages," Julie guessed.

"Of course we did. The Union never would have taken two boys into the same regiment. Passed me off as 17 and Will for 19 though he was only 15. We got the wages we needed but..." Forrest's voice went soft, and he looked away from her, his eyes trained on something she was unable to see. "We lost a lot of people we knew along the way. The things we saw were—well, no one should ever see what we saw or do what we had to do."

"What d—"

Forrest raised a hand, stilling the question in Julie's mouth. "I know what you're going to ask me, and I won't tell you the particulars of it all because I won't have that filth running around in my wife's head. Don't want it anywhere near our family. Understand?"

Julie closed her mouth and nodded. She wanted to ask, but she would respect Forrest's wishes. Instead, she threaded her fingers with his and asked, "What happened in the war made Will the way he is?"

"It did. He shielded me from a lot, being the older one of us. Always has taken care of me like a brother, though he never had any of his own. Will has a hard time letting people get close because of all the ones we lost. I think...I think that he's scared if he does that, that it's only a matter of time before he loses them." Forrest squeezed her fingers and smiled sadly at her. "I know him, and I know he cares for you, but he's a man with demons. It's why we came all the way out here. I—we, well, I thought if we had enough distance from Kentucky that he'd be able to quiet them for good."

"Did coming here help?"

Forrest nodded. "For a time, but it isn't so easy to get rid of a demon once it's deep in you. Something like that leaves a stain. Never leaves you."

"You have them too?" Julie asked she blinked back tears, thinking of Will and Forrest, boys leaving home out of necessity only to experience the horrors of war. How had two boys survived all that and gone on to become the men she now knew?

"No way a boy sees what we did and doesn't have 'em when he's grown."

"Oh, Forrest." Julie scooted closer to him, but he reached out and gently took her hands in his.

"Don't be sorry. I'm happy here in Gold Sky. Things are different with us because of the war, but it doesn't make life any less good. Having Will close by helps a great deal. It's why we knew we would have to find an exceptional woman who would have us both."

"I don't know how special I am," Julie whispered.

Forrest rubbed the back of her hand with his thumb. "Little bird, you are the most special thing to happen to me in a very long while. You've been here a day, and this place already feels more like a home than it ever did before."

"I hope...I hope Will feels the same way."

"Be patient with him. He can be an idiot, but he'll come around in his own time." Forrest kissed the tops of her knuckles. "Promise me you'll never doubt how special you are to us. I don't care how many Rosemary Stantons think they can show you otherwise. You're the one for us. That's a fact, Julie. Promise me you won't forget that."

"I promise," she whispered.

CHAPTER 7

*J*ulie let out a strangled gasp, her cries cut off short by Will's mouth, his kiss swallowing the moans. She leaned back against his muscular chest, and his hands tangled in her curly hair, turning her face to kiss him while Forrest's hands and mouth roamed over her.

They were in bed, all three of them, and bed was a place Julie witnessed Will become an entirely different person with her. Here among their soft sheets and pillows he was caring, passionate, tender, and most important, he wanted her. Of that she was sure. With her husbands' hands and mouths on her, no one else existed besides the three of them. It had been nearly a week now with just the three of them, and when they were in bed Will couldn't get enough of her.

Neither could Forrest.

The bed had become Julie's favorite place.

Forrest had just finished playing her body like an erotic instrument. She shuddered in the aftershocks of her orgasm underneath his gentle touch.

"My little bird," he murmured, leaning over her to paint her chest with gentle kisses. Her breasts ached, nipples puckered from the attention both of her husbands had given them. She wasn't sure if there hadn't been a part of her that hadn't been stroked, kissed, or bitten by them.

It was heaven.

Will lifted his head and gave her a tender smile. "Beautiful." He kissed her forehead.

Forrest reached forward, running a hand through Will's dark hair, his fingers tangled in the long strands. "Now this is a sight I'd like to get better acquainted with," he said, bringing up his other hand and cupping Julie's cheek. She hummed, content and relaxing back against Will. If these were the precious few moments that he felt comfortable enough to let her close, well, then she was going to make the most of them.

Forrest slipped out of bed with athletic grace, and a thrill went through Julie that she was able to stare at him freely. The man certainly wasn't ashamed of his nakedness. Neither of the men were, and after the discipline of finishing school and polite society's expectations of a young lady, Julie found it quite liberating.

Why should there be any shame in marriage? If they were tied to one another in mind, body, and soul for the rest of their days, then she intended to get her fill of looking at her beautiful husbands.

Will shifted to the side, pulling her close to him, a hand going down to caress her stomach. She looked up at him to see that he gazed at his hand against her bronzed skin, which was accentuated by the stark white of the sheets tangled around her.

"What is it?" she whispered.

He looked at her with as open a look in his eyes as she

had ever hoped to see since her talk with Forrest earlier in the week. Lord, she hadn't thought he would favor her with a look like that for another month, but here it was ahead of schedule and so much more than she could have ever imagined.

"Thinking about how you'll look carrying our baby."

Julie swallowed hard, her hand joining Will's. It warmed her, filled her with hope for the future about him opening fully up to her when he said things like this. Though she hoped her husbands would see fit to put her in a position where she would actually have a chance to become pregnant.

The men had spent every night since her arrival exploring her body and giving her pleasure the likes of which she had never dared to imagine in her wildest fantasies. She knew they did it for her sake, making sure she felt at ease with what was happening before they proceeded further, but Will's confession a moment before and the talk of a cradle with Stark earlier that week had her eager to push her husbands to the next step.

Forrest joined them back on the bed and pressed a kiss against her midsection. "Gonna look even more beautiful than you do now with our little one in there." He tapped his finger against her skin.

"You make me seem like an oven."

"The most beautiful oven this side of the Mississippi." Forrest winked at her.

Julie rolled her eyes at the playful expression on her husbands' faces. Deciding that the moment of levity was perfect for her next question, she pushed ahead.

"And when exactly are we going to get to the making part, hmm?"

Forrest pushed himself up on his elbow with an interested look. He shifted his eyes over her shoulder to Will, who still had a possessive hand over her stomach.

"Little bird wants to go further."

Will grunted but said nothing.

"What does that sound mean?" Julie angled her head to the side to look back at her husband, seeing that his eyes were on the ceiling above them.

"Just want to make sure you're comfortable with it all. Comfortable with the pair of us," Will said, lowering his eyes to look at her.

"I'm perfectly comfortable with you both. I knew what I signed up for when I agreed to your arrangement and I wish—"

Forrest cut off Julie's words with a sudden kiss. "When you get worked up it makes me want to put you on your back and give Stark a reason to get that cradle done on time," he said against her lips.

Julie's eyes widened, and she threw her arms around his neck, pulling him close for another kiss. She surprised herself when she swiped her tongue across his bottom lip in a mimic of the move he had demonstrated on her before. Forrest's arms tightened around her as he kissed her back, a strangled groan in his throat when one of Julie's hands wandered down to stroke his manhood.

He pulled back, blue eyes dark with passion, and gave Will a dazed look. "She's ready."

Will raised an eyebrow at his friend. "Oh, is she?"

Julie was still trying to kiss and touch every part of Forrest that pushed up against her. She blinked in confusion at his statement. "What are you talking about?"

His eyes darted back to her. "I was just testing the mettle of your words."

Julie's eyes widened, and she let out a gasp of outrage

when she understood his meaning. "You were testing me?!"

Will huffed out a laugh when she swatted at Forrest, and he wrapped his arms around her, dropping a kiss on her shoulder. "Shhh, Jules. He's always been like that. You're going to have to get used to it. Always pushing things." He tugged the sheet over their bodies while Julie gave Forrest a sharp look.

The blond held up his hands. "I needed to be certain you—"

"That I wasn't lying? Hmm?" Julie frowned at him, crossing her arms over herself, a difficult task given how Will still held her close.

"I didn't think you were lying, sweetheart." Forrest sighed and touched her hand. "Just didn't want you to feel like you had to take us both to bed, not so soon, just to please us."

"What do you mean by 'have to'? I was raised a Baptiste! I've never had to do a thing I didn't want, and this marriage is no exception to that. I'm here because I want you both, you pigheaded man!"

Will laughed. The rich and melodious sound of it rumbled against her back, and the sensation warmed her through and through. Forrest paused in speaking, his eyes taking on a soft look at hearing Will laugh, and before long he was chuckling along so that Julie was the only one still frowning.

"What's so funny?" she demanded, twisting to look back at Will, who grinned at her.

"You when you get riled. Have to make a note not to let it happen too often," Will replied. Forrest hummed in agreement, slipping beneath the sheets on her other side.

"I didn't mean to make you feel I doubted your honesty. I'm sorry," Forrest apologized.

"He meant well, Jules. Go easy on him, hmm? Forgive your idiot husband this time?" Will asked her, fingers stroking her arms.

Julie blew out a sigh. "This is not fair." She looked between the men and rolled her eyes at the puppy dog looks on both of their faces. "Most women have just one man to endure, but the Lord has seen fit to bless me with two. I'll never have order or a moment's rest with you two."

Her husbands smiled in unison at her. There wasn't anything she wouldn't give to have those smiles directed at her.

"That sounds about right, little bird," Forrest replied. He kissed her forehead, smoothing away the furrow of her brow. She opened her mouth to protest, but Will shushed her and reached for the quilt Forrest had begun to unfold over them.

"You need rest. Tomorrow is your first day teaching," he said.

Forrest nodded, his arm going over her waist. "He's right. We've kept you up long enough as it is."

"Oh, all right." Julie smiled in spite of herself. She closed her eyes, the secure and warm feeling of being between her men and the promise of their future more than enough to send her to sleep with a smile on her lips.

"Eat."

Will's terse voice pulled Julie's eyes away from the book she had open in front of her. It was a titillating gothic romance, which prompted her to clasp the book to her chest when Will leaned close, trying to see the pages. Tilting her book so that it was angled perfectly for her eyes only, Julie lowered her gaze back down to read the last sentence on the page, prompting an exasperated sigh from Will.

"Eat. Now, Jules."

"I just needed to finish the page. If I don't get to, it'll be absolute mayhem when I pick it back up, since I was in the middle of a scene. You just cannot leave your novel willy-nilly. There must be continuity!" She put down the book, well out of his reach, and picked up her fork.

Will rolled his eyes and sat down beside her at the table with a cup of coffee for each of them. She had just taken a bite of her pancake when Forrest walked into the room, still buttoning his shirt.

"You about done? If we leave in a few minutes, I can take you in the buckboard if you like."

Julie brightened at that and took a hasty sip of her coffee. "Just let me get my things!"

"She's not done eating," Will replied, putting an arm out and barring the way.

"Will, it's just one meal. It's not important," Julie replied, pushing on his arm. When he didn't so much as budge an inch, she looked at him and sighed when she saw the determined set of his jaw. There was no way this man was going to let her up.

No way. No how.

"I'll take her. You take the horse," he told Forrest, sipping at his coffee before he gestured at her with the mug. "You finish your breakfast. I'm not having you faint on your first day teaching."

"But W—"

"What is it? Don't want me takin' you into town?"

"No, it's not that." Julie tilted her head in confusion over his words.

"Then eat."

With a sullen expression, she picked up her fork again, giving Forrest a longing look. He finished buttoning his shirt while giving her a shrug.

"He's right about breakfast," he said, leaning down to kiss her cheek.

Julie glared at him. "Traitor."

Forrest grabbed an apple off the table and laughed, walking backward toward the doorway. "Oh, I'll take you by the lake another morning. Promise." The door banged shut after him, and Julie pursed her lips one more time before she resumed eating the pancakes Will had made her that morning.

"So that's what this was all about?" Will asked her, setting down his cup.

"I've wanted to see the lake since he—well, you both wrote me about it."

"Plenty of time to see the lake, Jules. You're not going anywhere anytime soon."

She took another quick bite of her breakfast. "So you've made apparent." Though she pouted, there was a part of her that relished Will's concern over what she ate that morning. It was nice to be thought of, for her health to be a concern for Will. She smiled at him then, touched by his effort to look after her.

"What?" He gave her a look of confusion when he caught her staring at him with a silly grin on her face.

"Nothing." Julie looked away quickly with a blush at having been caught staring at him like a lovesick girl, but then again, she supposed she was.

After a hasty breakfast, Julie grabbed her books and followed Will out to the buckboard. He settled her on the bench seat with as much ease as Forrest and before long they were off down the road, heading toward the school. Julie leaned back in the seat, content with her morning and happy for a ride to the school on her first day.

A few minutes into the trip she sensed a change in Will and bit her lip, shooting him a glance. It was hard to pinpoint when the shift in energy had happened, but she knew it wasn't her imagination that her husband was turning into someone else on the drive into town. He had already scooted an inch or two further away from where Julie had been pressed against him at the start of the ride.

A definite change from how wrapped around her he had been the night before in their bed. Where was that man? Sighing at the thought, Julie looked down at her hands and tugged her coat tighter around her. They might have only been inches apart, but it may as well have been the expanse of the Montana Territory.

Will looked over at her and cleared his throat. "Will you need a ride home?" he asked, voice calm and even.

"I can make my own way back," Julie said, meeting his gaze. "I'm not sure how long I'll be today with needing to take inventory and sort things out for the remainder of the term. There's a lot to do but not many days left to do it."

"Ah." He nodded but said nothing else. Julie could see that the gray eyes which had been so open and warm in their home were now shuttered. The feeling of distance only amplified the closer to town they got, and by the time they pulled up in front of the schoolhouse, Julie could practically see the walls Will had erected around himself to keep her out.

It was a painful experience.

Without a word, Will handed her out of the buckboard and then stood there awkwardly in front of her.

"Have, ah..." Will shifted uncomfortably. "Have a good day, Jules."

"Thank you for the ride," Julie said, forcing her tone to stay bright despite her disappointment at losing the closeness she had shared with him. She had to remain patient with him, to allow him time to come to her on his own. She had to trust Forrest that this wouldn't be forever.

"'Course," Will said, and then he surprised her by leaning forward to kiss her cheek. She smiled up at him, a real genuine one that he returned, albeit briefly.

Buoyed by the kiss, Julie's smile stayed in place and she gave a cheery wave when Will drove off in the direction of town. Once her husband was out of sight, she turned and practically bounded up the steps of the schoolhouse. She unlocked the heavy oak doors with the key that had been given to Forrest for safekeeping and took a hasty look around the space.

It was a single room, in which desks and chairs sat in rows of five. Julie rubbed her hands against her arms and made for the stove in the corner. Thought it was late spring, the mornings in Montana could still be downright chilly, and today looked like it promised rain. She would have to get to work immediately if she wanted her students to have a comfortable classroom.

Windows lined the room, providing plenty of natural light. Cubbies sat underneath the windows to the left and a small, rudimentary library of books occupied the opposite wall. She pursed her lips, taking in the collection. She would have to supplement the books on her own if she wanted her students to have access to quality resources. A blackboard took up the wall behind the large oak desk at the back of the room, and she painstakingly wrote her name in her neatest handwriting across the chalkboard.

Mrs. Wickes-Barnes.

She smiled at that. It looked nice and official.

No sooner had she put down the chalk than the school doors flew open with a bang. Julie jumped at the noise and turned to see a crowd of children bursting through the doors.

They froze when they caught sight of her.

"Hello." She gave them a warm smile, hands clasped in front of her. "Good morning and please take your seats." She gestured towards the row of desks.

A blond boy of about ten stumbled forward with wide eyes. "They were right! She's beautiful! Like a queen!"

A tittering of laughter escaped the students, and Julie blushed at the boy's comment.

She gave him a smile. "Thank you."

He nodded at her, still wide-eyed, and then shuffled toward his seat with furtive looks toward her. Julie waited while the rest of the students hurried to their seats. Her smile grew a bit more when she caught sight of Rhodes's daughters, girls of about ten and twelve with cascades of dark curls and dark eyes. They, she saw, regarded her as closely as she regarded them, and at her smile, they burst into happy expressions of their own.

Her promise to Rhodes on her wedding night came back to her and Julie straightened up a tad more.

"If you'll open your arithmetic books. Page 57, please."

The sound of pages rustling filled the room as the students obeyed. She had a job to do, and she had no intention of breaking her promise to Rhodes. He trusted her with his girls, and she would do her best to honor his trust.

Julie's first day at the school passed much like the previous two days: in a blur. It was, however, the most enjoyable blur she could remember experiencing in all her life. The children were eager to learn and absorbed her instruction. She wasn't sure exactly why the last teacher had fled the post, but Julie's opinion of the children was that they were angels.

Yes, the children were rough around the edges—she'd had to march out a pair of boys for sneaking in a toad, and then there had been the roughhousing during recess that had turned into an actual bout of fists—but it had all blown over with a few quiet apologies as soon as Julie had sent them a stern look.

She was eager to see just how much progress her students would make by this time next year, and smiled at the thought. Life in Gold Sky had promise, and today was a shining example of how much she had already gained by settling in the town. There were other bright spots, primarily in the form of her gentle blond husband and his mercurial brunette counterpart.

Julie played with the cuff of her wool coat, a bright blue garment that hung to mid-thigh. It was a pretty coat, something she had picked up while shopping with her mother, and it complimented her darker complexion perfectly, but it didn't do much for her in the way of protection against the Montana elements. She hadn't been wrong in her guess at rain, and a rumble of thunder in the distance had her hurrying toward the ranch. Shoving the novel she had hoped to continue reading from that morning into her bag, she hurried down the road, mindful of the rapidly darkening sky.

It was because she was staring so intently at the heavens above that she was surprised by the form of a woman rounding the corner just before the last stretch of road before the ranch.

Rosemary.

What was she doing this far out?

A quick look around her told her there was no reprieve from the niceties she would have to make with the other woman. Julie had to repress a sigh when she saw that Rosemary had dressed perfectly for the weather and even had an umbrella tucked under one arm as an extra precaution. A wry smile escaped Julie when she saw the moment Rosemary recognized her. The blonde stood just a bit taller, holding herself more elegantly, and walking with more confidence that she had moments before.

At least her presence had enough of an effect to push Rosemary to be at her best.

Julie took it upon herself to be the first to offer a greeting, and when they were only a few feet apart, she smiled.

"Rosemary. How nice to see you again."

Rosemary gestured a hello with occupied hands. Julie raised an eyebrow, taking in the bright and sunny yellow tea towel wrapped around what looked to be a small platter.

Curious, that the woman was out here on a lane that only led to Julie's home carrying such an item.

Were there other homesteads further on Forrest and Will had forgotten to mention?

"Same to you, Mrs. Wickes-Barnes." The stiff tone of Rosemary's greeting sang of propriety.

Julie's lips twitched. Hardly fitting for a woman who had been breakfasting with her husband the morning after her wedding. She raised her eyes from the yellow-swaddled dish Rosemary carried.

"Call me, Julie. Please," she said, taking another step closer. Why keep up with formal etiquette when Julie knew there was more to Rosemary's interest in her husband than being a good neighbor?

"Certainly, Julie." Rosemary inclined her head. "On your way home from the schoolhouse?"

"I am."

"I hope you found the children in good spirits. I was their substitute until recently. They can be a handful."

Julie nodded. "They can be, but I thoroughly enjoyed my first day."

"How wonderful! It takes a special kind to teach, you know. Some do and those that cannot, well, they teach."

Julie gave her a brittle smile. "Is that how the old adage goes?"

Rosemary gave a delicate shrug. "So I've heard."

A fat drop of rain on her shoulder had Julie looking up with a frown. She'd wasted too much time speaking to Rosemary. "I should be going. Goodbye, Rosemary."

"Doesn't seem like you're dressed for the weather." Rosemary tutted, unfurling her umbrella with a barely concealed smirk. "Don't catch a cold, Julie!"

Julie waved a quick goodbye to Rosemary on her way down the road. Though she was now stuck in the rain, she was glad that she had been provided with an excuse to make a quick exit. She would gladly walk through a monsoon if only to put distance between her and the other woman.

There was something unkind in Rosemary's eyes that made Julie uneasy, a feeling that had nothing to do with her dislike of Will's relationship, or very near relationship, with the blonde. The trek home was blessedly uneventful, and before long the ranch came into sight. Julie ran the last few steps as the rain turned into a raging thunderstorm, and icy water fell with abandon from the sky.

She dropped her keys twice from her shaking hands, fingers numb from the rain, before she got the door open. When she did, she was grateful for the warmth. Forrest and Will must have come home before her. She hadn't seen the buckboard outside, but with the rain, she supposed they had taken it to the barn around the back of the house.

Sagging against the door, Julie closed her eyes while she flexed her fingers, trying to work some feeling back into them.

"Julie? Is that you?" Forrest's voice floated to her from the parlor.

"Yes. It's me." Julie called out, eyes still closed.

"Was worried when you didn't come home sooner." Forrest's voice grew louder as he spoke. Julie opened her eyes when he came into the foyer, but from the dark look on his face, she almost wished she had kept them closed.

"What happened?" he asked, his voice sharp.

"Got caught in the rain." She gave him a sheepish smile, but Forrest didn't look amused.

"You could get sick standing there in your wet clothes! Julie, you're soaked through. Why is this all you're wearing? Where's your umbrella?" He came to stand in front of her. He reached out to touch her cheek, his hand warm on her. "Your lips are practically blue."

Julie touched them. "They do feel a bit cold now that you mention it."

"A bit?!" Forrest exploded, already propelling her up the stairs to their bedroom.

"I—I'm fine, really." Julie stumbled along after Forrest, her feet clumsy from walking in the cold rain. It was hard to keep up with Forrest's determined stride.

He swung her up into his arms with a barely repressed sigh. "I'm going to have to go by the schoolhouse now when the weather looks bad, aren't I?"

"It was just an accident!"

"And how many other women were out and about in this weather? None. That's how many. And dressed like you are! You aren't in the city anymore, Julie. Everyone knows to be indoors when a storm rolls in."

The boom of thunder in the background only served to drive his point home, and Julie said nothing. She was silent all the way to their room.

"I ran into Rosemary. She was out on the road."

"What?"

"You said no other women were out in the rain and that's just not true. Rosemary was."

"Don't care. She's not my wife. You are, and I'll not have you getting sick by being reckless." He went over to the fireplace and set about lighting it. "Get undressed. We have to get you dry and warm you up."

Julie huffed but did as she was told, pulling her jacket off with a wince when it came away soaked through. Forrest turned and cursed when he saw the once pretty garment dripping in her hands.

He stalked over to her and held out a hand. "Give it here."

She obliged and toed off her boots. Her fingers fumbled with the buttons on her dress, and she had just

125

changed her angle, hoping to have better luck, when Forrest stepped forward.

"Let me do it." His hands pushed hers to the side. She looked away, feeling like a scolded child while Forrest worked the buttons on her dress loose. When he was done he wasted no time in slipping her dress from her.

Forrest looked up at her with hard eyes. "You are going to promise me that you will not walk home in this weather again."

"How else was I supposed to get home?!" Julie exploded, unable to contain her temper any longer. Her run-in with Rosemary had her fit to be tied, and now Forrest's anger at her was more than enough to push her over the edge. "Would you have me stay at the school-house all night? You're overreacting about this, Forrest."

"I assumed Will was with you," Forrest shot back, running an angry hand through his hair. "Apparently, I was wrong about that. I was about to take off to the schoolhouse when you came home."

"Will's not home?" That explained why she hadn't seen the buckboard, at least.

"No. And if you think I'm overreacting about you walking home in the rain, then you're lucky Will wasn't home to see it." Forrest gave her a dark look before he pointed at her wet corset. "Keep getting undressed."

Julie blushed at her husband's forceful tone. "I'll do it on my own and in my own time."

"Julie, if you stay in those clothes you'll get sick."

"And that's my decision."

She took a step away from Forrest, intent on leaving the room. Where she planned on going she wasn't sure, but she was set on making her way there with as much dignity as she could manage in a soaking wet corset and underthings. Trail of waterdrops and all, she would hold her head high.

Julie had only managed a few of steps when Forrest caught her by the arm and rounded on her. His eyes blazed with anger, and his jaw was set.

"I'm not playing around with you, little bird. Get undressed," he ordered in a low voice, and this time when he said her nickname, there was nothing playful about it.

Julie wrenched her arm out of his grasp and put her hands on her hips. "Make me."

The words shocked even her as they slipped from her mouth, but like Lady Pim always said, 'Loosed words cannot be collected once given away. A young lady should stand firm but take care with her words.'

Well, Julie hadn't been careful, but she could at least stand firm. Getting half the equation right was better than not at all, wasn't it?

She tossed her head and stared back at her husband, whose eyes had widened in surprise at her show of defiance, but then Forrest drew himself up to his full stature. It was then that Julie realized she hadn't truly appreciated Forrest's sheer size and muscle mass.

She'd known he was athletic and toned, that he was a strong man, a big man. What she hadn't realized was just how small he made himself around her.

Forrest absolutely towered over her by half a foot. His blue eyes were electric.

"I ought to put you over my knee with the way you're behaving."

Julie quivered at his words because she believed what he said, but her bravado would not let her back down. Not when the turn of events hadn't been her fault. She couldn't anticipate how the weather would change, and why had she allowed herself to get distracted by that tart Rosemary for as long as she had?

The thought of Rosemary put a glare on Julie's face.

"Is that so?" Julie asked with a raised eyebrow. She was challenging him. They both knew it and it hung in the air between them. The space around them became fraught with tension, so heavy she could scarcely breathe from the weight of it.

Lord, how she wished she could take back the past few minutes. This was all going so wrong, and in record time as well. If she wasn't about to panic, Julie might be impressed with herself. Swallowing, she licked her lips, waiting for Forrest's next move in this tug-of-war they had somehow found themselves in.

His eyes tracked the movement of her tongue, and his jaw clenched as he did so. Her husband looked deeply conflicted. Julie could tell he was deliberating on what to do. What she did know was that she wasn't being fair, not in the least, but neither was he. For the love of God, why wouldn't he just touch her? Why hadn't he made love to her yet? How much longer would they dance around the issue?

So frustrated was she that she would welcome going over his knee if only to have his hands on her in a more intimate manner.

She drew in a breath that caused her corset to thrust her breasts higher. Forrest's eyes fell to her cleavage, and Julie had an idea. Perhaps she could use the heightened energy in the room to her advantage in tempting her husband.

Such a bold move would require her to be wanton. Too bad Julie hadn't the slightest inclination of what that entailed. Though that wouldn't prove to be an issue, because suddenly Forest moved. His athletic body, so tightly coiled a moment before, was now in motion, and before she could discern the intention of his movement, Julie found herself face down in the mattress of their bed.

Perhaps her plan to seduce her husband would be simpler than she imagined. He seemed determined to carry out more than his fair share of the seduction plot she had only just thought up.

"Oh!" Julie gasped, turning her face to the side. When she went to push herself up, she couldn't. Her hands, held fast by Forrest, were crossed behind her back.

"What are you doing?" she whispered, voice barely louder than the crackling and popping of the fire that now burned in the dim room. The firelight illuminated only their bed, with all else around them falling into shadow. It was as if nothing else on earth existed but the two of them and their bed.

"Getting you undressed," he said.

Julie swallowed hard. "Why?"

Forrest didn't answer as he yanked off her stockings and drawers. When he had the garments off, Julie felt the drag of his calloused fingers along her bare backside. For a solitary moment, Julie thought he was going to follow through on his promise to discipline her, but after another slow caress from her husband's palm, the energy in the room shifted.

Tension morphed from frustration to physical want that Julie felt down to her toes, prompting a moan muffled by the comforter on the bed. Her eyes drifted closed when she felt the rough material of Forrest's denim against her legs as he shifted behind her with a groan of his own.

Forrest still held her wrists in one of his hands while

he supported himself on his forearm by her cheek. He leaned down to whisper in her ear.

"Want you so bad, little bird. It's torture with you feeling so sweet under me."

"Then have me," she whimpered, fingernails scraping at the hand that held her wrists. "Please. I need you. "

Forrest's hand ventured further up, pushing the thin wet material of her slip as he went. When he reached the back of her corset, he hesitated before pushing himself back onto his knees to unknot her corset strings. Julie held herself still, a shiver moving through her as she anticipated Forrest's next move.

Forrest let out an appreciative sigh at the sight of her now undone corset. He reached out and trailed his finger along her spine in a featherlight touch, so light Julie half wondered if she had conjured the sensation from her overactive imagination and hormones.

Smoothing his palm against her back, Forrest then flipped her over onto her back with ease. Julie felt like her breath had been knocked out of her from the sudden gesture and she stared up at Forrest with wide eyes. The quick rise and fall of her chest drew his eyes down, and this time it was he who licked his lips. He smiled when he saw Julie's gaze fixed on his mouth.

"Are you still with me, little bird?" he asked, knees on either side of her legs, caging her in, his denim-clad thighs rough on her sensitive skin.

Julie gave the barest tip of her chin. "Yes."

Forrest blew out a deep breath through his nose, nostrils flaring as he stared down at her with eyes full of want. There was no mistaking that he genuinely did want her. His gaze moved over her with a heat that set her core on fire, and Julie couldn't speak.

Never in her life had anyone looked at her thusly. Wanted her in this way. Julie found she was desperate to be had.

She felt like a goddess.

The gentle, almost reverent touch of Forrest's hands on her body made her feel as if though she were meant to be worshipped. Oh, how she prayed he didn't stop himself.

Not this time.

Wordlessly Forrest continued unfastening the front of her corset, and it felt like a second later when he tossed the garment away from them to join the rest of her soaked clothes on the floor.

"You're beautiful," Forrest murmured. He pushed his palms against her sides and gave a slight shake of his head. "Most beautiful woman I've ever seen." He leaned close and pressed a kiss against her lips. "Inside and out."

Julie whimpered as Forrest kissed her, his fingers rucking up her slip. The now sheer material of it fit like a second skin on her thanks to the drenching she had suffered on her way home. She squirmed under Forrest's touch, fighting the urge to tug the material down past her waist where it had been shoved.

Trailing his fingers upwards, Forrest drew back and gave the ties at the front of her slip a gentle tug. "Raise your arms."

Her arms flew up, complying with his request. When her slip came off, she shivered, feeling the chill Forrest had warned her about.

"Cold?" he asked, blue eyes moving over her with a hunger that stilled her shaking. There was no way she could be cold with such a hot, desirous look from her husband.

"Yes," she told him with a nod.

Forrest bit his lip and yanked the comforter up and around her. Julie held her breath.

This was the moment she had been trying to skirt. She could see in his caring eyes that he was going to leave her now, pull away and take care of her from arm's length. Julie could not have that. She would not endure another night laying between her husbands without knowing what it was like to be made love to. She reached out, catching his wrist as he wrapped the thick material of the quilt around her.

"There is another way to warm me up. A more...physical way," she breathed, raising her whiskey-colored eyes to his. "Husband."

Julie had hoped to nudge him along in giving in to his need for her, but what she hadn't expected was the full-blown look of lust that swept over his face. Forrest's blue eyes darkened, pupils dilated, and he surged forward, capturing her lips in a passionate kiss. Julie whimpered when Forrest rolled his hips, the rough denim of his pants touching her just so in her most sensitive place.

"Forrest!" she gasped when he pulled away with a positively feral look on his face.

"I'll warm you up, little bird," he murmured to her, his voice low and full of promise. He shoved his suspenders off his shoulders while he toed off his boots. "Is that what you want?"

Forrest pulled his shirt off, and his undershirt and pants followed close behind. And then he pulled Julie under his muscular body in an embrace that left her breathless.

"Please, Forrest," she begged, though Julie hadn't the faintest idea what she begged him for. To kiss her? To not kiss her? Touch her? Whatever it was, she was desperate for it, and the only remedy for the tumult was her husband.

"Shhh, shhh," he whispered, nuzzling her neck, hands reaching down to squeeze her hips before trailing up her sides. Julie sucked in a breath when his thumbs brushed the underside of her breasts. Forrest noticed her quick intake and smiled, dipping his head to kiss the top of one breast while he palmed the other, first gently then more firmly, his palm grinding down onto her nipple.

"Mmm." Julie's hands flew up to grip his shoulders. His touch was nearly enough to make her dizzy, and she wanted more. Arching her back, she hooked a leg around his hip, seeking the friction she craved. When she felt his thick shaft pressing up against her inner thigh, she let out a moan of approval and fixed Forrest with a stare of pure wanting.

"I—I want you. Forrest, make love to me. I need you. Please!"

He swallowed hard, fingers digging roughly into her hips as he positioned her beneath him.

"God, Julie," Forrest whispered, sliding a hand down to hitch her leg higher against his side. "We have to go slow, darlin'. Don't," he breathed, ducking his head kissing her breast, this time his tongue sliding over the top of her nipple," want to hurt you."

Forrest's mouth continued to work her nipple. A bite from him had her gasping his name.

"Julie…" Forrest moaned, drinking in the sight of her reaction to his touch. "So beautiful, darling. Want to keep you safe. Never want to hurt you. You have to tell me if you need me to stop."

Julie closed her eyes and nodded. "You won't. I trust you."

"You have to tell me if I do," Forrest insisted.

Julie opened her eyes. "You won't hurt me. I know it. That's why I married you." She opened her eyes and smiled up at him, her fingers combing through his blond hair which glinted like burnished gold in the crackling fire. "I knew you were a good man from the first letter."

"Little bird..."

Forrest kissed her, silencing her from speaking any further. The hand at her thigh kept her leg where he wanted as he pressed forward, the head of his member pushing against her core. Julie let out a shuddering sigh when he kept pushing forward, and the head of his shaft slid inside of her.

At long last. Oh, yes.

"Forrest." Her hands tightened his hair, but she said nothing else as he began to drag his hips back and forth. That inch inside of her slid out, but a moment later slipped back in with a little more length added. Julie had heard that losing one's virtue as a new bride could be a painful and disagreeable experience but that was not the case with Forrest. He was gentle and attentive.

Julie rolled her hips, trying to take more of her husband inside of her. Forrest sighed against her skin, lips, and tongue moving up her neck as he thrust up into her again. A short cry of pleasure escaped her when Forrest suddenly snapped his hips forward until his hips rested flush against her.

"Jesus..." Forrest went still, his head falling forward against her neck, using his proximity to cover her chest in kisses, while one hand massaged her breast, twisting and pulling her nipple. Through all this he didn't move, his hips tense against her.

"Relax, little bird. We won't—I won't move until you tell me to." He kissed her, his hands moving almost lazily up and along her body. Forrest touched her arms, her neck, and face as he deepened the kiss. When they drew apart, Julie smiled up at him and tentatively raised her other leg until it was at his waist.

"Move, Forrest."

"Are you sure?" He pulled back, looking down at her.

She nodded, drinking in the sight of her beautiful husband above her, his eyes full of love. "Make love to me."

Forrest groaned low in his throat and at her request moved his hips in a gentle rocking motion that had Julie eager for more. Every roll and shift of his body had her feeling more on fire, and she reached up, running her hands over his muscular chest. Julie hesitated before she leaned close and gave one of his nipples an experimental squeeze of her own.

He sucked in a breath at that and grinned down at her.

"More." Julie dug her fingernails into his biceps. "I need more."

"God," Forrest said, voice barely above a whisper at her direct request. "My little wife likes sex."

Julie nodded. "With you."

"And Will," Forrest whispered, breath ragged. He thrust into her with more strength, his movements causing her body to quiver in his arms.

"A-and," Julie gasped from the sudden snap of Forrest's hips, "and Will." Her head fell back when Forrest picked up his pace in earnest.

"Yes, sweetheart." Forrest leaned over her, his body

blanketing her, every part of their bodies touching. He kissed her deeply."Say that again. Tell me you want this with Will and me."

"I want you and Will."

"What do you want from us?"

"I want—want you."

Forrest's thrusts had picked up in earnest, and he slipped one hand between them to capture that sensitive bud of nerves Julie was quickly learning to revere.

"Tell me you want us to have you like this. That you want us inside you. Only us."

"I want you inside me." Julie gave up trying to match Forrest's thrusts and gripped his shoulders, simply trying to hold on to her sense of where she was. Her husband had dropped all pretense of gentleness and moved into her with deep strokes, the muscles beneath her hands coiling and bunching as he took his pleasure. Though Julie found that she had not been forgotten in that regard, and gasped as wave after wave of ecstasy rolled over her.

"I want you to make love to me every night. I want you to have me in every way you want. The both of you. I want the both of you t-to bed me at once."

Forrest closed his eyes and clenched his jaws at her last statement. The words pulled to mind an obscene picture that was enough to nearly send him to his climax. He increased the pressure against her clitoris and before long he beheld the sight of Julie writhing beneath him, her eyes clenched shut.

"Look at me," Forrest bit out, his voice hoarse as he worked her toward her orgasm. Dutifully Julie opened her eyes to look at him. "So beautiful, Julie. I love your body, little bird. Mmm," he purred, nodding approvingly at her as he felt her start to clench around his shaft.

"That's it, let me feel your pleasure," he praised her when Julie's body shook with the throes her orgasm. Her fingernails dug into his skin, and she let loose a sob at the sensation of free-falling into the pleasure Forrest's body gave her.

After a shuddering gasp, Julie tensed and finally went pliant in Forrest's hands as her husband continued to thrust into her. Each buck of his hips was stronger than the last until Forrest threw his head back with a shout as he emptied into her. He groaned, his arms shaking as he leaned down to kiss her.

"You were beautiful," he whispered against her lips as another shudder ran through his body. "So lovely, so perfect for us."

"I love you," Julie whispered back.

Forrest smiled down at her. "I love you too, little bird."

CHAPTER 8

$\mathcal{W}$hen Forrest and Julie descended the stairs hand in hand, they caught sight of Will sitting at their kitchen table eating a slice of pie. He leaned back in his chair, balancing on the two hind legs with his feet up on the seat next to him.

Julie's eyes caught on the bright yellow material of the towel tossed to the side. It was identical to the towel wrapped around the dish Rosemary carried with her when they had crossed paths on the road. So that was what she had been carrying. Their, no, *her house*, had been Rosemary's destination that afternoon.

A flame of anger ignited in the pit of her stomach, though Julie tried to squash the feeling. She was being irrational. It could have been any number of things Rosemary had carried with her and yellow was not a unique color.

Who was she turning into out here on the frontier?

"And what have you two been up to?" Will asked, not looking up from the plate of pie.

Julie took a moment to collect herself from her self-reflection. There was something tense about the way Will held himself. The lines of his body were rigid and sharp. He wasn't looking at them, but Julie didn't have to see his eyes to know he wasn't happy. His tone was tense, his words clipped, and she bit her lip, casting a sidelong glance at Forrest whom she saw had also registered the almost accusing tone in Will's voice.

He wasn't happy, and it was because of them.

Forrest stood to his full height, bulk comforting at her side, and squeezed Julie's hand. "You know what we were doing."

Will looked up from the pie, a cruel smirk on his lips. "I suspect I do from the bounce in your step, Forrest."

Julie sucked in a breath at that. Oh, he was mad. He was very mad.

Forrest narrowed his eyes. "Treadin' heavy. Careful."

"I wouldn't say that." Will put his plate down on the table with a thunk and turned his eyes to Julie. "What do you think, Jules? You think I'm treadin' heavy?"

"What?" She crossed her arms in front of her and stepped closer to Forrest as Will leaned forward in his chair, regarding her as he rubbed a hand along his jaw.

His eyes landed on her hand in Forrest's for a moment before he asked, "Forrest make you feel good?"

Julie blushed, her fingers tightening on Forrest's hand. "I-I—"

"You don't have to answer that," Forrest interrupted her, shooting Will a glare. Will's eyes slid over to Forrest and Julie was suddenly worried about the consequences of her begging Forrest to take her to bed without Will.

She had made a terrible mistake.

Damn her libido.

She hadn't been thinking of how Will would feel at being

139

left out, and that was her error. And now that Will was upset, she wasn't going to hide behind Forrest while her husbands exchanged tense words over an act that she had pushed for.

"It's my fault." Julie stepped forward, letting go of Forrest's hand. "I asked him to do it."

"To do what?" Will asked, leaning back his chair.

"To make love to me." She held a hand out to Will. "Please don't be angry. I wasn't thinking about how this would affect you. I'm sorry."

Will cracked a thin smile. "I'm not angry, Jules. We already had decided he'd be the first to bed you."

Julie frowned and glanced back at Forrest, who looked at Will like he wanted to strangle him. "Then why…" She paused and took a quick breath before plunging ahead. "I mean, y-you just seem upset."

"M'not," Will replied smoothly. He stood, letting the chair fall back onto all four legs with a thud. "I'm not upset."

Forrest snorted, coming to stand close to Julie, but he said nothing else. He just put his hand on her waist and gave her a gentle squeeze.

"Are you sure?" Julie asked.

"Did you enjoy it?" Will asked her. He walked forward, the lines of his body softening as he came to stand in front of her, his gray eyes searching hers.

Julie swallowed hard and nodded, glancing over her shoulder at Forrest. "It was perfect."

Will nodded. "Good. Perfect is what you deserve."

Julie blushed at his words and reached out to take his hand. "Having you there would have made it far more perfect. I didn't think when I tempted him. We—I should have waited for you to come home."

Will turned his hand up to take hers. "No, Jules. It's better there was only one of us. We didn't want to overwhelm you your first time."

"But I want you," Julie said, emboldened by her earlier admission to Forrest during their lovemaking. "I want the both of you."

Will's fingers tightened against hers at her words, his gray eyes darkened.

"Be careful, Jules," Will said, his voice low. He raised his other hand to cup her cheek. "I already want to take you right back upstairs for the rest of the night. You talk like that, and I'm not going to be able to keep myself from it. From you."

"Maybe, well...maybe you shouldn't stop yourself," Julie said, doing her best to give him what she hoped was an enticing look. If she had gotten Forrest to crack, then surely there was a way to elicit the same response from Will.

Or maybe not, she thought with a frown as Will shook his head and let go of her hand.

"You don't want that. Not with me," he said, taking another step back.

"Why not?" Julie asked, moving forward, trying to close the space that Will was rapidly putting between them. Will cleared his throat, turned, and snatched up the plate he had been eating from before moving toward the sink with a jerk.

"I'm not like Forrest. Not gentle in bed, darlin'. Don't have it in me anymore."

"I won't mind," Julie said, voice soft.

"I will," Will bit out.

Julie stepped forward and put a hand on Will's arm.

The muscles beneath her hand were rock hard from how hard he was squeezing the sink. "Will?"

His jaw clenched. "What?"

"You'll be gentle enough with me. I know it," Julie said, placing her other hand on his arm so that she was holding onto him. "And if you aren't, I won't break."

Will's eyes cut to her, and she almost took a step back from the glare on his face. "You don't know that. I could hurt you."

"I trust you."

"You shouldn't."

Julie frowned. "You're my husband."

He barked out a dry laugh and nodded. "Still don't know how that happened. Not fair to you, tying yourself to someone like me."

"Stop it," Forrest said. He stepped up behind them, a hand going to the back of Will's neck. "You aren't going to talk like that. I won't allow it."

Will's eyes closed at Forrest's touch, and he let out a sigh, his body relaxing, the muscles under Julie's hand gradually loosening as he unclenched his fist.

"What we have is good," Forrest said, rubbing Will's neck as he spoke. "You need to accept that."

"Oh, I do?" Will asked, but his tone wasn't tense any longer. The corner of his lips pulled up in a half smile. Forrest slipped his arm around Julie's waist and leaned his chin against Will's shoulder.

"Yes. And that's final. No pushing us away or acting like you're not jealous when I know how badly you want our sweet little wife. And let me tell you, she is sweet."

Will let out a strangled moan and opened his gray eyes to look down at her. "I'm sorry."

"It's okay. I'm sorry too." Julie slipped her arms around

Will's waist and smiled when he relaxed against her. It was a gift to feel the tenseness in his muscles dissolve beneath her hands. "You should have been there, Will." She turned her face, pressing her cheek against his chest.

"No, no." Will shook his head. "Wanted that to be normal for you. Your first time. Because none of this is normal. Our marriage is—"

He stopped short as both Julie and Forrest pinned him with glares.

"It's what?" they said in unison.

"Unique," Will supplied.

"Doesn't mean it's not right," Forrest muttered.

"Amen," Julie added in, her voice muffled against the front of Will's shirt as she laid her head back on his chest. Will chuckled, his fingers carding through her curly hair with a sigh. She smiled, squeezing him tighter before she stepped back and looked up at her husbands.

"I should get dinner started."

Forrest kissed her. "*We* should get dinner started."

Julie nodded at his words, and after another quick hug and kiss to Will's cheek, she moved past him to the icebox. There was a roast that Forrest had picked up earlier in the week. She glanced out the window and saw that the sun hadn't yet set, so if she worked quickly then she could have dinner coming out of the oven within the hour.

Though a knowing smirk from Forrest had her accepting his help without protest, and she let him take the roast from her. Will surprised her by working on chopping carrots and potatoes, and she let out a sigh.

"I feel useless," she said, her hands on her hips.

"Never expected you to be a cook," Will replied, methodically quartering potatoes.

"Advert said as much." Forrest nodded.

She raised an eyebrow. "Are you trying to give me a hint that there's a problem with my cooking?"

The men exchanged quick looks but remained silent on the matter.

Julie pursed her lips. "Fine. I'll put out a notice for a cook tomorrow." She tried not to notice the relieved sigh from Forrest, and she outright glowered at Will when she picked up the bright yellow towel that had been wrapped around the pie he had been eating. It was apple, and it looked divine, with its flaky golden crust and perfectly set filling.

She was positive it was the same yellow towel that Rosemary had been carrying. There was no mistaking it, and now she knew exactly what the woman had carried.

A pie, of all things.

She frowned, looking at the dessert. It didn't sit well with her that Rosemary had been coming from the direction of the ranch. It was now abundantly clear that she'd been on her way to give Will the pie.

If it was so innocent, then why hadn't she told Julie about the pie? And how had he ended up with it even after Rosemary had found him absent from home?

"What's got you frowning?" Forrest asked, rolling his sleeves up as he got ready to prepare the roast.

"Where did this pie come from?" Julie asked, doing her best for nonchalance, but she knew from the look Will gave her that she had failed.

"Rosemary," he answered her, looking back down at the vegetables.

"I ran into her just before it started raining. She didn't tell me she'd gifted you a pie."

Will shrugged. "Not much to tell about a pie."

Julie let out a harrumph and took the pie to the walk-

144

in pantry, just to have it out of sight. She didn't like the other woman's presence in Will's life, and her little cutting remarks only added to Julie's dislike of her. The past week had been rife with the woman, and it was enough to make Julie see red. She knew without a shadow of a doubt that Rosemary hadn't given up hope on Will. And that was the true root of Rosemary's ire toward her.

"Not my fault they didn't want you," Julie muttered to herself. "Giving my husband pies and having breakfast with him. The little chit." She may have put the pie down with a little more force than necessary, which amounted to her slamming it down on the pantry shelf, prompting Forrest to call to her.

"You okay in there?" he asked.

"Yes, yes." Julie walked back out with a bright smile on her face.

"What was that sound?" Will asked her, hitching a hip against the counter and giving her a curious look.

"Slipped," she blurted out. "Not me, the pie—it slipped. Flew right out of my hands."

"Slipped or slammed?" Forrest asked, stoking the fire in the oven with a barely-concealed grin.

"Slipped," Julie insisted, pulling an apron on with a determined set to her shoulders. "Strangest thing."

"What are you doing?" Forrest asked her with no small measure of trepidation when he saw her begin to measure out flour and sugar.

"Making," she said, pulling a large mixing bowl and pie tin out of the cupboard, "a pie."

"Do you know how to make pie?" Will asked.

"Well, not necessarily. But how hard can it be?"

The men exchanged looks again, but they didn't stop her, not when Julie had as determined a look in her eyes as any general they had followed in the war. It was best to let her go ahead. They nodded to one another in agreement and kept their eyes down as their wife began to mix and beat for all she was worth.

An hour later, Julie had the answer to her flippant question. Turned out making a pie was very difficult. In fact, it was damn near impossible without the proper proportions.

'Baking is a science unto itself,' *The Lady's Cooking Compendium* informed her when she pulled a still raw in the middle pie out from the oven with a groan. Julie had been so excited to showcase her own baking that she couldn't quite remember if she'd put baking soda or baking powder in, and had she used salt?

It turned out that she most likely hadn't, or that if she had, it had been too generously.

"It looks...interesting," Will offered when she looked ready to burst into tears at the sight of the mess in the pie tin. It wasn't at all like Rosemary's apple pie with its golden crust and flawlessly formed filling.

"It's a disaster," Julie whispered, dabbing at her eyes with her apron.

"We don't need pie," Forrest said, squeezing her shoulder. "We have the other pie."

"I don't want that pie," Julie protested. But her husbands didn't listen, and before long they had cut up and served the pie, and she reluctantly sampled a forkful.

It was delicious. So delicious that it made her want to stamp her foot in frustration. She absolutely could not stand Rosemary. Not her, or her pie.

"It's good," Julie had muttered mulishly with a pout. Will and Forrest had kept eating, not understanding why she was upset, and she hadn't wanted to bring attention to the reason for her consternation, so she had choked down the cursed pie without another word.

"Might ask Rosemary if she'd like to help out here a few days," Will said while they washed dishes after dinner.

The suggestion had her back stiffening. "I don't think that's a good idea," Julie said quietly.

"Why not?" Will pressed, earning a warning look from Forrest.

"I'd rather not have her in the house."

"Julie…"

"She doesn't like me." Julie sighed, drying her hands on a towel. "I'll write her a thank-you note for the pie. I'll make sure to take it to her when I place the advert for a cook tomorrow."

"That's not true," Will told her, crossing his arms over his chest. "She likes you fine."

"All the same." Julie took her apron off and hung it up. "I would prefer someone…" She hesitated as she scrambled for a way to explain that the men would understand. "Ah, someone older."

"Older?" Forrest asked.

"I could learn a lot from an older woman. Someone that I choose myself, if that's all right with you both," Julie said, throwing herself into her excuse with as much conviction as she could manage.

Will sighed but nodded along with Forrest, who was still motioning for the other man to back down. "Ah, housekeeping decisions are up to you, Jules."

"Thank you." She nodded to the pair of men, already focused on going to the parlor to read her book when Forrest's arms shot out, catching her around the waist. "What are—"

Forrest kissed her deeply, cutting her off. She blinked up at him when he drew back from her.

"Where do you think you're going?" he asked her.

"The parlor?" she whispered, feeling short of breath from the kiss.

"What's so interesting in the parlor?"

"Well, my novel..." Julie breathed out her answer, though a heat had started in her belly and begun spreading through her body to her fingers and toes. The memory of their lovemaking was fresh in her mind, making her breath come quick.

Forrest caught Will's hand and pulled the other man close. "I can see how the parlor would be interesting, but I think we should stick to the bedroom for the time being."

"Oh." She bit her lip, cheeks warming.

Her book was suddenly looking *dull*.

"Forrest..." Will's voice held a note of warning, but the blond paid him no mind.

"She wants you," Forrest told the other man with a nod toward Julie, whose eyes were wide and mouth parted as she struggled to keep her breathing even. "Don't you, little bird?"

"Yes. Very much," Julie whispered. She reached a hand out to Will and hesitantly placed her palm on his chest. The man sucked in a short breath at her touch. "I want you inside me."

Will let out a strangled groan and took a quick half step toward her. "Jules, I don't think we should."

"Please." She licked her lips and put her other hand on his chest, fingers pulling at the material of his shirt. "Please, Will."

His resolve may have held if Forrest hadn't stepped behind their wife, his hands on her shoulders as he started

148

to work down the neckline of her dress. He kissed her neck and looked at Will.

"She's so sweet, Will. Feels like heaven, just like the daydreams we talked about in the war. A woman like this between the two of us. Enough to bring you to your knees."

"Son of—" Will's hands clenched and unclenched.

"Language," Forrest admonished him, kissing her bare shoulder. Julie leaned her head back against Forrest's chest while he kissed her, and she let out a happy gasp when Will moved forward, pressing himself against her front and kissing her as he did so. His fingers joined Forrest's at her waist, and she trembled while both men worked her dress off.

When they had the fabric pooled around her feet, Will swung her up into his arms and carried her toward the staircase. She continued to kiss him as he walked, her fingers threading through his long hair, which she pulled free from its tie.

"Gonna love you sweet," he promised her.

She hummed at the words. "I didn't think you would have any other way."

"Won't always be sweet," Will told her, turning his gray eyes on her. They were at the top of the stairs, and he surprised her when he dropped her legs down and pressed her against the wall of the hallway, one of his hands sliding down to cup her between her legs. "Sometimes, I'll be rough with you." He kissed her hard then, teeth nipping at her bottom lip, but when he drew back, Julie surprised him by leaning into him.

"And I'll like that too," she whispered, kissing him back as fiercely as he had her.

Forrest came up the stairs, chuckling as he did so.

"Forgot to tell you. She's taken a liking to the pleasures of the flesh."

"Good Lord," Will moaned, picking her up once again, this time with her legs wrapped around his waist. "Perfect." He kissed her lips again before he lowered his head to nuzzle her cleavage, his tongue painting delicious paths along her skin.

"So perfect for us."

Julie wiggled her hips, trying to get closer to him. When he put her down on the bed, she let out a keening sound in protest, but Will was back at her side within a heartbeat.

"Shh." He cupped her face in his hands, shirtless now. "Right here." He kissed her then, his lips following the trail his fingers mapped out for him.

"Will…" Julie arched her hips the way Forrest had taught her hours before, and when she made contact with his rapidly hardening manhood, she knew Forrest had guided her for a reason. Will grunted and buried his face in her mass of dark curls which now tumbled free from her braid.

"Jules," he rasped out against her skin while working off her slip. His hands lifted her hips up again to press against him, and she let out a satisfied sigh when he allowed her to undo his belt and unbutton his pants.

The time that had passed from the moment they entered the room slid by in a slow dance of touches, kisses, lips, and cries of pleasure. They came together slowly, Will taking his time with every part of her. It was different than it had been with Forrest but no less lovely, and Julie felt every bit as much love and care under Will's hands as she had with Forrest.

The only difference in her feelings was that in the

afterglow of their lovemaking she didn't utter the words she had with Forrest, nor did her husband make any romantic overtures of his own. He held her close, her back to his chest, stroking her sides and kissing her neck.

She barely stirred when Forrest joined them in bed later that night. And when she fell asleep it was to two pairs of arms cradling her, not one, and that was Julie Wickes-Barnes's idea of perfect.

CHAPTER 9

*J*ulie sighed and shifted from foot to foot. Despite her assurances to act quickly, it had been nearly a week since she'd promised to put the advert in the newspaper for a cook. And if left to her own devices Julie might have played for more time, anything but come face-to-face with Rosemary Stanton. She'd successfully avoided the other woman and had congratulated herself on her skills of evasion, learned from her personal collection of novels portraying wily detectives and the criminals they stalked.

She owed so much to her books, now including this bit of fortune and peace in Gold Sky as well. Never let it be said that a well-read woman wasn't worth her salt.

Except that all of her careful avoiding and turning a blind eye to the other woman's continuous presence in Will's life all came to a halt today, a pleasant Saturday morning, until Forrest had loaded her into the buckboard with a pointed look.

Julie could take a hint, and no matter how hard she worked like a supplicant in front of *The Lady's Cooking*

Compendium she just couldn't manage to turn out anything edible. To her consternation, she had failed at making a pie no less than ten times. It was a sore issue in the house, especially when Will kept returning home, day after day, with some baked good or another from Rosemary. The desserts tasted like ash in her mouth each night after the less than edible or identifiable dinner she had prepared.

Seeing as a majority of their meals ended up turning to ash, Julie had to hire a cook or her husbands would either waste away into nothing or plan a mutiny in which they hired one for her. And letting the men choose the cook ran the risk of finding Rosemary in her home, so here she was trying not to glare at the unsuspecting door of the newspaper office.

She could do this.

She had come out during one of the most maddening and scandalous seasons on record for The Four Hundred, and she had managed to do it all with her nose firmly ensconced in a book. Julie nodded to herself, sucked in a fortifying breath, and pushed open the door into the office.

She would do this.

Though no sooner had she set a foot over the threshold than she heard her name called out. Julie froze, still as a statue, and turned her head to the side. If the Lord were merciful, it wouldn't be Rosemary, though knowing her luck...

"Julie!"

Prompted by the voice, Julie turned to the side entirely, and she let out a relieved sigh when she saw Alice hurrying toward her with a smile on her face.

"Oh, young lady, I see those men of yours finally let

you out on your own." Alice paused and wagged a finger at Julie. "Hmm, maybe I shouldn't call you young lady, as no doubt those men have made a woman out of you by now."

Julie blushed. "I, ah, well—"

"I'm being crass. I'm sorry, I'm sorry." Alice looped her arm through Julie's and gave her a sweet smile. "Forgive an old woman?"

"You're hardly a day over thirty."

Alice pulled a face. "I'll have you know I'm nowhere near thirty."

Julie blanched, her eyes going wide, as she began to stutter, "Oh, I didn't mean to say that you—"

Alice threw her head back and let out a peal of laughter. "Julie, I'm kidding! I'm kidding!" She waved her hands with another merry laugh. "I'm nearly fifty, you know."

"Really?" Julie gaped.

"Truly."

"How sensational. What is your secret?" Julie lowered her voice to a hushed whisper.

"That, my blushing bride, is a story for another time." Alice bumped her shoulder against Julie's in a good-natured tease. "Now that you're away from the ranch, how are you? Tell. Me. Everything. Have your virile husbands taught you much in the way of the intimacies of marriage?"

"Alice!" Julie clapped a hand over her mouth. The words set her cheeks aflame, but mostly because she was bursting at the seams with things to tell her friend. There was no denying that she had gotten a thorough education from her husbands, or that her life had consisted mainly of the schoolhouse and her place at the ranch. It was hard not to make a beeline for the ranch as soon as she was able, not with Forrest waiting on her with the buckboard outside the schoolhouse, and certainly not when she knew what waited for her behind the doors of their bedroom.

Julie's pulse raced at remembering the passionate exploration she had engaged in, which had not been relegated to their bedroom as of late. Just last night she had been taken by surprise on the dining room table when she had wandered downstairs looking for a snack.

Will had given her something far more tempting than the chocolates she'd been after.

"A lady never kisses and tells." Julie smiled brightly, pushing away the thoughts of her husband and their dining room table.

Alice threw her arms around Julie. "You would be proper, but that's all right. I forgive the virtue and good breeding. What are you doing here, hmm? I came this way to pay for next week's advertisement."

"Just placing an advert for a cook." Julie held up the piece of paper with the small ad she had penciled in.

"Oh, let me take a look at that. I might know a gal." Alice already had the sheet of paper in her hand before Julie could so much as protest, but she didn't mind. Alice's energy was infectious, and she welcomed it wholeheartedly.

"That would be helpful." Julie clasped her hands and watched as Alice scanned the notice.

"You're being generous with pay," Alice said after reading the small advert.

"Just want to give what's fair."

"Twenty dollars a week is more than fair." Alice wagged the paper at her. "And not even to clean? Just cook? I'd add in cleaning as well."

"I've been managing the cleaning but...it would be nice to rest a little more." Julie sighed, thinking of how she wanted to spend less time scrubbing floors or doing laundry and more time working on new ways to engage her students.

"You're a teacher. That's hard enough work. I say add in the cleaning bit. Here, let me." Alice snatched up a pencil from a passing clerk's hand and ignored the man's startled look. "Definitely the wash as well," she hummed, staring down at the paper as she wrote. "That's hell in the winter, and while we are warming up now, it never hurts to have someone used to it when the time comes."

"Alice—" Julie tried to take the sheet back, but the other woman suddenly stood up with a jab of the pencil.

"You know what? I know a woman, fantastic cook, housemaid, the works! She'll show you how to mend like a dream." Alice nodded, tucking the notice into her reticule. "Don't you worry about a thing. I'll send her over this afternoon. Her name is Leslie."

Julie blinked at the speediness of Alice's action. "Are you sure?"

"Oh, quite. You'll love Leslie. She's a mother hen sort of woman and very deserving of this kind of pay. She lives in town and helps me when I'm in need. You won't regret taking her on."

"Alice, thank you so much!" Julie bounced on her toes in excitement.

Alice looped her arm through Julie's and pulled her close. "Plus, she's an older woman. You won't have to worry about her sniffing around your husbands like a certain citizen," she said, her voice now barely above a whisper.

"Alice, I don't know wh—"

Alice pursed her lips. "Don't lie to me. I thought we were friends. I see the way she looks at Will. We all do. Have for a while."

The other woman turned her head, prompting Julie to follow her gaze, which landed on Rosemary. The blonde woman moved about the office with a stack of papers in one hand and a cup of tea in the other. She looked at ease in the hustle and bustle of the newsroom, which irked Julie because she realized that she had never seen Rosemary with a hair out of place. She self-consciously smoothed a hand over her own curls, which made Alice smirk at her.

"You're much prettier," she said.

Julie sighed. "Thank you. But that isn't the point. Women shouldn't have to...tear one another down to feel better."

"That's no fun when the other one is an utter monster."

The corner's of Julie's lips turned up in a smile. "Thank you nonetheless."

"What are friends for?"

"Evidently placating insecure wives," Julie muttered, turning to leave the newsroom now that her business of hiring a cook has been seen to. The relief of not having to engage with Rosemary put a happy smile on her face and a spring in her step. Perhaps today could still turn out to be the perfect Saturday Julie had envisioned upon waking.

Alice stepped beside her. "You're not insecure. She's wanted Will since before her husband died. God rest his soul."

"Are you serious?" Julie hissed with a wide-eyed look at the new bit of information. Alice gave her a quick nod, but before she could say more Rosemary appeared at their side, blocking their access to the news office door.

"Well, look at you two!" Rosemary smiled at them. "Tell me, what has the two of you whispering like schoolgirls?"

Alice gave a small shrug. "Oh, you know, the secrets of the newlywed bride."

Rosemary's smile faltered at that. She cleared her throat before cutting her eyes to Julie. "Ah, yes, what happy days you must be experiencing."

Julie inclined her head. "Thank you. I am."

"Hard not to, with such fine men for company," Alice added with a wink.

"Alice!" Julie swatted at the other woman, which only made Alice giggle and Rosemary scowl, an expression that Julie wasn't upset to see after all the vexation the blonde's baked goods had caused her that week. She considered it just desserts.

"So, tell me, how is the dance planning going?" Rosemary asked, turning the conversation away from talk of Julie's newlywed bliss.

"Excuse me? Dance?" Julie blinked in surprise.

"The spring dance," Rosemary said, one hand at her chest with feigned innocence. Something in her words had Julie wary, like she was about to have some very unpleasant news dropped in her lap.

"What spring dance?"

Rosemary held up a hand. "Sorry. The school has put it on for the past three years. It's become a Gold Sky tradition. One of the biggest events in the entire town."

Julie's eyes darted to Alice to see if Rosemary was telling the truth, and the wince she saw on her friend's face had Julie letting out a sigh.

"When is it supposed to be put on?" she asked,

resigned to her fate of planning a spring dance. If it was a tradition, there was no way around it.

"Next Thursday," Rosemary said with a shake of her head. "Did no one tell you?"

Julie gritted her teeth. Now she knew the other woman played at concern. There was no mistaking the patronizing tone in Rosemary's voice, and she put on a tight smile.

"No, not a word."

"Odd, doesn't the newspaper send out a reporter to get the full story on the preparations at least two weeks before the dance?" Alice asked, pinning Rosemary with a disapproving look.

"Oh, yes, I suppose they have in the past. Funny thing, that. We've just been so busy around here!" Rosemary tapped her chin with a sigh and then shrugged. "Well, that just means you'll have to work doubly hard to ensure we have the best spring dance yet, isn't that right, Julie?"

Julie's fingers tightened on her reticule. "Of course. The absolute best Gold Sky has ever seen." She cleared her throat and stepped toward the door. "And that means I should be heading out now. Alice, please send Leslie by as soon as you can. I suspect I'll be needing the extra set of hands sooner than I realized."

"Of course. Here, let me walk with you." Alice once again was at her side and helping her push open the door.

"Goodbye, ladies!" Rosemary called after them with a little wiggle of her fingers.

"Is it safe to say that I abhor that woman?" Julie fumed as they walked along the storefronts.

"Not in the least, and that's not even because she wants your husband," Alice replied with a shake of her head.

"It's that apparent?" Julie frowned, pausing to give a

cautionary look over her shoulder toward the newspaper office. The last thing she wanted was Rosemary sneaking up on them again.

Alice gave her hand a squeeze. "It is, and you're right to feel like you do. She's always been a forward woman, and after her husband died, well, she just does as she pleases. Doesn't care who gets hurt."

"I see."

"I wouldn't worry," Alice told her. "Your husbands are smitten with you. They barely leave your side. It used to be that they were in town so much, but since you arrived, that's changed."

Julie nodded, but she couldn't shake Alice's words. It had been one thing to blame her jealousy on travel nerves or being tired, or on the simple fact that she couldn't cook or bake while Rosemary did so with little effort. It was another thing to know that her suspicions about Rosemary were correct and that knowledge of it was public.

"Speak of the devil." Alice nudged her in the side, and Julie looked up in surprise, but she smiled when she saw Forrest and Will ambling down the boardwalk toward her. Though her smile faltered when she noticed Will raising his hand in greeting to someone inside the newspaper office.

She had a guess as to who had caught his attention through the window.

"Don't pay her any mind," Alice told her, seeing her reaction. "What you need to do is focus on planning the dance. I'll have Leslie by at about two today, and you can discuss a satisfactory routine at the ranch."

Julie jerked her eyes away from Will stopping to talk to an excited Rosemary, who had bustled out of the newspaper office to chat, and gave Alice a nod.

"I should stay busy."

"Yes, you should." Alice gave her shoulder a squeeze. "I've got to run back to the boarding house before Peter sets the place ablaze. Left him making breakfast while our cook is in Butte."

Julie nodded and waved at her friend, but the moment Alice left she looked back at Will and wished that she could believe Alice's words about not worrying over Rosemary, because at the moment the petite blonde woman didn't seem to have any problem holding Will's attention.

"Get the advert placed?"

Forrest's question pulled her attention away from watching Rosemary and Will talk.

"Ah, no. Alice knows a woman who would be perfect. She's having her come by at two." Julie did her best to recover from her displeasure at seeing Rosemary and Will together.

It meant nothing because he was, she reminded herself, married to her. Not the blonde.

"Well, that's great news. Alice knows wonderful people around town, and she'd only send the best our way. Always been kind to us." Forrest smiled at her, though he cleared his throat when he noticed the pinched look on her face that she hadn't quite managed to wipe away. "Something wrong, little bird?"

"No, it's nothing." Julie took his arm and gestured towards the mercantile. "Shall we see if the curtains and extra linens for the upstairs have come in?"

Forrest glanced behind him. "Will wanted to come with us…"

"Will seems to be otherwise occupied," Julie replied, already walking along, tugging her big husband along behind her. "And I need to get by the grocer as well for more supplies. I know you wanted to hire on a few hands, and meals are a requirement for labor. Plus, I just found out about the spring dance. Not much time to spare."

Forrest made a face. "Spring dance? They have you planning that? Usually there's a committee working on it for months ahead of time."

Julie's steps faltered. "Months?" she asked, giving him an aghast look.

"Least that's the way it was last year. Rosemary headed it up. Assumed she would again this year."

"So the school is only the venue for the dance? Not the planner?" Julie asked, glaring over her shoulder at where Rosemary had one hand on Will's shoulder. They were standing too close together, and it had Julie's teeth on edge. She had half a mind to march over there and say something, but she refused to give Rosemary the satisfaction.

"Not that I recall, but I never paid much attention to it. Only did last year on account of that being when—" He stopped short and suddenly looked uncomfortable. "Well, I just did last year, is all."

Julie raised an eyebrow at him. "Why did you last year?" she asked as they walked into the mercantile.

"Doesn't matter, little bird." Forrest shook his head and stepped past her to the counter. "I'll check on the order if you want to take a look around."

Julie nodded, confused at Forrest's lack of an explanation. She didn't understand why he wasn't answering her question. It didn't seem like a big one to ask, but she could tell it made him uncomfortable to talk about. Julie didn't press the issue, and Forrest looked relieved for it as they made their way to the grocer's. Only when she saw a beautiful display of apples did her thoughts turned from Forrest's odd behavior.

"We'll take a bushel," he told the grocer when he caught her looking at the fruit longingly.

"Really?" Julie asked excitedly.

"Of course. And I almost forgot. We got two telegrams waiting for you from your family. We can go get them after this."

"Oh, I hope one is from my mother. I know she has so many questions at this point. Do you think my letter got there yet?"

"Could be if things went smoothly." Forrest smiled at her excitement as he watched her hurry around the store, picking out their groceries for the next couple of weeks. Forrest added on his own list of staples to Julie's, and she practically skipped down the boardwalk to the sheriff's station.

News from her family was almost enough to stop her from noticing that Will was still absent from what was supposed to be their first shopping trip as a trio.

Almost.

That was, until she found out that her letter had indeed made it to New York City. All thoughts of her consternation at Rosemary and Will left her as she devoured news from home. Julie sat at Forrest's desk, scratching out a reply to her mother's inquiry after the social scene in Gold Sky and what her husband was like.

The simple question had Julie tapping her chin with her pencil, thinking of a truthful answer.

Her mother didn't know about Will, and it seemed the best course of action was to keep it that way. Not until she had more time to explain the situation to her family.

Perhaps a visit to Gold Sky would be the best time to do that?

She had just finished describing how kind Forrest was when the door banged open, causing both Forrest and Julie to jerk toward the door in surprise.

"Julie?!" There was a wild look in Will's eyes that bordered on panic.

"Yes?" She put her down and stood from the desk. "Will, are you all right?"

"What? Where did you go?!" Will shut the door with a shove of his hands, and in an instant stood in front of her. He reached out and took hold of her hands. "I couldn't find you."

Julie swallowed hard, giving Forrest a sidelong look where he shined his boots while he waited for her to go through her messages. There was a scared look to Will's grey eyes that urged Julie to provide comfort, though she knew not what from.

"Shopping," she said, trying to keep her voice as soothing as possible.

"Already?" Will frowned.

"Well, yes." She pulled her hands away from his. Her instinct to soothe him was at odds with the one thought that paraded through her mind: what if he had touched Rosemary with those hands? Her eyes fell to his elbow where the other woman had latched on earlier.

Will looked like he wanted to snatch her hands back, but he didn't move any closer to her, and said, "I thought this was our family trip into town. Why did you go on without me?"

"Little bird has a lot on her schedule this week. Even getting a cook in an hour," Forrest added, looking back down at his boots.

Julie nodded and let out a frustrated sigh. "This dance is going to be the death of me. I'm going to make coffee. I'll need it if I want to make any headway on the planning for it. Do you think I could talk Alice into helping?"

"She'd lend a hand," Forrest said with a thoughtful look on his face. "You should also ask Rhodes's wife. She has been dying to help with the dance."

"Perfect!" Julie grinned at him and busied herself with stoking the fire at the stove. "Will, do you want any coffee?" she asked, looking over her shoulder at him. Though she might not be able to bake, she knew her way around a percolator.

He stood behind the desk, his eyes trained on the letter she had been writing. "Writing home?" he asked her quietly.

"Yes, there were messages from my mother. She's curious about Gold Sky." Julie smiled at him and turned back to the coffee in front of her. "Seems her interest in the frontier was piqued by my last letter."

"Mm." Will picked up her letter with a raised eyebrow. "And your husband."

Julie bit her lip at the look in his eyes. They weren't the warm gray she had started to grow accustomed to, but were a cold, hard, flinty shade that she had never had fixed on her before.

"Husbands," Forrest corrected without looking up, his blond head bent over his boots.

"Not according to this letter home. Isn't that right, Julie?" Will gave the letter a little shake before he let it fall back onto the desk.

Forrest's hands stilled, and he put his boot down with a frown. "What does he mean?"

"Well, ah." Julie's hand toyed with the percolator she

had been preparing. "My family doesn't know that I married you both."

"What do they think?" Will asked, leveling an unblinking stare at her.

"That I just—just married Forrest." She bit her lip and looked to the side.

Forrest winced at the news. "Little bird..." His voice was soft, and his blue eyes were far kinder to look at than Will's, so Julie took a hesitant step in his direction as she struggled to find the words to explain.

"They wouldn't have let me come. And I wanted to do it, I wanted the both of you." She looked over at Will. He still stood motionless by the desk. "And isn't it my life? Why shouldn't I get to pick whom I marry?"

Forrest let out a sigh and held an arm out to her. "We understand, we—"

"Oh, we do, do we?" Will's voice cut Forrest off so sharply that Julie flinched.

Forrest stood up, his hands on his hips in exasperation. "You heard her, Will. They wouldn't have let her come."

"Well, she's here now, and she's fine with lettin' them think it's just you." Will tapped a finger on her letter. "Says you're kind, gentle, a good man. That you make her happy. Not even trying to set them straight."

"Will, I just—I don't know how yet, but I will." Julie's hands twisted in her skirts. "Please, believe me. I know you're angry."

Will scoffed. "Angry about what? That you're ashamed of me?"

Julie's mouth dropped open. "I am not ashamed of you! Take that back this instant."

"No." Will crossed his arms over his chest as he glared at her.

"Will. Ease up." Forrest came to stand beside her. "This isn't an easy situation to explain. Not everywhere is like Gold Sky—not as accepting—especially not high society in New York."

Will's eyes moved between them. "You would say that. You're the one she's telling them about. She wants them to know all about you."

"Will, I'm sorry. Please." Julie lowered her eyes to the floor. "You're my husband. Nothing can change what I promised in front of this entire town and God."

"You're damn right nothing can change that," Will said, striding toward the door with angry steps. He paused and looked back at her. "You're my wife, Julie Anne, and so long as you remain in Gold Sky, I'll make sure you don't forget it for a second." Will's eyes flashed at the both of them before he slammed the door behind him.

"Oh—oh no," Julie moaned, her eyes filling with tears. She covered her mouth and shook her head while Forrest wrapped his arms around her.

"Shh, shh, little bird." He kissed her forehead and led her over to the desk to sit down. "He'll calm down. I promise. Will's always been the emotional one. He's just angry, but it'll blow over. Everything will be alright once he's had some time."

"He was so mad," Julie whispered, looking down at her hands where tears had begun to fall onto her skin. "I just... This is my fault. I should have said something before I wrote the letter."

"No, it's not. This is an unconventional marriage, even for Gold Sky." Forrest crouched down in front of her and wiped at her tears with a handkerchief. "I know it can't be easy to explain to your family about us. You're from a proper family. A real debutante. And this is something ladies like you don't even think about, let alone do."

"I just want them to understand. I want them to love us as much as I love us." Julie took the handkerchief and dabbed at her eyes, trying to stop the tears, but it was no use, and a sob escaped her chest. "I made an awful mess of things with this letter." She snatched up the sheaf of paper and tore it up in frustration.

Forrest caught her hands as she threw the paper scraps into the trash. "It's all right. This is just one of those things. It's no one's fault."

"One of those things?" Julie shook her head. "Did you see the look on his face? He hates me."

Forrest snorted. "Julie, that couldn't be further from the truth. Give him time, and he'll come out of this."

Julie nodded, trying to cling to the little bit of hope that Forrest's words inspired in her. The look of betrayal in Will's eyes had been nothing short of gut-wrenching.

If she lived to be a hundred years old, she never wanted to see that expression again.

CHAPTER 10

*J*ulie was thrilled her afternoon meeting with Leslie O'Brennan had gone over well. She had taken to the older woman's motherly vibe. It would be nice to have Leslie's calming presence in the house, especially with the chaos of the dance looming overhead.

Leslie was in her early fifties, with burnished red hair and laughing blue eyes. She had come to America in her youth from Ireland, and had never regretted it for a moment. After living in New York for two decades, she had made the move to Gold Sky, and all of her efforts went toward working hard to help support her daughter's children after their father had died in the winter of the previous year.

It was gratifying to be able to help give back to Gold Sky by employing Leslie. The woman had nearly burst into tears at discovering the proposed wage for the position.

"This is a godsend," Leslie had wept, clutching her hand. "Thank you! I'll not disappoint you. I swear it!"

Julie had shown Leslie the lay of the house and had set up a washing and cleaning schedule along with the cooking duties. Though, when she really looked at the sheer size of the house, she began to toy with the idea of hiring on an additional pair of hands, but Leslie would hear none of it and assured her that she was more than capable.

When asked if she had any special requests, Julie had only been able to think of one thing.

"Can you show me how to bake?"

"Bake what?"

Julie sucked in a deep breath and said, "A pie. An apple pie."

Leslie raised an eyebrow. "That's all?"

"That's all." Julie gave a curt nod.

"Oh, missus. Your husbands won't want any other pie in the territory. You have my word."

Julie's heart soared at the promise. "When can you start?" she asked, beaming at Leslie.

And it had been as simple as that. Julie was happy at the idea of having a delicious meal for dinner the next day when Leslie would begin working. Her husbands had been patient with her lack of culinary expertise, and it comforted her that they would have a meal they deserved.

Though a moment later her smile faltered.

Her husbands.

Plural.

A sour taste permeated Julie's mouth, and she sagged forward in her seat at the table with a heavy sigh. How she wished she'd been direct with her family about her plan to marry both men.

Why had she put off telling them about Will?

She would have to work on a letter that explained her

unique marriage arrangement to them as soon as she was able to get a handle on the spring dance planning. She hadn't had so much as a spare hour to devout to the pile of books she had purchased on her arrival in Gold Sky.

Disgraceful. Who was she becoming?

At the realization that she had neglected her reading, Julie resolved she would go by Alice's home and speak to her about being on the committee, and Rhodes' wife as well. Between the three of them, it should be doable. And that meant she would be able to get back to her novels at some point, which was all she could really hope for.

Snatching up a piece of paper and pencil, Julie had only just begun to write a list of possible supplies and necessities for the dance when she heard the front door open and close.

Julie closed her eyes and took a deep breath as she wondered which of her husbands it would be. Forrest had left to mend a fence with two of the men he had just hired on at the ranch, and she hadn't a clue where Will had gone after he had left the sheriff's station that afternoon.

"Little bird?" Forrest's voice called out to her, and she let out a breath, relaxing when it wasn't Will. She wasn't quite ready to face him just yet.

"In here!" Julie called out. A minute later Forrest appeared in the kitchen with a crooked smile on his face.

"You don't know how nice it is to see you in here. Well, just in our home." Forrest kissed her cheek. "Makes me feel complete."

"Forrest." Julie blushed, putting her pencil down.

"Planning for the dance?"

"Solid logistics ensure a victory."

Forrest laughed at her, tweaking her nose. "Sound like a general with that talk."

"I'm going to have to be if I have any hope of putting this dance together in a week. I can do it, I think. Plus, I'll have you to help me if I get stuck."

Forrest's smile fell, and he rocked back on his heels with a sigh. "I wish I could help you. That's what I came to find you about."

"What is it?" Julie bit her lip at the suddenly morose look on Forrest's face.

"I'm being called out on an assignment. There's a gang of robbers causing havoc on the line into Butte City. They are calling in a posse to help with setting it right."

"Oh." Julie gripped his hand tightly. "How long will you be gone?"

"Could be days. Could be weeks. As long as it takes to put them down." Forrest rubbed a hand along her cheek. "I just got the message that I'm being sent and wanted to come tell you as soon as I was able. I'm leaving tomorrow."

Julie sucked in a deep breath at the sudden news. "Is Will going too?"

Forrest shook his head. "No. They won't leave this area without a gun. Will is staying behind."

Julie nodded, though her stomach twisted at the thought of being left alone with her moody husband. She was nervous about how to act around him after today. What if she made a bigger mess of their marriage before Forrest returned to help fix it?

"That—that's good," she said softly.

"Don't worry, little bird." Forrest hugged her tight. "You'll be safe with Will. I know he can be gruff, but he loves you. This will be good for both of you. When I get back, the two of you will be like two peas in a pod. I know it."

"Are you sure?" Julie looked at him doubtfully. "I'm scared I'll make him angrier with me. I don't—I just can't seem to find my footing with him."

"That's just his way. He'll settle into things, and when he does, you'll be the first and last thing on the idiot's mind."

Julie smiled at the thought of Will treating her as gently as Forrest did. "I'd like that. You're both already the first and last thought I have."

"Oh, darlin'." Forrest sighed and kissed her. "You're so easy to love."

Julie leaned into Forrest with a smile. "So are you."

They held each other for a bit before Julie spoke again. "We have a cook. She's promised to show me how to bake the best pie in the territory."

Forrest chuckled. "Now that is worth the wage we are paying. I'll keep that in mind when I'm eating beans out of a can and salt pork."

"That sounds…awful." Julie sniffed delicately.

"It's what I signed up to do." Forrest shrugged, his hands stroking her sides. "Not where I want to be, though, when I could have you pressed up against me."

Julie blushed. "Flattery will get you everywhere, sir."

"Good, because I intend to have every part of you." Forrest kissed her jaw, earning him a sharp intake of breath.

"I'm not sure if that's what the saying means," she rasped out, letting Forrest draw her toward the foyer. She knew he wanted to take her upstairs, and there wasn't a bone in her body saying otherwise. Not when she had a roast ready to be put in the oven. Leslie had been gracious to put it together for her with specific instructions. Dinner was all but taken care of, which meant that Julie was free to take care of her husband...and herself, for that matter.

"It isn't?" Forrest gave a mock look of disbelief. "And to think I've been doing it wrong all this time."

Julie laughed, following him up the stairs. "Trust me. There isn't a thing you've done wrong by me, and that is the honest truth."

Forrest let out a groan and before she knew what was happening, he had her up in his arms. "Well then, little bird. Allow me to continue to do right by you one more time before I perform my civic duties."

Julie giggled at her husband's playfulness, but her laughter died away the moment Forrest carried her inside their bedroom. No sooner had he kicked the door shut than Julie realized that Forrest had no intention of doing right by her just once more, but rather several more times. The pair spent the rest of the afternoon wrapped up in one another, and Julie had a flash of worry that Will had come home during their lovemaking, but when they descended the stairs, it was to a quiet house.

Will still hadn't returned by dinnertime.

Forrest kept a smile on his face, though it seemed strained as he reassured her that Will would be home before long and that there was nothing to worry about.

Try as she might, Julie was unable to believe Forrest's words as she had done earlier in the day. It did indeed seem as if there was a reason for concern, because Will didn't return after dinner, nor after, and not even by the time Julie had fallen into a troubled sleep that night with Forrest wrapped around her. Not even his warmth at her back had set her mind at ease. Not with Will missing.

"Just out thinking. Does it from time to time," Forrest told her over breakfast the next morning.

Julie gave him a tired nod. She hadn't gotten much sleep, waking at every sound thinking it was Will returning, but each and every creak had been nothing more than the house settling.

"I'll let him know you've gone if he misses you," Julie told him.

"He knows. We got the telegram at the station," Forrest replied, surprising her. "Thought he'd be home by now to discuss the particulars, but it'll all work itself out. Let's get you to the schoolhouse. I don't want to see you late with all this planning you're doing. You already look tired, darlin'."

"Not tired over the planning," Julie muttered.

"I know," Forrest sighed, helping her into her coat. "I didn't sleep much either over the idiot."

Julie cracked a smile. "At least we are in agreement with what he is."

"Unequivocally." Forrest winked at her, opening the front door. He stopped short when they heard the sound of hooves, and Julie peered around him to see Will making his way down the lane toward them.

Forrest's lips pressed into a thin line as they watched him approach. He swung down from the horse, and Julie was startled when he barely gave them a look on his way toward the door.

"Where you think you're going?" Forrest asked with a clipped tone.

Will froze and looked at them. He was now a foot or two away, and Julie felt the hot heat of anger flushing her face when she smelled the sickly sweet scent of cheap perfume wafting from him.

"To wash," he said, narrowing his eyes at them.

"Where were you?" Julie asked, forgetting her trepidation. There was no mistaking the cloying smell, and she found she wanted to rip every garment from him that stunk of it and scrub him until it was gone.

If her husband had touched anyone…

"With a friend," Will told her, his gray eyes cutting through her dispassionately.

Julie flinched, but she pushed her way past Forrest who had already moved toward Will.

"Who?"

Will shrugged. "Not important."

"Oh, it's not? I was worried sick over you last night. I didn't sleep a wink, and you were out with a 'friend'?" Julie's hands tightened into fists, and Will smirked when he saw it.

He cocked his head to the side. "Bothered, wife?"

The way he said wife wasn't lost on Julie. It sounded like a curse, and she felt some of her fight slip out of her spine at the way Will spit the word out at her. It was awful. Forrest didn't miss the tone either, and he reared on Will like an avenging angel.

"Don't you talk to her like that," Forrest growled, stepping in front of Julie. "You got hurt, and that's fine, but don't you come home to us smelling like a whore."

"Language," Will chided with a mirthless laugh.

"I'm not going to let you push us away, and I'm sure as hell not letting you treat Julie like this. When it was just us, that was was one thing, but you will not do this to her." Forrest jabbed a finger at Will. "I'm taking her to the schoolhouse. She's got a dance to plan, and you're going to do right by her and help. When I leave, you will take care of her. You will honor her. Now go wash that filth off yourself."

Forrest gave Will one last angry look before he

wrapped an arm around Julie and led her toward the buckboard. "Come on, little bird."

Julie followed him, but she couldn't help but glance at Will over her shoulder as they went. He still stood where he had been a moment before, but he watched her now. His gray eyes weren't the same cold flint they had been before, and he took a hesitant step toward them.

"Jules..."

"Wash up," Forrest ordered, voice snapping like a whip, not stopping in his march toward the buckboard with Julie in tow. "Now."

Will snapped his mouth shut and gave them a quick nod before he ducked into the house. Julie let out a shaky breath when Forrest settled her in the buckboard. She bit back tears; all she could think of was the smell of the sweet perfume on his skin.

"How could he?" she whispered, blinking through her tears. She felt sick to her stomach at just the thought of him near anyone else but them.

How could she ever have his hands on her again?

"He didn't break his marriage vow to you," Forrest said woodenly. He eased the buckboard into motion with a heavy sigh. "Will is a lot of things, but a liar isn't one of them. He'd never take another woman to bed while you're married to him."

"But he smells like—like a bordello!"

"I suspect he was at the Yellow Rose brothel." Forrest nodded along at her words. "But that doesn't mean he made use of the women there."

"Then how do you explain the smell?"

"Brothels smell like the inside of a penny perfume drum, darlin'. The minute you set foot in there you stink of it. No helpin' it," Forrest said with a sure nod. "Men get hurt, and they run to where their ego will be stroked. I know him. He spent the night drinking, talking about you, and licking his wounds."

Julie dabbed at the tear that slid down her cheek. "Are you sure?"

"Positive."

"How do you know?"

"Because it's what I would have done," Forrest told her.

"You better never do that when we fight." Julie crossed her arms over her chest. "I can't take this. I want to burn his clothes this moment."

Forrest smiled. "I know. I saw it on your face the second you smelled it on him. Don't blame you. I'm just sorry that I have to go. I'd like to stay here and help put this to rights."

"It's just poor timing."

"Poor is putting it mildly," Forrest muttered. They had come to a stop now in front of the schoolhouse, and he turned to face her, catching her hands. "Trust me. He wasn't unfaithful to you, or us. He was an idiot. A hurt idiot who needed to blow off some steam."

Julie bit her lip. Everything in her screamed at her to not listen to Forrest, everything but her heart. Her heart said to trust her husband's assessment.

"I'll talk to him."

"That'd be for the best." Forrest kissed her gently before hopping out of the buckboard and pulling her down beside him. "I'll send word when I can. And I know you're going to pull off this dance even if Rosemary threw you to the wolves."

"Caught that, did you?"

"She's not as subtle as she likes to think." Forrest rolled his eyes and then gave him a warm smile. "But I know my little bird is resourceful, and she doesn't quit. You're going to do this, and it's going to be done in fashion."

"Thank you, Forrest." Julie smiled at his vote of confidence. "That means a lot."

"Of course. Now go on inside before you catch a cold." He leaned forward, kissing her, and Julie found herself throwing her arms around him before he could pull away.

"I'll miss you," she whispered against his chest.

"I'll miss you too."

"Come back to me. Safe." Julie pulled back, giving him a stern look.

"Of course." Forrest saluted her, which made her giggle despite the morning's earlier drama. She kissed him one more time and then turned to go up the stairs, except instead of hurrying inside like she normally did, she stood on the steps of the schoolhouse and watched until Forrest disappeared from sight.

She prayed he wasn't gone long, but most of all she prayed that he came back to her safely. She couldn't handle the thought of losing one husband when it already felt like she had lost Will.

JULIE TURNED HER FACE UP INTO THE SUN AND BREATHED out. It was a beautiful day, with the longer daytime hours providing plenty of warmth and light when the school day ended. She had just sent the last of the children home with arms of ribbons and string. She had assigned an "art project" to the students, allowing each of them to choose from the collection of random fabrics she had found when taking stock of the school's inventory. If she added a little twine to the fabric, then she had the raw materials for fabric garlands which could be used as decorations.

The students knew they were for the dance, and Julie knew the parents would as well, but that wasn't something a little handwritten note, a task in itself that she somehow accomplished over lunch, couldn't take care of.

This year's dance would have the theme of celebrating everything Gold Sky, and that most certainly included the children.

It was a stroke of genius, really. But Julie wasn't able to enjoy her quick thinking, not with the morning's heaviness hanging over her. She should be happy with her progress, but all she could think of was Will and the mess that lay in front of her.

Any thoughts where she felt sorry for herself would have to wait, because right now Julie was on her way into town to see Alice. Hopefully, she would find a partner in Alice for planning the spring dance. There was something so self-assured about the other woman, and Julie knew she couldn't fail with Alice at her side.

She had just knocked on the door when, again, like the very first time she had been in front of it, the door flew open.

"I was wondering when I would see you today." Alice gestured for her to follow after her, already moving down the hallway.

"You were?" Julie asked in surprise. She closed the door and hurried after Alice, who was halfway down the hallway by this point. "How did you know?"

"Kind of hard to miss Will when he's on a rip about something." Alice tossed over her shoulder. "Was in fine form last night."

"Oh, that." Julie sighed, fingers twisting in her skirts.

She went into the room Alice had entered and glanced around the cozy kitchen.

Alice looked up from fixing a kettle for tea. "What do you mean?" She raised an eyebrow.

"I mean, that's not what I'm here about." Julie sighed, taking a seat at the kitchen table in the corner of the room.

Alice's hands stilled. "It's not?"

Julie shook her head. "No. I came to ask for your help planning the dance. I was hoping you would agree to co-chair the committee for it?"

Alice closed her eyes and blew out a sigh. "And I just went and—" she bit her lip with a grimace— "brought up Will."

"Indeed."

"I'm sorry, Julie." Alice sighed.

"It's all right."

"It's not, but you should know that Will didn't do a thing with anyone last night." Alice came to the table and took a seat. "He drank his weight in whiskey and passed out in one of the girls' beds. A feat only accomplished after he passed out at the bar. Wouldn't go near their rooms beforehand on account of him being 'married to the prettiest woman in town.'"

Julie sat up straight and looked up at Alice. "He said that?" she asked, her voice barely above a whisper.

Alice nodded. "He did. Repeatedly." She grinned at her. "And often."

"How do you know this?"

"Julie, I suspect there isn't much in this town that I don't know." Alice smiled at her and squeezed her hand. "Thought you were coming to see what I knew."

Julie shook her head. "Forrest told me Will wouldn't

have, ah, taken liberties in breaking our vows at the brothel. That he had just needed to lick his wounds."

"He did do that. When I came by to check on him, I thought he was going to cry."

Julie's eyes widened. "What?"

"Whiskey makes a man get in touch with his feelings." Alice winked at her. "You want to know what's on in a man's mind? Just fix him a stiff drink...or four, and you'll know soon enough. Will was torn up about whatever happened. Wouldn't say what it was. Other than that he loved you."

"He did?"

"Mm, while I was there checking up on him, let's see... what did he say?" Alice held up her hand and began to tick off fingers. "He didn't deserve you. You make him happy. He wants a family, and you're the smartest woman he's ever met, and he adores you—oh, and he loves you. Did I say that one already?"

Alice tapped her chin before she added, "I think he may have tried to wax poetic about your, ahem," her eyes dropped to Julie's chest, "assets, but then he almost got into a fistfight when one of the miners agreed."

Julie clapped a hand over her mouth and laughed at the thought. "I just, he's very reserved around me."

"I bet so, but he does a lot of thinking when he isn't talking." Alice stood from the table and went back to the stove to finish preparing their tea. "He cares for you. I know you know this, but it's tough for him to relax. To accept a good thing. To think he deserves the best in life."

"I know," Julie sighed, looking out the window as Alice moved around the kitchen, setting teacups out and fixing their brew for them. "Forrest asked me to be patient, but it's just difficult when things like yesterday happened. I saw him with Rosemary and went about our day without him. I didn't want to think about her and him, together. And now this, all because I didn't know how to tell my family about my two husbands."

"They are not together." Alice fixed her with a stare. "Did you miss that I said the best? You are the best for Will, for Forrest. The only woman they'd have. He's just scared. The words for your family...those will come. Just be patient with Will, but most of all with yourself."

Julie nodded along and took the cup of tea with a grateful smile. "Thank you. You're a true friend."

"Which is precisely why I'm going to help you put on the best spring dance this town has ever seen."

"Really?!"

"Truly." Alice smiled at her over her teacup. "Rhodes's wife, Lily, will want to help. And I think I know of a few other women in town who would be more than happy to help us. You might be new in town, but you're bringing joy to the men that keep us safe, and that means you have us all in your corner when you need us."

Julie blinked back tears. "That's more than I could ever ask for. I don't know how to repay everyone."

"Just teach and be you. You are part of Gold Sky." Alice smiled, putting her cup down onto her saucer, and patted Julie's hand. "It's what we do out here. We're a family on the frontier."

Touched by Alice's words, Julie let out a shaky breath. There had been something missing in her relationships with the other socialites of her age. Theirs had been friendly smiles cultivated with calculating moves, smiles that didn't quite reach anyone's eyes. It had been stifling.

Gold Sky was the opposite of the controlled and reserved life Julie had found herself being pushed into, and not for the first time she was grateful that she had answered Forrest's ad.

She shuddered to think of where she would be if she hadn't decided to marry. Her sudden role of wife to both men had put her in a new position of having two men who made it their business to ensure her comfort and happiness.

Gold Sky indeed was her home.

"Thank you." Julie gave Alice a genuine smile. "Thank you so much."

JULIE SMOOTHED HER HANDS OVER THE FRONT OF HER skirts. It had been a whirlwind day for her which hadn't stopped the second she had set out with Alice to seek the help of Lily Rhodes, a woman with brown eyes and an infectious smile that had Julie grinning ear-to-ear in the span of a heartbeat. Lily had been delighted upon asked to join the spring dance committee, a feat she had not been invited to do in the four years she had lived in Gold Sky. It didn't matter if they had only had a day to plan the dance, Lily assured her, it would be done and done with flair.

From there, the women had split up in different directions to enlist the help of the town's women in pulling off what Julie hoped would be a dance to remember.

So far they had secured a live band and flowers for the evening. Alice was confident that she would be able to handle the food for the evening, given her connections with the restaurants of the town. Dessert had even been sorted out as Julie had promised Leslie a handsome bonus if she would work her culinary magic to produce pies and cakes for the occasion. Leslie had agreed, and had already begun to draw up a list of ingredients she would shop for the following day in preparation of the dance.

Considering how blindsided she had been just 24 hours before, Julie was pleased with the day's efforts. Now she waited for Will to return home for the evening. Leslie had made a meal sure to please.

"It's his favorite. Trust me. Perfect for a man on the mend." Leslie pointed out the fried chicken, mashed potatoes and gravy, fresh bread, and sweet potatoes she had left warming in the oven. A frosted chocolate cake sat on the counter, waiting for dessert.

Biting her lip, Julie took in the veritable feast Leslie had made and wondered just how public Will had been in his night out.

All that was missing was said man, and Julie's eyes darted to the grandfather clock in the foyer. She paced from the front door to the stove where she paused for a few minutes, fussing with this and that, before turning on her heel and returning to the front door, hoping to hear the approach of Will's horse.

It seemed an eternity before Julie heard the sound she had been waiting for. The sound of Will's boots on the porch had her scurrying back to the kitchen where she began to pull the dishes and platters from the oven where they had been stored. She had just set down the platter of fried chicken when Will entered the dining room.

He cleared his throat and hesitated on the threshold for a second before his eyes darted up to her.

"Julie."

"Will."

His eyes moved down to the take in the fried chicken in front of her. "Dinner?"

"Ah, yes." Julie licked her lips and gave him a small smile. "I'll finish setting the table if you would wash up—or we can wait if you like."

"No, no." Will gave a quick jerk of his head, already rolling up the sleeves of his shirt. "Now is good. I'll just be a minute." He strode through the dining room on his way to fetch water for his washing.

Julie sucked in a deep breath. She had to keep calm. This was her husband, not a stranger, but the feeling of nervousness sweeping over her was like nothing else she had ever known.

It was hard to imagine her curt and reserved husband publicly declaring his love for her. She would have to believe Alice on the matter and hope that there was a side to Will she hadn't seen just yet.

Julie went into the kitchen behind Will to bring another serving dish to the table, pleased when Will grabbed the rolls and gravy to help.

"Thank you." Julie smiled at him, but Will only shrugged.

"Ma raised me to help."

"I see."

Will shifted, suddenly uncomfortable. "Looks great though."

"Leslie assured me it was your favorite."

Will gave a rare grin. "She's observant."

"And a dream with the house. She's even offered to help with the desserts for the dance," Julie said. She glanced back at the table, glad to see that everything had been brought out. "Please, sit down." She pointed to the chair at the head of the table. "I'll just be a minute."

Will nodded, sitting at the table while Julie hustled

into the kitchen. She was looking for the small bottle of lager that Leslie had brought with her to complete dinner.

She poured a glass just as the older woman had instructed her and then carried it, along with a glass of wine for herself, back to the table.

"Here you are." She set the glass down next to him and took her place at his left.

She startled when Will took her hand, his fingers gentle on her skin, his palm warm against hers.

"Dear Lord, we thank you for this bounty," Will said, eyes closed and head bowed. Immediately, Julie's cheeks burned with embarrassment at mistaking Will's touch as romantic. When grace was finished, Julie was grateful for something to do with her hands, and she began to dish out the food.

Only when Will had a heaping plate in front of him did she take a breath.

"Jules—" Will sighed when she had just added another scoop of potatoes to his plate with a look of concentration.

"Hmm?" Julie poured a river of gravy over the potatoes, steadfastly avoiding Will's searching gray eyes.

"I'm — I shouldn't have stayed out last night."

Julie froze. "What?"

"Darlin', look at me."

She looked up at him and felt her mouth go dry at the intense look in his eyes. "Yes?"

"Didn't touch anyone," he said, his voice low.

"I didn't think you did," Julie whispered.

The corner of Will's mouth lifted up in a wry smile. "Liar."

She shook her head and opened her mouth to protest,

but he stopped her with a sigh. "Saw it in your eyes the second I hit the porch. I smelled like a cheap night."

Julie lowered her eyes. "Yes."

"There's only you." Will touched her hand again, and this time it was anything but chaste. "I'm never going to break the promise I made in front of God, Julie Ann. You're my wife."

"Will, I'm sorry." Julie clasped his hand to her with a frown. "I'm so sorry I made you feel like I was ashamed to be your wife. I'm so proud of you and Forrest. My family, I just want them to understand how much I love you and—"

"Say that again," Will said. He gazed at her mouth, and when Julie ran her tongue along her bottom lip, his fingers tightened on hers.

"I love you," Julie whispered.

"Jules." Will shook his head, but then he stood up and moved toward her with a groan. He pulled her out of her chair and claimed her mouth in a hot kiss that she felt down to her toes.

"Will," she gasped, throwing her arms around him with an eager mewl of pleasure.

"So beautiful," Will murmured against her skin, his hands already grabbing her skirts. He jerked them up to her thighs as he pressed himself against her. The rough feel of his pants against her stockinged legs made her moan in pleasure.

"Need you." Will's hands pushed beneath Julie's skirts, and she gasped when he cupped her sex in his large hand. "I— God, Julie, I need to be inside you."

"Yes." Julie rolled her hips, earning her an approving sigh from Will. "Yes," she said again, following Will's direction and sliding to the floor with him in a tangle of limbs and skirts. She kissed as passionately as she could. This was where she wanted to be, and she welcomed the hardwood of the floor at her back.

"Ride me, Jules." Will's command had Julie blinking in confusion.

"How?" she asked, feeling out of sorts but eager to learn what it was he was asking her to do.

"Take your drawers off," he husked out, yanking his pants down past his muscular thighs and revealing his proud and erect manhood. Julie nodded, hurrying to comply with his instructions. Anything to have him inside of her.

Once she had slipped her undergarment past her feet Will surprised her by yanking her close.

"M'gonna kiss you."

"Okay." Julie closed her eyes, leaning forward, but Will shook his head.

"Not there." He pushed her skirts up past her now bare thighs and nudged her to slide up his body. "Here," he said, sliding a finger through the folds of her wet sex.

"Oh!" Julie's hips jerked at the contact. She was nervous about what he asked her to do. It wasn't something young ladies were told was permissible, but then again, she wasn't a young lady any longer. She was a married woman, wasn't she? Julie slipped higher until she felt the ghost of Will's breath against her core and then under the guidance of his hands she sank down until she felt her husband's lips and tongue working against her.

Lord.

How misled she had been about the pleasures of marriage. No wonder so many married, and so young. Julie let out a startled cry, her hands coming out to brace her before she fell forward in ecstasy.

"Will!"

His fingers tightened on her thighs, and she heard a moan in answer to her cry. Julie moved her hips against her husband's skilled tongue and let out a shuddering gasp at the sensation. It was a feeling unlike anything she had experienced before, and though her husbands had lavished her body with attention she had never before been in control of that pleasure. Now she was able to do as she pleased and she gasped, falling into a rhythm that felt best to her. And she was going to chase that feeling for all she was worth.

Her hips undulated as she sobbed out her relief. She wasn't sure if it was minutes or seconds, but before long she felt the familiar ache of her orgasm gathering in her.

It was wantonly sexy to be with her husband like this. Fully clothed and on the floor of their dining room while their dinner sat forgotten only feet away. The thought of Will wanting her so badly he would take her so suddenly had Julie climaxing with a shout before long, her body sagging forward slightly as she hit the peak of her pleasure.

Will shifted her to the side before he settled her on her back and slipped between her thighs.

"Look so pretty like this." He kissed her cheeks and hiked her legs up around his waist. "You going to take all of me, darlin'?

"Yes," Julie moaned.

Will's hips snapped forward, and he entered her with a grunt. "So sweet." He sighed, beginning to pump in and out of her.

She pulled at his shirt, suddenly feeling wild and needy. She needed more of everything, so she canted her hips up to take her husband deeper and gasped, "More, Will."

"Always so good to me." Wil's eyes shut as he leaned forward over her, a hand braced on the floor on either side of her head. He thrust into her harder now. It straddled the border between pain and pleasure for Julie, but it was exactly what she needed.

Will caught one of her hands and pressed a kiss against her palm as he continued to move in and out of her with ever-increasing desperation. His rhythm was erratic, a far cry from the slow and measured way he usually made love to her.

Julie bit her lip, a keening sound escaping her mouth. This didn't feel like making love, not with the grunts from Will, her wild desperation, the way his hands now gripped her around her thighs as he settled back on his knees to thrust up into her. Will's hands slipped down to cup her behind and he let out a muffled curse as he began a brutal pace that Julie knew he would be unable to sustain for long.

He was close, and so was she.

"Touch yourself, Jules," he groaned, looking down to meet her gaze.

"I don't know how."

"Just pretend it's me," Will told her with another thrust of his hips. "It's all right to enjoy this. And I'm too close. I need you to climax one more time. Can you do that?"

She loved seeing the look in his eyes. It was wild and passionate, and in turn, it made her feel that way, so she reached down and slipped a hand past the skirts bunched at her waist and touched that bundle of nerves Will and Forrest seemed to understand in ways that she couldn't dream of. After a moment of tentative stroking, she gasped at finding a rhythm that she liked.

"Feels good, doesn't it?"

"Y-yes," she gasped, her head falling back when she successfully mimicked the way her husbands touched her. She knew that she might blush later when she remembered how she had touched herself while Will made love to her on the dining room floor, but now was not the time for that. Now she was doing exactly what her body demanded she do as Will took her.

She groaned at the thought. This wasn't lovemaking, this was being taken, and her husband was taking her in spectacular fashion.

"You're mine," Will told her as he thrust into her with enough force to make Julie's body shake in his hands. She looked up at him as he sped up his pace. "You're mine."

"Yes!" Julie cried out, her fingers between her legs moving faster now. "I'm yours. Take me! Take me, Will!"

Will threw his head back with a shout as he came. His calloused hands on her delicate skin clenched painfully. There was no way that she wouldn't have bruises the following day where her husband had grabbed her, but Julie didn't mind it. It would be a reminder, and that was something she found she quite liked.

She moaned and shook through her own release and slumped back against the floor with a little laugh.

"Oh, my."

"Jules." Will set her on the floor and looked down at her with a dazed expression. "God, you make me forget myself."

"That's okay," Julie told him, reaching out a hand for him as he began to tuck himself into his pants.

Will looked at her with an almost apologetic expression when he reached for her skirts. "No, it's not. You deserve feather beds and sweet words, not..." His eyes shifted to the side. "Not to be taken on the floor."

"Don't say that." Julie sat up abruptly. "Don't you dare feel bad about this, William."

He bit his lip at the use of his first name. "Julie, I—"

"What? Feel like your delicate wife can't handle it when you give it to her rough? Well, I can, and I like it. How about that?" she asked with him a defiant lift of her chin. "I want everything you have to give me, William Barnes, and that's final."

Will cracked a wry smile. "Is that so?"

"Yes, And now that we've sorted that out, help me up. I'm afraid the dinner has gotten cold." Julie reached a hand out to him with a frown at the dinner table, still sitting laden with their untouched dinner. Will let loose a deep laugh, one so big that it bounced off the walls and put one on Julie's face.

"You really are something else, Julie Wickes-Barnes," he said, sweeping her up into his arms, and when she gave him a surprised look, he kissed her and sat her down at the table. Julie blinked at her sudden change of position, but she said nothing and fell into companionable silence as they began eating.

There was no tension in the room anymore, and all the nervousness that she had felt before was gone. It was just an enjoyable dinner—Julie hoped it was the first of many to come.

CHAPTER 11

*T*he night following their impromptu lovemaking on the dining room floor proved to be absolutely magical for the couple. Julie found that it was the most relaxing handful of hours she had experienced since moving to Gold Sky, and she cherished the sweetness of it.

Will had bathed with her, his hands moving over her as if he wanted to reassure himself that she was real while he kissed every last place that wasn't submerged underwater. The physical intimacy of it all had been a welcome reprieve from the previous tension, but what Julie treasured the most about that night was how freely Will spoke his mind to her.

The couple had spent hours in bed talking about his life before the war, about what it had been like after, and how he and Forrest had managed since.

Julie treasured the vulnerability Will offered her and drank it up like a dying woman in the desert. What Forrest had told her about their partner was true. He would, in his own time, open up to her, and Julie was delighted that the time was now. It filled her heart with promise for the future, and she fell asleep content and at peace with her place in Gold Sky.

The next morning she awoke to Will wrapped around her, his nose buried in her hair, legs twined together, and arms around her with his hands splayed possessively over her stomach. It had been a lovely way to wake up, and she smiled, remembering how gently Will had kissed her good morning, how he had made love to her, rocking his body into hers over and over until she had sobbed out her orgasm against the pillow.

"Our family is going to be beautiful," Will whispered to her while she trembled in the afterglow of her climax.

It had been a truly memorable morning, and now Julie was busy ordering school supplies for the students. They had been overjoyed at learning that they would all be given the opportunity to personally write the President of the United States. It was an opportunity afforded by her familial connections and Julie was, for once, happy to use her father's social and military station to get what she wanted. Each child who wrote would receive a personal response. Whether the President replied himself or not she wasn't sure, but it was worth the excited smiles on her students' faces to assure them that *someone* would.

"Now, how many sheets of paper are you going to need?" Mrs. Harris, the mercantile owner, asked Julie with a pencil tap.

"Well, I'm not sure, so let's go with an even 500, shall we?" Julie smiled at the shocked but pleased expression on Mrs. Harris' face.

"You know, the other school teacher never ordered supplies like this," the woman said as she placed the order and gave Julie a gentle smile. "Are you sure about the amount? It won't be cheap."

Julie nodded. When she had arrived, the schoolhouse had been all but bare in the things a child needed to learn, and Julie had resolved to remedy it as soon as she was able. And due to her family fortune, she was able to afford any and all amount of supplies her students might require.

"My students deserve the best I can give them," Julie said. She paid for her order before she paused and added, "Throw in at least two more boxes of pencils as well, please."

"You really do care for them." Mrs. Harris handed her back her change with a nod. "You'll let me and Mr. Harris know if we can help with the dance this week, won't you?"

Julie grinned and nodded, taking her money. "Of course! I'm so touched with how much the town is helping put together the celebration. It means so much, and it will mean the world to the children."

"Well, we all know it got dumped on you by our lovely Rosemary." Mrs. Harris rolled her eyes. "We would all like to make it as easy as we can on you. You're doing a wonderful job. I can already tell the difference in my Miles's reading, and I have you to thank for that."

Julie ducked her head. "Thank you. I'm delighted to be Miles's teacher."

"And we're pleased to have you as his teacher." Mrs. Harris waved her out of the store, and Julie stepped onto the street with a smile on her face. The sun was bright and shining, not a sign of the sudden spring storms that had been sweeping through the areas as of late. It was even warm enough that Julie felt like she could shed her jacket without worry, though she didn't for fear of disrupting the new peacefulness of her relationship with Will.

The man wouldn't, she knew, take kindly to her being underdressed for the weather. He'd hadn't wasted an opportunity to throw in his two cents on her walk in the rain, and Forrest had been right: she was lucky that that Will hadn't been home that day. Though he would be home tonight, and Julie flushed at the prospect of spending another night in Will's arms.

If things continued as they were, then the dance wouldn't be the only thing put to rights by Thursday. Forrest would be pleased by the progress made in his absence, and the thought put a happy smile on her face. Lost in her thoughts and still smiling, Julie rounded the corner and collided with someone else.

"Oh, I'm sorry!" she exclaimed, reaching out to steady the other person.

"Oh, that's all right. You're just the person I wanted to see!" Rosemary laughed, straightening her hat with a little shake of her head. "You really do need to watch where you're going. This isn't New York, but no nevermind that!"

Julie grit her teeth, her cheer evaporating like mist in the sun. "Rosemary." She forced a smile on her lips. "What was it you wanted to see me about?" she asked, doing her best impression of civil.

Though it was taxing.

Thank the Lord for all her time in finishing school, or she might not have managed it.

"Oh, yes, yes, that." Rosemary waved a distracted hand and then nodded up ahead to the newspaper offices. "If you'd walk with me? I was just on my way in."

"Of course." Julie forced her feet forward. "Lovely day, isn't it?"

Rosemary hummed in agreement. "It is, but I won't waste your time with pleasantries." She opened the door to the newspaper offices, which were quiet and empty save for the two women.

"Pardon me?" Julie blinked in surprise.

"Oh, I know you were raised well, which is the only reason why you're trying to engage me in mundane prattle. There's no need for that here." Rosemary closed the door behind them and smiled brightly at Julie. "I'm going to save us time, since we are both busy women, and get right to the matter at hand."

"Which is?" Julie asked, recovering from the blonde's directness.

"Your marriage," Rosemary said, putting down her reticule on her desk. "Or rather, Will."

"What about Will?" Julie asked, her voice going quiet.

"The poor dear isn't happy," Rosemary said without ceremony.

Julie felt like she had been punched in the stomach. She swallowed hard, already feeling sick at the prospect of whatever Rosemary had in store for her that afternoon.

"Excuse me?"

Rosemary gave Julie a smile that she supposed was meant to pass for sympathetic. "William isn't happy with the marriage."

"I'm sorry, but I fear you are mistaken in your observation. We are all very happy. Will included." Julie drew herself up to her full height, glad that she was taller than the other woman by a few inches.

"Oh, Julie," Rosemary tutted, pulling a glove off with a look of dismay, "I wish that were true. I truly do."

"Are you sure about that?" Julie raised an eyebrow.

"Yes, I want nothing more than for Will to be happy. He deserves it after everything he's been through. You do know about that, don't you?" Rosemary inclined her head, giving Julie an assessing look.

Though she was able to keep her face composed, Julie's cheeks burned, and she cursed her inability to stop the reaction.

Julie looked down at her hands, feigning indifference. "I know well that my husbands deserve happiness."

Rosemary sighed and laid her gloves on her desk. "That's saying the least about that poor, beautiful man." Julie's eyes snapped up to Rosemary, and the blonde shrugged her delicate shoulders.

"I've never been a good liar, and anyone with eyes can see that Will is gorgeous."

"I'd prefer it if you didn't speak about my husband in such a manner," Julie bit out, face no longer composed.

Rosemary sighed and sat down at her desk. "My apologies, Julie. Now," she said, and dipped her chin, giving the other woman a small smile, "shall we get back to the matter at hand?"

"Please do."

"Will is unhappy. The marriage is not what he imagined for himself."

Julie pursed her lips. "Your speculation—"

"He told me as much."

Julie went still, the blood draining from her face. "What?"

Rosemary leaned back in her chair and had enough grace to look slightly uncomfortable as she said, "Will told me himself just this weekend."

"Why would he confide that in you?" Julie asked, and

though she fought to keep her voice calm, even she heard the slight waver of doubt in it.

"As you know, Will and I have a very special relationship," Rosemary said, and Julie didn't miss the woman's emphasis on *relationship*.

"I do. But you know," Julie said, and put her hands on her hips, "now that we are disposing of the required niceties, why is that? Why is that you have such an intimate acquaintanceship with a married man?"

Rosemary didn't so much as blanch. Instead, she leaned forward and gave Julie an almost apologetic smile.

"We have a common bond you wouldn't understand."

"Which is?" Julie challenged, crossing her arms.

"We both know what it's like to lose a spouse," Rosemary told her.

"Excuse me?"

"You don't know about Will's first wife?" Rosemary asked with a raised eyebrow.

"I-I," Julie stammered, shocked by the news that Will had not only been married before her but that he had been a widower. There was no hiding that she hadn't known about his first marriage, so she shook her head.

"No."

"Doesn't surprise me he doesn't speak of her. First love is so hard to revisit once it's lost so tragically." Rosemary shrugged as she gave Julie a shrewd look. "You're nothing like her, you know?"

Julie's heart sank at the observation. This was not what she needed to hear. Not when she had made so much progress with her husband.

They were on the path to discovering one another. Whatever Rosemary spewed was only going to tear down the beginnings of something beautiful.

"I need to go." Julie stood up straighter and moved toward the door, but she stopped in her tracks when Rosemary spoke again.

"That is probably for the best. By the way," the blonde said, making Julie freeze, "what I had my heart on discussing is simply this: I aim to have Will."

Julie swallowed hard, turning to look back at Rosemary. "What did you say?"

"I can give Will back what he lost. Unlike you," Rosemary said, giving her a disdainful look, "I am every bit the woman he lost. She was even a blonde, you see." Rosemary ran a hand over her curls and gave Julie a mean smile. "You're not even the sort of woman he would pick for himself, so unlike his past physical wants. Forrest only saw the ghost of Will's past in me. That's why you're here." She jabbed a finger at Julie. "They received responses to their advert in the matrimonial newspaper by the sackful. Countless women wanted them, but all the promising ones were so like her that they kept searching until they came across you. A woman so different that there would be no confusion for Will."

Julie felt like she was falling through the floor at Rosemary's words. They explained why and how she was here with the two of them in a way that made logical sense to her. Julie now understood why Will hadn't immediately embraced her as Forrest had, why he was often closed off to her in a way that she couldn't reach.

"You, Miss Stanton, are mistaken," Julie told her, opening the door with a jerk of her arm. She forced her eyes straight ahead of her. She would not give the other woman the satisfaction of seeing her distress, and not one tear would fall in her presence.

"I wish I was." Rosemary got up from her desk with a

swish of skirts that made Julie pause in the doorway. "But I'm not, and you know it. I'm going to take Will from you, and when I do, it will be for the best, for his happiness. Don't you want that?" Rosemary shook her head and threw her hands out. "How can you be so selfish? Why would you force him to stay with you in this mockery of matrimony? Keep Forrest, but William will have his happy ending, and I aim to make that a life with me. I'm giving you the option of bowing out gracefully, and if you care for him at all you won't make this harder than it has to be!"

"You're a vile woman," Julie whispered, her voice cracking, the tears she vowed not to shed shining bright in her eyes.

Rosemary jabbed a well-manicured finger at Julie. "The only way you're keeping Will is if you've managed to fall pregnant. Forrest believed that the deciding factor when it came to choosing between us." She flicked a finger between them to emphasize her words. "A baby is the only way he would he stay with you. The man is far too honorable for his own good," Rosemary's eyes lowered to Julie's stomach. "And Forrest wants a family more than anything, something the Lord hasn't seen fit to equip me to do. My body just cannot handle the stress." Rosemary lowered a hand to her own abdomen. "But Will doesn't care about a baby. He only cares because of Forrest."

"Just stop," Julie ordered. Her voice snapped through the room like a thunderclap, and she worked to look stronger than she felt. "I am very sorry that you feel the way you do, Rosemary. Stay away from my husband," she all but growled, her eyes hard and cold enough to make the calculating socialites of New York City proud. She had survived them, and she would survive Rosemary, who was, after all, only one woman.

Only then did she step through the door and back into the shining sun of the day, but this time the sunshine didn't quite warm her through as it had before, because before the door slammed shut behind her, she caught Rosemary's parting words.

"Let him be happy. He deserves it."

~

"JULES?" WILL'S VOICE STARTLED JULIE OUT OF HER thoughts at the dinner table.

"Hmm?" She blinked at him, trying to keep her face composed, though she was still in shock from her earlier confrontation with Rosemary. Immediately following their interaction, Julie had fled home and hidden in the kitchen with Leslie. Her mind had been abuzz with what she had learned, and she wasn't quite sure what to do.

Most of the time had been spent drinking tonic water to calm her roiling stomach, something Leslie insisted upon. Julie had shrugged it off as nothing but exhaustion over planning the dance.

"You'll run yourself into the ground with all of this dance planning. I say let the cow who dumped this on you handle it!" Leslie said while she cooked, her eyes flashing with indignation on Julie's behalf.

"I can manage a dance, but thank you for your succinct description of the situation," Julie said with a wry smile on her face. She had remained in the kitchen, sipping her drink and picking at the toast Leslie had prepared for her until she heard the familiar sound of Will coming home. She had nearly fallen from her perch on the stool, which caused Leslie to insist upon serving them dinner, though she was busy with baking desserts for the spring dance.

Now she was at dinner with a very concerned Will looking at her over the dinner table. He reached over and caught her hand.

"What's wrong?"

"Nothing. I'm, ah, just busy planning away." She tapped her temple with a finger.

Will looked relieved at her answer. "Ah, the dance. Do you need me to do anything for that? Already got Stark on board with making sure there's enough outside seating. Talked to the mercantile about lights, too," he said, looking down at the steak he was currently eating.

"You did all that for the dance?" Julie asked in surprise. A glow of happiness at his interest and involvement bloomed in her chest.

"'Course. Under strict orders from Forrest, remember?" Will winked at her before going back to cutting into his steak.

"Oh, yes, yes." Julie bobbed her head, toying with her napkin. The small sparks of happiness she had felt warming her extinguished almost as suddenly as they had ignited. She knew it didn't make sense that she had wished Will had claimed complete ownership over his motivations for helping her with the dance, but after Rosemary, it did.

It did, so very much.

"You sure you're all right?" Will frowned at her as he chewed. He placed a hand on her forehead. "Not feeling ill?"

"I'm fine," Julie lied, lowering her eyes to her plate as she pushed her peas around.

"Don't look fine," Will frowned at her. "Leslie said you

got sick when you came home. Pastor Bruce asked after you. Said you looked out of sorts on your way through town. Is teaching wearing you out? Because if it is, you don't have to keep doing it."

Her fork clattered to her plate, and she looked up at Will in shock. "What?! No! I love teaching. I'm just tired." Julie paused and then added, "And not from teaching, either. The dance planning is just wearing me thin."

"That's why you have a committee." Will put his silverware down and eyed the glass of wine Julie was nursing in favor of eating her dinner. "Delegate to them — I will take over the whole thing if you need more rest."

Julie worried her bottom lip between her teeth at the anxious look on Will's face. Why did he seem so determined to make sure she rest more?

"What's wrong?" she asked, turning his question back onto him. She leaned back in her chair and watched as Will's face flitted between concern and annoyance at her inquiry.

"Worried about you." He tapped the wine glass in her hand. "Are you sure wine is a good idea right now?"

"Why wouldn't it be?"

"Jules…" Will sighed, her name hanging between them like a warning. Julie looked away from the depths of her wineglass to see him studying her.

"What?"

Will cleared his throat and looked away. "Nothing. Finish your dinner. Taking you straight to bed after."

At that, Julie perked up. Her lust was stronger than her anxiety over Rosemary's threat to take her husband, but Will shook his head at her.

"Taking you to bed to sleep."

"Fine, fine," Julie grumbled, picking back up her silverware under the watchful gaze of her husband.

The rest of the dinner passed by fine enough, with Will looking appeased at Julie's clean plate. Though no sooner had she ascended the stairs to their bedroom than she began to feel queasy. She paused, one hand bracing against the wall as her stomach roiled.

"I don't feel well," she told him with a grimace. Will reached for her to help her down the hallway, but a second later Julie batter at his hands and pushed past him, running toward the bathroom at the end of the hallway with her hands over her mouth. She only just managed to make it to the bathroom before she vomited.

"Oh no," she gasped as her body shuddered from the heaving of her stomach. She winced, seeing that she hasn't made it to the toilet and instead had only made a mess. A choked sob escaped her when she looked down at the vomit on her skirts.

"Jules?" Will burst into the bathroom behind her. "Are you sick? Darlin'?"

"I'm fine. Ju—just go back to the bedroom." Julie held a hand out to him and then snatched it back when she saw it was covered in sick. "It's fine."

Will's eyes scanned the bathroom, taking in the state of the room, and he sighed, walking toward her. "Nothing about this scene is fine. Get undressed and in the tub. I'll clean this up."

"No, no." Julie grabbed for a towel to begin cleaning the mess. "I can manage. You should not have to put up with this."

"Put up with what? My sick little wife, who won't listen to reason?" Will asked, taking the towel from her hands and opening the window at the foot of the tub before he switched on the water taps. "I quite agree with that, so do your husband a mercy and get in the bath." He gave her a pleading look. "Please."

"Fine, fine." Julie sighed, working on undressing. She was grateful Will let her slip her dress and undergarments off on her own while he worked on cleaning up the bathroom. He did, however, help her into the bath and only looked satisfied when Julie had settled in the bathtub with water to her chest.

"Let me," Will said, dropping to his knees beside the tub and taking a bar of soap in hand. Julie nodded at his request before Will began to wash her hair. He didn't, as she had anticipated, pull needlessly. Before she could stop the thought, she wondered where he had learned to wash hair just so, but then she bit her lip because she had an idea of how he had gotten his education.

His wife.

His *first* wife, Julie's mind stressed to her.

She fought against that voice that whispered to her that Rosemary was right. That her husband wasn't happy.

That wasn't true, and now she was his wife, and that was what mattered the most.

"Still feeling sick?" Will asked her, his fingers going still against her scalp. He leaned close to look at her. "Do you need me to go make you tea?"

"No, I'm fine." Julie gave him a tight smile and looked down at the soapy water. "Thank you for taking care of me."

"You're my wife," Will said simply, as if that explained everything.

"Mmm," Julie hummed, but said nothing else as Will continued to wash her hair, strong fingers moving through her tresses. When he was satisfied that she was clean and not feeling sick, he allowed her to stand, hands braced on his shoulders as he wrapped a thick towel around her.

"Don't even think about it," Will told her sternly when she went to step out of the tub.

"I can walk," Julie protested, but Will wouldn't hear it.

"You can walk later," he said gruffly, and swung her up in his arms. "Now, stop giving me that look." He nodded at her and turned toward their bedroom. "Let me take care of you."

"Fine." Julie sighed, leaning her cheek against his chest. Will pressed a kiss to the top of her forehead, which had Julie's eyes stinging with unshed tears. She wrapped her arms around his neck and turned her face into his chest. How could there be any truth in Rosemary's words when he took care of her like this? When he handled her like she was made of glass? Will was happy. He had to be, didn't he? Why else would he be treating her like this?

"Jules?" Will looked down at her with a raised eyebrow. It was then Julie realized he had been speaking to her.

"Sorry?"

He nodded toward their bed. "Was asking if you could stand while I got the bed ready."

"Oh, yes." Julie nodded and stood by the bed as he turned down the quilts for her. When he was done, he reached a hand out to her and helped her slip into bed.

"Comfortable?" he asked with an anxious bite of his lip. He was busy fluffing pillows and pulling the comforter up around her chin with a worried look in his eyes. "Can't have anything happening to you."

"Nothing will." She caught his wrist and smiled at him. "I just caught a little something. It will pass."

"Forrest would kill me if he came back to you sick," he said, sitting down beside her on the bed.

Julie's smile faltered at that.

"I'll be fine." She turned on her side to stare out the window at the darkening sky. She wanted to hear that he would be a wreck if she were sick, because he cared for her, because he was in love with her, not because of Forrest's displeasure.

"I'll go get you tea," Will told her, kissing her shoulder before he stood up and headed out of the bedroom.

Julie sighed and closed her eyes. Even if Rosemary were right in asserting that Will was unhappy, she couldn't let him go. There was no way she was going to stand aside and let the other woman have her husband.

He cared for her, Julie knew that much.

She could see it in the way he handled her, even if he cited Forrest as his reason for concern. She could live with that, and she would do her very best to make him happy each and every single day she had as Mrs. Wickes-Barnes.

CHAPTER 12

The next two days were a veritable whirlwind of activity, though Julie was able to rest as much as she needed. Will had very nearly taken over the planning for the dance. How he managed to do so without abandoning his post as sheriff's deputy for Gold Sky she wasn't sure, but she suspected it had something to do with how remote the area was. If Forrest was out chasing the last known gang of thieves, then what action was there left for Will to deal with?

Even if he was under the strain of double duties at work, Will never let on that the task of acting in Julie's stead planning the dance taxed him in any way. Alice assured Julie that everything was right on track, and she trusted Alice to take over the planning from Will if there was the chance of it interfering in his duties.

In those couple of days, Will's decision to relieve Julie of planning the dance was fortuitous as her energy levels that week had nosedived to nearly nothing. By the end of each school day, she found that she was ready for sleep with no appetite. Will made her sit and eat, but it didn't matter as the food never managed to stay down for long. Thankfully she had gotten better at making it either to the bathroom or outdoors in time, and there were no repeats of the messy events of earlier in the week.

Her earlier wish to have time to read was granted as Will ushered her to bed early and the alone time proved both a blessing and a curse. It was a boon in the sense that she was able to finally make her way through her waiting novels, but in the moments that she put down her books, she had far more time than she liked to dwell on Rosemary's words.

In those evening hours, while Will was out of the house and hard at work over the dance preparations, Julie nearly went mad analyzing how he touched her, wondering if the smile reached his eyes when he laughed at her jokes, what he could possibly mean when he bid her a good day after dropping her off at the schoolhouse...

All of it pushed her nerves to the brink, and she devoured her novels like a starving woman in a bid to stay her thoughts. Torturing herself over her interactions with Will only gave way to her worries over Forrest. She hadn't heard from him in nearly a week, with his last missive assuring them that all was well and he expected to be home soon, but the positive words mattered not one whit with her nerves and body betraying her.

Not even her time alone with her books had provided comfort as usual. The characters on the page had seemed thin, their concerns trivial. Life on the frontier was exhausting. And by the night of the dance, Julie was a nervous wreck.

Despite all that, the spring dance was a success. Or at

least it appeared to be in Julie's estimation. The schoolhouse overflowed with the citizens of Gold Sky, and the canvas pavilion hastily erected around the makeshift dance floor for the night spilled over with merrymakers. It was enough to cheer her heart after the stressful week.

Julie breathed in and smiled at the scene of merriment from her position outside the schoolhouse, which was festooned in brightly colored ribbons and lanterns for the occasion, every last window open to the warm breeze of the night.

It was lovely, and she was proud to have played a part in bringing this type of magic to the small town she had come to think of as home.

"Mrs. Wickes-Barnes?" a voice called to her, and she turned to see Rhodes walking toward her with a bucket of ice in his arms.

"Rhodes! Hello there." She smiled as warmly as she could despite the familiar feeling of nausea making her nervous.

"I was directed to ask you where you would prefer the extra ice." Rhodes nodded at the large bucket he carried.

"Oh, I thought..." She bit her lip and looked around for Will, who had insisted on organizing all the necessities for refreshments. Her heart plummeted when she spotted him at the center of the dance floor with Rosemary in his arms.

"Ah, that would be around back. Lily said she was setting up the bar there." Julie strived for nonchalant, but she knew she failed when her smile wavered, and Rhodes's eyes narrowed at the sight.

His eyes flicked to the dance floor and his lips pressed into a thin line. They stood together in silence for a moment before he turned to her with a worried expression.

"I'm fine," Julie said, holding up a hand when Rhodes opened his mouth to speak. He snapped it shut with a sigh and gave her a nod.

"I know better than to question a woman when she uses that tone," he joked, making her blush.

"I'm sorry." Julie sighed. "I've just been rather tired lately. It's been affecting my mood. I didn't mean to use a tone with you, Rhodes."

"It's no worry at all. Would you like me to fetch Will?" He nodded at the dance floor where Will spun a laughing Rosemary. As much as she hated it Julie was able to pick out the other woman's laugh above the music and chatter of the dance.

Julie shook her head. "No. That won't be necessary, but thank you, Rhodes. I'll just come along with you and have a refreshment to perk me up. I'm sure a treat is all I need."

"If you're sure," Rhodes said, but his expression said he was doubtful a cool drink was the answer. She was glad when he didn't press the issue and she gratefully took a glass of cold lemonade from the refreshment offerings.

Julie idly sipped her drink and continued to watch the dance proceedings under the tent. For a moment she thought about going inside the schoolhouse where there was a plethora of foodstuffs for the evening, but she found the mere thought of food turned her stomach. Food was not something she wanted, even if her corset and dresses were beginning to fit her a tad too loosely.

With a shake of her head, she nursed the sweet drink in her hand, grateful her stomach didn't object, and walked toward the dance floor. She liked seeing so many happy faces, even if Rosemary's was one of them, even if the source of the woman's happiness was her very own husband.

Glancing around the dance floor, Julie frowned when she didn't see the other woman's familiar figure in the crush of people. Biting her lip, Julie looked for Will. After a few frantic seconds of searching, her body went tight when she realized he was also missing from the celebration. Julie sucked in a deep breath and tried to keep a composed smile on her face while she began to walk the length of the pavilion, her eyes moving furtively over the crowd.

"He just needed to step out for a moment," she said to herself as she walked. "Nothing to worry about."

Yet the second time Julie made the circle of the pavilion and even ducked into the schoolhouse for a quick look around, she began to panic. There was no way to stop the flood of adrenaline that had her breath coming short when she could find neither Rosemary nor Will.

It was like they had vanished into thin air.

Julie sighed and walked out toward where the buckboards and horses of visiting families waited, about to give up hope of finding her husband when she heard Rosemary's voice from somewhere nearby.

Holding her breath, Julie poked her head around the buckboard she had been leaning against and frowned when she didn't see anyone immediately. She could clearly make out the agitated tones in Rosemary's voice, so she crept forward.

"That doesn't mean anything," Rosemary exclaimed.

Julie stepped around the buckboard, careful not to make any heavy sounds, and felt her breath catch when she finally caught sight of the couple. Will stood with his

214

back to Rosemary, arms crossed over his chest while the woman stood at his back with a pained look on her pretty face.

"You don't owe her anything! No one made her come out here!" Rosemary reached out, catching one of Will's arms, and pulled him around to face her. "She's no one to you."

"She's my wife," Will said, his voice gruff.

Julie waited for him to continue on, but when he said nothing she leaned her forehead against the back of the wagon she hid behind. A sinking feeling in her stomach pulled at her, making her feel like she was drowning. Her worst nightmare since her confrontation with Rosemary had come true in front of her, and she had no clue what to do.

Lady Pim had never prepared her for what to do when discovering an assignation between one's husband and another. And all she could find the strength to do was tremble while she listened to the couple and prayed for the best.

"And? I could be your wife," Rosemary countered. "I almost was your wife except—except for my failings at childbearing."

"Rosemary, don't say that." Will took a slight step back, pulling his arm away from her.

"It's true, and we both know it! You wanted me." Rosemary crossed her arms, closing the space between them with a single step. "You still do. You're just scared of losing Forrest, so you gave him Julie. When are you going to see that he isn't going to walk away from you just because you don't love that woman! He's going to stay with you no matter what woman you choose."

Will took another step back. "Don't bring Forrest into this."

"Why won't you let yourself be happy? Why is it so hard to let yourself love after Clarissa?" Rosemary caught his hand in hers, pulling it to her chest. "We both know I can give you that back. You said I reminded you of her."

"You do." Will sighed. "That's the problem."

"That isn't a problem! This is your, no, *our* second chance at happiness. We could be so good together and—"

"Julie's pregnant."

"What?!" Rosemary froze. "What do you mean?"

Will tugged his hand away from Rosemary. "Just that. She's pregnant. Figure she's about a month along." He rubbed a hand along his jaw. "That's the way it is, Rosemary. I'm sorry, but you need to move on. There is nothing here for you. I'm married to her, and she's pregnant. She's my family now. I'm not walking away from that. I swore in front of Forrest, this whole town, and God."

Julie struggled to breathe. This wasn't her husband turning away another woman because he didn't want her.

It was him sticking to his word.

This was him not breaking the vows he had made in a church, to not just her, but to Forrest.

Julie squeezed her eyes shut, suddenly feeling dizzy. Her ill feelings weren't just a product from the shock of finding her husband having a less than proper conversation with another woman, but the news he had so casually delivered.

She was pregnant.

Had been for the past month.

A month.

Suddenly all of Will's overprotective behavior made

perfect sense. His unwillingness for her to wear herself out with planning the dance and the fact that he watched over her eating and bouts of nausea with the attention of a mother hen. She had mistaken all of it for him caring, an outward proof that he was happy as her husband, happy in their marriage.

That he loved her.

None of it was real. It had only been because she was pregnant.

Julie blinked at the hot tears that threatened to fall from her eyes and pushed herself away from the collection of wagons with a deep sigh. No longer caring if they heard her, she took off at a fast walk back toward the dance, but then at last second she veered toward the lane that would take her home.

Julie had to get home.

First to mourn what never was. And then to plan her next move.

There was no way she could stay in Gold Sky and sleep in the same bed as a man who didn't want her. Her pride wouldn't allow it.

Julie clapped a hand over her mouth to stifle the sob that wanted to burst from her. All she could think of was how fixated both her husbands had been on her becoming pregnant, even from the first. How, when she fell asleep in Will's arms, his hand always came to rest against her stomach. All of it threw the tenderness and closeness she had experienced with her husbands into sharp relief, and even Forrest's gentleness suddenly seemed suspect.

It made Julie feel sick in a way that her nausea could never touch.

Though she guessed that was how Will had known she was pregnant, when she hadn't even thought of it herself.

How terribly naive of her, with her husbands' regular talk of a family and children. Somehow Julie had thought they had wanted her for who she was. Their original advert for a wife had stressed the need for their future wife to be skilled as a teacher, but how could she not have realized her womb proved just as valuable as her talent in the classroom?

She had fallen in love with them. Yet they viewed her as an asset, as something to be laid out in pros and cons versus the other women. Over a hundred other women.

Will's conversation with Rosemary proved just as much.

How can you be so selfish, Rosemary had asked her.

Julie swallowed hard. The last statement from Rosemary repeated in her mind until it became a mantra, and Julie paused in the foyer, her eyes going to the mirror that occupied the wall beside the door. She looked tired, the hollows of her cheeks more pronounced, the skin beneath her eyes all but bruised.

Gone was the girl from New York City. She didn't recognize the woman in the throes of grief who stared back at her.

"You don't deserve this," Julie said, though she wasn't talking to herself. Her hand rested against her stomach. "You deserve better. A family who loves each other for the sake of love." Her fingers flexed on the material of her dress.

"You deserve a mother who isn't content to be a duty to the men she loves."

There was no world in which Julie would allow her child to see her slighted. If she didn't provide an example, if she didn't demand more for herself, then how would her child know what they were worth? What they deserved? And though Julie was heartbroken at how she had found out that she was with child, she knew one thing for certain, and that was that she already loved the little soul with all her heart.

"You deserve better," Julie said again, "and I intend to give it to you."

CHAPTER 13

*B*y the time Will came home Julie was already in bed and fast asleep, or at least she pretended to be. It took everything in her not to stir when she heard him moving around as quietly as he was able.

Two hours had passed since she had returned home, and she began to wonder what had occupied his attention during that time. She clutched the quilt that lay over her tighter and squeezed her eyes shut. This was madness, and she would drive herself crazy if she let herself think about those missing two hours.

Whatever it was, Julie forced her thoughts from it and concentrated on keeping her breathing even. A feat that became herculean when Will slipped into bed and pressed a kiss to her shoulder before he tugged the quilt up and over them.

Thankfully, she had fallen asleep not long after because she had finally decided on a plan. Though it was a plan that required she be as rested as possible, especially when she wasn't sure how long it would be until she was able to lay in a bed again.

It would be a rough journey on the train back to New York City.

Julie shuddered, thinking of the weeks she had in front of her on a train as she packed her bag with the essentials she would need for the trip home. The two trunks she had brought with her would have to stay, as there was no way she would be able to load them in the buckboard without help, and she had no intention of giving herself away by asking for it.

What she would say when she arrived back home in New York pregnant and heartbroken was anyone's guess, but Julie suspected she would be able to think of something on the nearly month-long journey.

Julie shook her head, thinking of what her mother would say, or what the press would have to say, but she pushed the thoughts away. It was best to approach her obstacles as they came because if she thought too far into the future, it all seemed impossible.

Closing her bag with a snap of her hands, Julie walked over to the bedroom window that faced the lane in front of the ranch. There was no one in sight, though Will had left just a few minutes before. She planned on having breakfast, a simple meal of black tea and dry toast, before she hitched up the buckboard and left Gold Sky forever.

Which seemed like a well-enough and simple plan until she stood with the horses and realized she had no idea how to hitch up the buckboard.

"Don't suppose *The Lady's Cooking Compendium* has anything to say to this, now does it?" she asked the horses.

It was just as well, she supposed, stabling the horses again. She would have worried about the horses being left alone at the train depot, but if she moved quickly enough, she might be able to catch passage on the coach straight to

Butte City, or even farther than that given Butte City was anything but gentle.

Grabbing her bag, Julie walked as briskly as she could down the lane and into Gold Sky. She did her best to appear inconspicuous, but it was difficult with so many of her students' families out on the bright and happy weekend. She had just managed to duck around the corner from a favorite student when she heard a voice call out:

"Coach to Butte City! LAST CALL! LAST CALL!"

Daring to step out into the open, Julie raised her hand and waved at the coach driver. "That's me, sir! How much?"

"Ten dollars," he said, giving her a friendly smile.

"Certainly." Julie pushed the currency into his hand and returned his smile when he swung down from the driver's perch and grabbed her bag from her.

"We'll be off soon as I get this tied up," he said, already scrambling up the coach's side with her bag in tow.

Julie nodded and stepped into the coach, which was blessedly only occupied by one other person. An elderly woman she didn't recognize dozed away in one corner. Settling on the opposite bench, Julie let out a little yelp at the sudden lurch of the coach as it sprang into motion. She adjusted her bonnet and leaned back against the soft cushion of the bench seat, soothed by the gentle rocking motion of the coach as it began its journey out of Gold Sky. She peeked out of the window and bit her lip, seeing the town she had come to love as her home start to slip away.

Before long they were on the outskirts and speeding toward the open plains of the Montana Territory.

Julie's heart clenched, seeing the stretch of road she

hadn't been on since she had arrived with her husbands at her side.

Now she was seeing it alone...no, not alone. She smiled, putting a hand on her stomach. She had a bit of them with her and that, she supposed, would have to be enough.

Bracing her arms on the window, she pulled up the shade and let out a sigh as daydreams of what could have been if she stayed in Gold Sky played out in her mind's eye. In that world she was happy, she had four more children, Forrest cooked with her, Will gave her gentle smiles meant only for her. It was absolutely perfect and helped dull the ache in her heart.

In this fictional world, they would tell her they loved her, they would stop her from leaving, swearing she was the first and only woman in their hearts. It was enough to make her romantic heart weep with joy.

So lost was she in staring out the window that she didn't see the rider coming toward them until he was almost in front of her, which was why when the man jerked up in his saddle suddenly and called her name out she sat in stunned disbelief.

"Julie?" the man exclaimed again before he jerked off his hat and yelled at the driver. "Stop this couch now!"

"Says who?" the driver yelled back. Julie blinked, trying to figure out if what she saw was real or a mirage.

"Says her *husband!*" Forrest roared, wheeling his horse around to stare at her in disbelief. "Where do you think you're going, little bird?" he asked as the coach slowed and came to a stop.

"I—I..." Julie jerked back from the window when she realized she hadn't imagined Forrest, but that he was really in front of her, really leaping off his horse and wrenching open the door.

"Home," she said weakly.

"Funny thing about that," he said, pulling her forward and into his arms, "Home is that way." He nodded toward the direction of Gold Sky. "You want to tell me where you're really going?"

Julie remained silent the entire ride back to Gold Sky. Wedged as she was between Forrest and the pommel of his saddle, she kept her gaze down when they encountered curious looks from the townsfolk along the way. She knew their interest was piqued because while Gold Sky had expected to see Forrest riding into town at any time given the uncertain nature of his work, it was quite another thing for Julie to be with him when he did so.

Julie only turned to look at Forrest over her shoulder when he directed his horse towards the sheriff's office and not the lane that led toward the ranch.

"Where are you going?" she asked.

"To check in with Will," he said, looking down at her with a frown. His normally bright blue eyes were clouded now, full of an emotion that Julie couldn't quite place, but she had an inkling that it was akin to betrayal.

"I can stay here," she said, toying with the cuff of her gloves. Anything but look up and meet those troubled eyes of his.

"Rather you not." Forrest rubbed a hand along the bridge of his nose and reached up for her with a pinched look on his face.

"But—"

"Not going in without you and that's final." His big hands closed around her waist, pulling her close. He didn't trust her. It was all over his handsome face, and Julie found it broke her heart to see.

"Very well." Julie tipped her chin down. She was content to follow Forrest up the stairs, just a step behind him, but he surprised her when he caught her hand and tugged her close, a calloused thumb rubbing the back of her gloved hand. She looked up at him at the tender gesture, but Forrest's eyes focused on the door ahead of them, his jaw firmly set, so she said nothing and entered the sheriff's station with him.

Julie wasn't sure what she would feel when she looked at Will. She hadn't anticipated ever doing it again, having feigned sleep when he had set out for work that morning. It had been torture to have the last image of him, in her memories, being of him in conversation with Rosemary. She had thought she might be angry with him, but she wasn't.

Instead, Julie felt an overwhelming sadness when she took in his handsome face. He drank a cup of coffee at his desk with a stack of reports in one hand. A smile spread over his face when he saw Forrest, Julie looked away before she could see what his face would do when he saw her. She didn't have it in her to take it if his smiled faltered even in the slightest. It was torture to analyze a husband's expression for evidence of real affection, and Julie found she had no taste for it after the week she had tried her hand at it.

"Forrest! Wasn't expecting y'all'd be off the case this soon. You just missed the dance." Will set his coffee cup on the desk with a jovial smile. "You go by the house already?" he asked, his eyes going to Julie, who still avoided looking at him.

"No," Forrest sighed, rocking back on his heels, "hadn't had the chance just yet. Barely got into town just a few minutes ago."

"Well, lucky you ran into Julie on the way in." Will came to stand beside her. "You feel better after a good night's sleep? I didn't wake you this morning, did I?"

"Ah, yes." Julie nodded, eyes darting up to his face for a moment before she looked away again. "Much better. Thank you."

"She hasn't been sleeping?" Forrest asked, his eyes moving over her face like he was inspecting her for damage. "What's wrong?"

"Just under the weather," Julie said, keeping her voice even. She wouldn't bring up her pregnancy, not yet. "And the dance, it's been tiring."

"That was last night." Will waved a hand. "I expect she'll settle back into herself soon enough."

Forrest crossed his arms. "There a trip planned in that settling?"

Julie barely dared to breathe at that, but said nothing while Will frowned in confusion.

"Trip? What trip?" he asked, his gray eyes moving to her in question. Julie took a small step away from the men as Forrest spoke again.

"I'm not sure on the particulars of that, to be truthful." Forrest turned so that he faced Julie. "Though Julie does."

"Wha-what is he talking about?" Will asked finally, taking in the uncomfortable posture Julie had assumed. She crossed her arms and sidled away from the pair of men, opting to put the desk between them as she spoke.

"I just thought a change of scenery would be beneficial."

"What?" Forrest and Will asked in such perfect union that Julie had to stifle a pained sigh.

"Came home and found her on her way out of town with a bag of clothes," Forrest said with a nod at Julie. A look of disbelief crossed Will's face at the news. "Took her right off the coach. If I hadn't, she would be halfway to Butte City by now."

"Where were you going?" Will asked. The question was like a dagger through her heart. He sounded concerned, worried even, so much so that Julie let out a nervous giggle at the preposterous thought.

"Home. I was going home."

"This is your home." Will waved an arm around the sheriff's office. "You belong here."

"No, I do not," Julie shot back, finally daring to meet her husband's eyes. "I belong back home in New York City and that—that's where I was going until—"

"Until I found you and ruined your plans to run off?" Forrest had both hands on his hips as he glared at her. It was startling to see such a hard look on his face, so tender were the looks he usually gave her, that she took a half step back.

"You don't understand," she told him, fingers twisting in her skirts.

"Then tell me," Forrest said, rounding the desk to stand before her. "When I left things were rough. That's true enough, but that doesn't mean you run from us."

"I wasn't running," Julie said, but there was no conviction in her words. She had been running scared, and they all knew it.

"Then what do you call being on a coach with a packed bag on your way to the railroad depot?!" Forrest exploded. Julie gasped in shock and backpedaled so quickly she stumbled when the heel of her boot caught on the lip of an uneven floorboard.

"Forrest…" Will surprised her when he stepped between them and put a hand on the other man's shoulder. "Take it easy."

"No!" Forrest shoved Will's hand off with a scowl, a scowl that pinned Julie to the spot where she leaned against the wall for support, her heart beating fast in her chest.

"Where did you think you were going?! You would—" His voice cracked, and he ripped the hat off his head with a shuddering breath. "You would be gone if I hadn't seen you in the window," he finished a slightly calmer voice.

"Yes," Julie swallowed hard and nodded. "Yes, I would be."

"But *why*, little bird?" Forrest dropped down onto the desk beside him with a thud. "Why are you trying to fly away from us?"

"I don't belong here," Julie whispered, her eyes on the floor. "It would be better, for everyone, if I left. If we annulled the marriage."

"Why would you say that?" Forrest demanded, lifting his head through his shoulders still slumped in defeat.

"I told you—I don't—" she began, and the blond man waved a hand at her.

"If you say you don't belong here one more time I will lose my damn mind, Julie." He clenched and unclenched his jaw. "When I left, you were happy, things were going well, we were—we were starting to be happy. All of us." He paused and looked at Will then.

"What happened? What changed that?" he asked the other man.

"Nothing." Will sighed crossing his arms. "I thought,"

he shook his head, "I thought I was making her happy. Doing what was needed to make her happy here."

Julie's cheeks burned hot. There it was again. What was needed. She was a duty to be managed, an offering to Forrest that needed to be maintained in his absence while Will denied his own desire for another woman.

"Well, you are relieved of your duty, sir," she said with as much pride as she could manage. "I aim to board the train in Butte City as soon as possible and return to New York City."

"The hell you are," Will told her with an arched eyebrow.

"You cannot presume to tell me what to do."

"I can and I will. We will." Will jerked his head between himself and Forrest before he said, "You aren't going anywhere, Jules. That's final."

Julie blanched at his order and straightened her posture.

"I do not have to listen to you," she said, her voice icy.

"That's not what the law says about wives," Will shot back, making her gasp in outrage.

"How dare you!" she yelled at him, throwing as much venom into her glare as possible, but the effect made Will throw his head back and laugh.

"You're beautiful when you're riled. Even more so when you think you've got a fighting chance against the pair of us."

"I am leaving for New York, and there isn't a thing you can do about it," Julie spat back, already bustling toward the door with a haughty toss of her head. "Good day, gentlemen. I trust you'll send along my things when it's convenient."

"Get back here this instant, little bird," Forrest

growled, standing. Julie didn't listen and threw open the door. It was now or never, and she didn't aim to allow the men to stop her a second time.

She descended the stairs, already working out how to pull her bag down from where Forrest had secured it on the saddle when a strong hand caught her wrist.

"Let go of me!" Julie jerked her arm back, but before she could gain any ground, she found herself being swung up and over Forrest's shoulder.

"Unhand me! Put me down!," she screamed, attracting attention from the other citizens staring at their school teacher and sheriffs' display of less than blissful matrimony.

"It'll be a cold day before I let you go, little bird," he told her, striding back into the station. He kicked the door shut behind him and set her down on her feet. Forrest jerked the deadbolt of the door in place and hiked a thumb at the empty jail cell in the corner.

"You keep trying to make a run for it, and I'll put you in a cell. Don't make me do it, Julie."

"You wouldn't dare," she gasped in outrage.

"Oh, I would, if it means keeping my wife safe and not running off to God knows where without me," Forrest thundered back at her.

"New York isn't God knows where and it's certainly more civilized than this town!"

"Not setting a foot outside of Gold Sky without us and that's final." Forrest took a step toward her and Julie willed herself not to move as he did so. She was angry with him for stopping her, for ruining her plans of escape, but she was also struggling not to burst into grateful tears and throw herself into her beautiful husband's arms, because he had come for her. He had stopped her. He refused to her let her go, and as much as Julie knew it wasn't fair of her to cling to the hope it gave her, she did with a fierce desperation.

And it was all she could do to stop herself from crumbling, to become weak when faced with those summer sky eyes that begged her for an explanation, that willed her not to say she wanted to leave, that reminded her that she loved him and vice versa.

It was a tall order, but she managed. She barely pulled it off with a glare and would have challenged him to make good on his threat to lock her up if Will hadn't spoken.

"You're not going any place with our child in you."

She snapped her mouth shut and focused all of her hurt from the night before at him. Suddenly, all the emotions she had been holding back escaped in a rush.

Julie let out a bitter laugh. "Do not pretend to care."

"I do," Will began, walking toward her now that Forrest had stumbled back half a step with a dazed expression on his face.

"You're with child?" he asked, voice full of wonder in a way that made Julie's heart ache.

"I—yes—I'm not sure." Julie shook her head, choosing to answer Forrest's question rather than meet Will's steady gaze.

Forrest shook his head as if waking from a dream with a smile spreading over his face. "This is a miracle." He laughed then, his eyes dropping to her stomach, though he froze a second later. "Oh, Christ! I threw you over my shoulder. The baby!" His hands went to his head, and he pulled on his hair in frustration. "I'm so sorry, are you all right? I didn't hurt you?"

"I'm fine," Julie told him, unable to stop the smile on

her lips at his reaction to the news. "I'm not even sure if I'm pregnant. I could be just sick."

"You're pregnant," Will told her with a sure look.

Julie raised an eyebrow in challenge. "How do you know?"

"Experience," was all Will said with an impassive look on his face.

"Clarissa?" Julie asked before she could stop herself, and if she had thought herself proficient in understanding Will's reactions, she was wholly unprepared for the look of fury that crossed Will's face as she uttered the name.

"What did you say?" he asked in a deathly quiet voice.

Julie looked to the side to see that Forrest hadn't heard her question or Will's answer. In fact, the other man gazed up at the ceiling with a wide grin on his face as he laughed to himself. "A baby!"

"I said, what did you say." Will took a step toward her.

"I, ah." Julie swallowed hard and cursed herself for not thinking before she spoke. "I asked if it was because of Clarissa."

"Where did you hear that name?"

"Rosemary," Julie whispered, feeling like prey caught in the stare of a predator. Will paced toward her, his body rigid, and she was nervous as to what he would do next.

"Last night, I just, I'm sorry. I shouldn't have brought her up." Julie lowered her eyes, not wanting to meet his gaze. Forrest's arms wrapped her up and pulled her against him.

"You want to see your Ma, don't you?" he asked with a gentle look on his face. "That's why you wanted to go home, wasn't it?" Forrest's eyes were warm, understanding, and Julie hurt at the sight.

"Forrest…" She bit her lip and looked away from her husband's earnest gaze.

"It's okay to be scared, but we'll make sure you're safe. Gonna take care of you and, the little one. Whatever we need to do to keep you healthy and happy. The both of you."

"Forrest, please, I have to go back to New York."

Forrest gave her a smile and kept speaking, ignoring Julie's protest. "I know the doctors out here aren't usually the best, but we'll fix that. I don't care if I have to put one on private retainer."

"No, Forrest."

"Darlin' it won't be any trouble to do it. And—"

Julie put her hands on his chest and pushed him back an inch. "I cannot stay here."

"Julie—"

"No!" The outburst startled even her, and she pressed a hand against her mouth with a ragged breath. "No," she said again, "I want to go home."

"I don't understand." Forrest gave her a confused look. "This is your home. What are you not telling us?"

His wounded blue eyes pierced Julie to her core, but she shook her head, forcing herself to stay resolved in her campaign to leave Gold Sky as soon as she was able. She couldn't stay here another minute with these men, or she wouldn't be able to do it.

"It's because of me," Will said, stepping forward next to Forrest. He put a hand on the other man's shoulder. "She's leaving on account of me."

"What? Why?" Forrest looked at Will in surprise.

"She found out about Clarissa."

Forrest's eyes briefly closed and he let out a silent curse. "How?"

"Rosemary told me," Julie supplied quietly.

"She had no right," Forrest snapped, his eyes hard. "It's not what you think, little bird. We swear it."

"I don't care that Will was married before, or that he— he has experience with," she paused, bit her lip, and gestured to herself, "knowing when a woman is with child because of it. That isn't why I'm leaving."

"Sister was a midwife," Will curtly cut in, his lips turned down in a frown. "That's how I know about women and babies."

"Oh." Julie nodded dumbly at that new bit of information.

"Oh," Will shot back with a tip of his head.

Forrest rolled his eyes and held up a hand, breaking the staring match the other two engaged in. "Now tell us again. Why are you leaving?"

Julie dragged her eyes from Will's unwavering stare and said, "I have never been one to keep someone from what they truly desire."

"What the hell does that mean?" Will blurted out.

"You know what it means," Julie shot back, earning a snort from Will.

"The hell I do, woman!"

This time Julie rolled her eyes. "You very well know what I mean, William."

"Oh, William is it? We're back to that?"

Julie opened her mouth to retort, but Forrest waved his hands, breaking up the sparring match between his spouses.

"She means Rosemary, goddammit. Stop being so damn obtuse, Will."

"What?" Will frowned in surprise and Julie's mouth

snapped shut. He looked at her when she said nothing else. "Jules?"

"What?" she asked, eyes still looking anywhere but at him.

"You're running off because of Rosemary?!" Will asked incredulously. A beat of silence passed before Julie sighed and met his eyes.

"Yes."

"That's—that…" Will took a quick step forward as he struggled with his words. "That has to be the most ridiculous thing I've ever heard."

Julie's mouth dropped open in shock. "Pardon me?"

"That woman isn't anyone to me," Will told her, still closing the space between them even as Julie continued to back up.

"She bakes you pies."

Will shrugged, taking another slow, measured step forward. "Got a sweet tooth. Everyone knows that."

"You have breakfast with her!"

"Couldn't eat a damn thing at our reception because I was too nervous looking at you. Next morning, I was desperate," Will countered, still moving forward.

"You were almost—the three of you." Julie flung a hand out at the men. "The two of you were almost a triad with her."

"Like hell we were," Forrest muttered, joining Will in his forward march toward her. Julie swallowed hard and took another step back until she hit the wall and shook her head at them, but Forrest added, "She wasn't the one for us. Didn't understand what we wanted. Couldn't accept us as we were. Not like you."

"Because she couldn't give you children…"

"Who said that?" Will demanded.

"She did," Julie whispered.

"Never been happier hearing you were pregnant but we never expected to find a woman who could love us both, let alone give us a child. Only started wanting a family when it was with you, little bird." Forrest smiled at her and Julie felt her resolve against the men begin to crack.

It was all too good to be true, too easy to give into and believe because that was what her heart wanted. She wanted them to say she was the only woman they desired, the only one they loved, but there was one last obstacle between Julie and believing that these beautiful men were only for her. It was almost too much to even entertain, and Julie found herself stripped bare and vulnerable under the sincere words and gentle looks her husbands gave her.

It frightened her to be exposed in such a way, and she scrambled to throw up the last defense she had at her disposal, the final wall to crossing the little bit of space that remained between them and offering her heart to them.

"I heard you last night with Rosemary," she said in a rush, looking at Will, whose eyebrows shot up at her admission.

"You were there?" he asked, rubbing a hand over his jaw, "Thought I heard something."

"Of course I was there. I went looking for you after I couldn't find you—or Rosemary." Julie pursed her lips.

"It was nothing."

"You danced all night with her."

Will shook his head at her. "One dance isn't all night, Jules."

"You didn't even take me out on the floor!"

He flung a hand out at her stomach. "Because you're not far enough along for it!"

Julie's mouth dropped open and then she snapped it shut. "That's not how babies work, Will."

"Better safe than sorry. I'm not risking it," he said with a determined set of his jaw.

"Where were you?" Forrest held up a hand, stopping the flow of conversation. "I'm not following the two of you."

"She heard me letting Rosemary down."

Forrest sighed, his eyes moving to the ceiling. "Again?"

"Yes," Will muttered. "Again."

"Again?" Julie was dumbstruck by the news, and the flicker of hope, real hope, bloomed in her chest. "I—she didn't—"

"She didn't tell you that, did she?" Will asked, his hands going to his hips in frustration. "Didn't tell you that I've been letting her down since she tried answering our ad herself."

"But, Clarissa—you said, I heard...that you said she reminded you of her." Julie shook her head, unwilling to give in to the hope that was no longer just a flicker but was as real and as tangible as her husbands.

"I did tell her that, but it wasn't meant as a compliment," Will told her with a grimace. "Clarissa was a love that could have only happened in my youth when I knew nothing and was ruled by my needs. She understood how men work and used it to get what she wanted from me." Will shook his head at the memory. "God, she was the most beautiful woman I had ever seen."

Julie looked down at his remembrance and hated that she was hurt by it.

"Until you, Jules," Will sighed, coming to stand in front of her, his hands cupping her face. "You're perfect."

"I'm not."

"For us you are." He smiled at her, thumbs caressing her cheeks. "You're the love I know better than to let go. Clarissa knew how to use me to get what she wanted. I loved her until her last day but she never truly loved me, not when things didn't get better after the war, and you, God, you are—-you've been my darling little wife since you laid eyes on me. You want me. Truly want me, and Jules, there's nothing more I want on this earth than to love you and have a family with you," he reached back and caught Forrest's hand, "and Forrest."

"Will." Julie's eyes filled with unshed tears, and her breath hitched when she let out a little hiccup of a sob. She closed her eyes, feeling the wall around her heart tumbling down around her.

"After Clarissa never thought I would love anyone again," Will told her before he smiled ruefully, "not anyone that wasn't Forrest, but then he found you."

Julie sniffled and nodded at him. "He did."

"Knew you were it from the minute I opened your reply." Forrest touched her cheek gently. "You're the soft we needed. We don't work without you."

Tears slid down Julie's cheeks, and she trembled as she cried, tucked between her two loving husbands. They wrapped their arms around her, hands linking together, and Julie let out a shaky laugh of disbelief.

"I'm sorry," she whispered and tilted her head black to look at the two men. "I shouldn't have tried to run from you. I became overwhelmed by what she was telling me, and I should never have believed her."

"Shh, shh." Will kissed her temple. "Things have been

unconventional between the three of us. We should have told you about Clarissa in the letters."

"It just felt like Rosemary knew a part of you I couldn't reach." Julie leaned her cheek against Will's chest and closed her eyes. "I desperately wanted to make you happy, and it was torture thinking another woman had your heart."

"That woman is you," Will told her.

"You've made us the happiest men in all the territory," Forrest said, hugging her close.

Julie sagged in her men's arms in relief, content to just be in the moment with her husbands. It was in that instant Julie glimpsed their future, that while it wouldn't always be easy, so long as they had one another, all would still be right in their world.

"Do you think it's a boy or a girl?" she asked quietly.

"So long as it's got all its fingers and toes I don't care." Forrest huffed out a laugh. "I do hope it has your eyes," he said, rearing back to look at her.

"Teacher's pet," Will muttered with a wry grin at the blonde, who only winked at him over Julie's head.

"Trying to make up for being away chasing vagrants," Forrest said, sliding his hands up to cup Julie's face in his hands, his fingertips lightly stroking the soft skin behind her ears as he did so.

"I missed waking up to you. Missing seeing that soft look in your eyes." He leaned forward and kissed her lightly. His lips pressed against hers in what felt like a chaste kiss, though at the tiny moan Julie let loose it didn't stay sweet for long, and before she knew it she was pressed, with her back against Will's chest as Forrest explored her mouth.

"Taste so sweet," he murmured against her lips before

he began to pepper her neck with kisses. Julie tilted her head back and gasped when she felt Forrest press himself against her through her skirts.

Eyes shut, Julie asked the question she had been too terrified to ask only moments before. "Do you forgive me? I'm so sorry, I shouldn't have run. I'll never do it again—"

Forrest silenced her with another passionate kiss, his teeth nipping her bottom lip before he leaned back and said, "Little bird, you're going to be the mother of our children. There isn't a thing you could do that we wouldn't forgive."

"He's right," Will said as his hands worked at unbuttoning her dress. "We will mess up, all three of us, but that doesn't mean we won't forgive and move forward together."

"That's what marriage is. Falling and getting back up together," Forrest said, slipping the dress down her shoulders once Will had unbuttoned it.

"Learning together." Julie's fingers caught in Forrest's hair before she leaned back and ran a hand through Will's longer brunette locks. "I'm so happy to learn with the both of you."

Forrest kissed the skin above her collarbone, his tongue lightly dragging across Julie's skin and making her squirm against Will, who let out a sigh at the pressure of her body against him.

"Well, you are the teacher." He grinned at her rakishly.

Julie rolled her eyes. "You did not just—"

Her words ended in a sharp gasp as Will pulled her skirts up around her thighs and no sooner had the material settled did Forrest drop to his knees and begin to work her underthings and stockings off. Words flew from her mind at the sight of her husband on his knees between her legs.

"Time for talking is done." Forrest's lips ghosted over her skin, and he pressed a kiss against her hip. "M'gonna show you how much I missed you, Mrs. Wickes-Barnes."

Julie only managed a quick nod before Will leaned her back against him, supporting her with an arm around her waist, as Forrest pulled her close and went about showing her just how much he had missed her in the month he had been gone.

Nothing much got done that day by the law, at least not anything outside the four walls of the sheriff's office, and the people of Gold Sky were pleased as punch to have their favorite family back together once more. It might not have been perfect, but it was home.

And that was more than enough.

EPILOGUE

Ten months later...

"Oh, give the little darling here!" Manon Baptiste held out her arms for the wiggling bundle of perfection her daughter held against her chest. Julie has been considering the safest way to get out of the buckboard while holding her daughter safely to her.

"Thank you, *Maman*." Julie let out a relieved sigh and handed the infant to her mother, who cooed lovingly at her first grandchild.

"You precious little gift," Manon murmured, arranging the pale yellow blanket of cashmere just so around the newborn, Seylah. The baby was all flawless soft tan skin, wiggling fingers and toes, with large hazel eyes, and had inherited her mother's riot of chestnut curls, being born with a full head of hair.

Seylah Wickes-Barnes was a treasure to Gold Sky, who greeted the addition of one more soul with love. The entire town had erupted in celebration when an excited Will had let loose a yell on the early morning of her birth, that after fifteen long hours of labor when Julie's water had broken at early that afternoon, they had been blessed with a healthy child.

"It's a girl," he had hollered, throwing open the door of the ranch. The front yard and lane of the ranch had teemed with concerned friends and citizens of the town who had camped out over the ordeal to be the first to welcome Gold Sky's newest citizen. There had been no shortage of love for Seylah, who had the good fortune of being blessed with three loving parents and many more immediate family members, when Jean, Manon, and Julian had arrived in town a month after her birth.

And while Julie had been nervous, even fearful, of telling her family of the life she had chosen—that she loved not one, but two men with her entire heart and soul —Seylah's presence was enough to diffuse and put aside the confusion of her family.

"I don't...understand it," her mother had told her with a shake of her head as Julie waited for a response from her family at the revelation that Julie had two husbands. Her family sat pressed in next to each other on a settee in the parlor. Julie stood with a hand each clutched by Forrest and William, who stood on either side of her. Their larger frames and warmth lent Julie strength during such a stressful time.

"*Maman*, I love them," Julie whispered.

Jean opened his mouth to speak, but the wail of an infant in need cut him off. And just like that, the focus of the entire room shifted to attending to Seylah's needs, and whether they understood it or not, all it took was the sight of Forrest and Will rushing to fuss after the baby girl to change their minds.

"She's hungry." Will held a bottle up.

Forrest shook his head. "No, she needs a change. I'll do it."

The pair of fathers rushed from the room to change the baby and Manon laughed sending Julie a knowing smile.

"I think I might understand your choices now, my darling girl."

Jean and Julian had taken a tad longer to warm up to the idea of Julie being wed to two men. However, that changed when they witnessed the care and concern both men expressed over Julie while she nursed. Julian had been particularly won over when Forrest set up a game of poker special for him.

Now a month later the Baptiste and Wickes-Barnes clan had settled into a comfortable dynamic, a world that centered on little Seylah, and Manon had already begun inquiring after a second grandchild.

"She will, of course, require a sibling."

"*Maman*, please," Julie moaned, rubbing her temples while her mother laughed at her daughter's consternation. It had been especially gratifying for Julie to see the ones she loved the most come together into one big, happy, family. She had never been happier. The smile on her face needed little help as the town was coming together to celebrate the fourth of July, an occasion that blessedly brought her husbands and father together in solidarity at having served in the Union Army.

Julie glanced their way and saw all three men laughing raucously over what she could only imagine was a bawdy limerick her father had informed her the men had often sung over campfire.

"Here, give me your hand," Julian said, suddenly appearing in front of her. He handed her down and nudged her shoulder with his. "Looks like a veteran cele-bration with how they are getting on now."

"I know. I'm glad." Julie grinned at him. "I'm happy you're here. When do you have to leave?"

Julian shrugged. "Who knows. I'm finding the drawing rooms of the city quite boring as of late. Perhaps I'll stay on longer than *Maman* and Papa."

Julie bounced. "Truly?!"

"Most likely."

Julie let out a screech and threw her arms around her brother. "We will have a wonderful summer! You'll see!"

"Oh, Lord," Manon sighed, stepping close to her chil-dren, "are the two of you planning some kind of uprisal?"

"Julian is staying!" Julie crowed with a laugh.

"Really, Julian?"

"Mm," Julian nodded at his mother as they walked along to the town center where everyone was gathering to watch the planned fireworks for the celebration. "New York has been...stifling lately. I think a change of scenery is just what I need to feel rejuvenated."

Manon cradled Seylah close and kissed the baby girl's forehead. "I would feel good about the two of you spending time together. How long will you stay?"

"Ah, now that is the adventure of it all." Julian winked at his mother. "We will just have to see how long I can last before New York calls me home."

"How bohemian of you," Manon told her son with a wry look on her face.

"Quite." Julian stuck his hands in his pockets with a smile. "Though I won't intrude on my fair sister and her happy home for the duration of my stay."

"You won't? Why not?" Julie demanded.

"Oh, men and wives need...privacy, especially if you are to grant *Maman* that second grandchild she craves."

Julie blushed but then said, "Fair."

"Where shall you stay then?" Manon gave him a curious look.

"There's a boarding house in town. It's lovely. My friend Alice Hill runs it, and I know Julian will find comfort during his stay there."

Julian clapped his hands. "Then it's settled! To Ms. Hill's I shall go!" He turned, looking around, "Which way would that be?"

"You're going now?" Julie raised an eyebrow.

"As father says, no time like the present. Besides, if I go now, I'll be practically settled by the time the real celebration happens."

"It's just down that way then." Julie pointed down the crowded street. "Alice might not be there but her cook, Violet, should be."

"Perfect. I'll return shortly, my fair ladies." Julian gave them an extended bow with a flourish that had Julie giggling and their mother rolling her eyes as she cradled Seylah.

Julian turned on his heel and sauntered down the block until he came upon a pretty Victorian with a wrap-around porch that seemed far too grand for Gold Sky. A white and blue sign painted with an elegant gold script read Gold Sky Boarding House: Proprietress, Miss Alice Hill.

"Nice, very respectable," Julian mused, sauntering up the small walk to the front door. He pulled the bell cord for the door and clasped his hands behind his back as he waited for entry.

A minute passed, and then another, and he wondered

if he had been ahead of himself in his excitement to get things done. What if everyone had gone to the square for the celebration? He supposed he could come back easily the next morning, and had just resolved to do so when the door opened suddenly, revealing a stunningly statuesque woman with raven hair, sparkling brown eyes, a tanned face full of freckles, and a broad, open smile that set Julian's heart racing and his palms sweating.

"Hello, I'm Violet Shield."

THANK YOU!

We hope you enjoyed Heart and Hand!

Julie, Forrest and Will's story is at an end but your time in the Montana Territory doesn't have to be over. There's so much left to fall in love with in the town of Gold Sky! We hope you will come along with us for Julian and Violet's love story featuring a male-order bride.

Yes, that was a pun. <3

Until then!

Turn the page and enjoy a sneaky peek at Julian and Violet!

EXCERPT: JULIAN'S STORY

*J*ulian stepped inside of the boarding house and cautioned a look around him. He knew the establishment was reputable. His sister's glowing recommendation of not only the facilities but the proprietress had made him hopeful for a comfortable stay, but a cursory glance around the well-appointed space had convinced him of it.

Miss Alice Hill's boarding house was entirely unexpected on the frontier but would have fit in among the businesses of the city's most affluent streets. The furniture was tasteful, luxurious drapery decorated the French style windows, the hardwood flooring gleaming and spotless... and then there was the woman who greeted him at the door.

Violet Shield.

Something coiled and tightened in his chest at just thinking her name. The woman was like a vision in the desert, the warm smile on her face touching a softer part of himself he'd turned away from. A part of him he hadn't realized he'd pushed away until the moment the door had opened and there she had been.

She'd been garbed simply enough in a starched apron and muslin dress of a shade of lilac that brought attention to her dark waist-length hair which had been pulled back at the crown of her head. She wore no jewelry or adornments save for a thin gold chain at her neck that caught the light when she turned toward him.

"How long will we have you in Gold Sky, Mr. Baptiste?"

Julian's eyes left the glint of the gold chain to meet the eyes of the smiling woman he'd been trying very hard not to stare at. It was impolite, ill-mannered, and—well, he wasn't a man who stared at women.

He was no stranger to beautiful women, women who donned only the finest fashions, possessed advantageous familial connections, and moved through the world with only the kind of grace a charmed life could offer.

It wasn't even that Violet was refreshingly unlike certain women who had scorned him, or even that she was like ones he found himself helpless to resist.

Violet simply *was*.

She spoke plainly enough but Julian warmed to her husky tone that reminded him of summer nights. Her Mexican accent, light as it was, brought to mind the sound of flint striking steel.

There was strength in her. He could see it. He could hear it.

Julian chanced a glance at her profile to see high cheekbones and full lips. Dark lashes rimmed large brown eyes flecked with gold—and he suddenly chastised himself. He should not have noticed that about her, that her eyes held an ochre color unlike he had ever seen, but here he was feeling unnerved by this woman and fighting the urge to gawk at her.

Julian Baptiste III had been brought up better than to stare at a lady.

Or at least until now.

He was gentleman enough to admit that he had been struck dumb the second Violet Shield had opened the door and greeted him with an easy smile, a genuine smile, so unlike what he was used to seeing from strangers.

Life in New York City, even as a man with means and an influential family, was still exhausting, because even if he was a gentleman, he was still a man of mixed heritage. Those who balked at shaking his hand or serving him were forced to bow before the Baptiste name, and so he'd learned to wrap that power around himself, clothe himself in it like the finest bespoke attire.

He clasped his hands behind his back, careful to keep his eyes trained just over her shoulder. The woman's dark eyes were too soft for him to trust himself with. Julian was no stranger to guarding himself around women who might seek to find themselves in a compromising position with an heir to a fortune, but this was different. Violet's looks were of the trapping sort, but were the kind that disarmed for all their promised safety; tempted one to relax, and that was dangerous.

If he wasn't careful, he'd forget himself and say something he would regret. He could feel it in his bones with the way she drew him to her.

He cleared his throat. "I'm unsure. Through the summer, possibly longer if the area suits me."

"You won't find our little town...lacking for entertainment?" Violet asked, scribbling in the ledger book the boarding house used to record guests.

He smiled, finally moving his gaze to meet hers, and felt his heart squeeze.

"No, I expect I'll have plenty of entertainment on account of my sister and her family."

Violet beamed at him and Julian felt himself go warm at her sunny expression. The coronary squeeze became nearly unbearable at the weight of such an expression. "Seylah is gorgeous. You must be very happy to have such a perfect little thing in your family."

Damn it all. He'd been right about the ochre in her eyes. He nodded, looking away from her. "Quite. Maman is overjoyed by the new addition. I expect to have spoiled her entirely rotten by the time I return to New York."

"Of course." Violet shut the book and picked up a key. "It's your right as her uncle."

Julian cracked a smile, steadfastly avoiding looking Violet in the eyes again, and instead focused on the key in her hand. "My responsibility, I suppose."

"One might say a sacred duty, even," she said, coming around the desk to stand beside him.

"Ah, yes, the age-old tradition of spoiling a sibling's progeny until they are ruined to the core. A time-honored tradition, and we Baptistes are nothing if not sticklers for tradition."

She was close enough now that he could smell the faint scent of rosewater. Sweet and light as the laugh that slipped from her mouth at his joke—sweet and light, just like her.

Or rather, what he supposed she was, Julian reminded himself.

He didn't know this woman even if it was like something had woken up inside him the moment their eyes had met. Like lightning, it was. Electrifying every part of him that had been put to sleep by the city and constraints of polite society. The shell around him had cracked, that perfect facade he kept in place that showed how unbothered he was by everyone and everything around him had splintered with a simple hello...and the mad thing was, Julian did not hate it.

Julian could think of only one time he'd ever heard anyone describe meeting anyone like that.

His father and mother.

He swallowed hard and took another half-step away from Violet, aiming to maintain his distance. It was only proper, no matter how much he wanted to walk closely to her as if they were familiar, not strangers newly met, but...intimate. His skin flushed hot at the thought and he bit back an angry groan at himself for letting his mind get away from him—again.

What was he? An untried boy in his first season?

"Are you alright?" Violet asked, stopping to look at him strangely, and Julian knew he had almost been found out.

"I'm quite alright—better than, in fact."

"But just then..." She pointed at him and tilted her head to the side, the movement causing her dark hair to slip over her shoulders. Julian's fingers itched to see if her hair was as soft as it looked. He clenched his fingers together for a second before he shoved a hand into his pocket.

"Just then?" he prompted with as guileless a look as he could manage.

Violet blinked at him. "You growled," she informed him.

"Ah, that," he said, and chuckled, turning away to examine a painting on the wall as if the watercolor landscape were the most captivating art he'd seen since the Louvre. "That was a cough."

"A cough?" Violet's brow furrowed. "Are you unwell?"

"It's a, well... it's a small condition I have," Julian said. One that apparently only took him when he was struck dumb at the sight of a dark-eyed beauty with a smile like the sun. He winced at himself.

Confound it.

"Did you have consumption?"

He well and truly coughed at that. "Consumption? Ah, no, no, it's nothing like that." He held his hands up, but Violet continued on as if he hadn't spoken.

"Because if it is we can put you in one of the southern-facing rooms for your health." Violet turned and made to go for the keys at the front of the boarding house with a worried look on her face.

"That won't be necessary. I'm quite fine."

She shook her head, giving him a pained look. "It wouldn't do to have your health put upon by your lodging conditions. I had no idea you were sickly, I—"

Julian's eyes widened, aghast. "I am not sickly."

How had this happened? *Sickly*. Of all the things this woman thought of him while he went moon-eyed over her? He did his best to draw himself up, posture snapping into place as he worked to project an air of perfect health.

There were many things Julian wished Violet thought of him.

Manly? *Of course.*

Virile and in possession of strength of will? *Certainly.*

He'd settle for well-read and debonair, but sickly? *No.* Under no conditions did he want that to cross her mind when she looked at him, as she was now with her big brown eyes full of concern.

He'd made an ungodly mess of this. One errant growl and suddenly he had been stricken with consumption.

"But your cough," she said.

"Is...a tickle, nothing more." He inclined his head. "Please show me to the rooms. It's fine, Miss Shield."

She worried her bottom lip. That full, pink, plump lip that begged Julian to come closer. He stood still, feet planted where he was, and gave her a tight smile.

"If you're sure."

He moved to give her a gallant bow, more at home in a ballroom than the hall of Miss Hill's boarding house. "I am. You needn't make a fuss over me, Miss Shield."

She shook her head, looking unsure, but her posture had relaxed somewhat, and if Julian didn't know better he would swear that her cheeks were dusted a pretty pink.

Was she blushing? His heart sped up, pulse hammering against his chest. Had he made her blush?

Violet swallowed and met his eyes, and this time Julian knew it was he who had put that dusky color on her cheeks. That was dangerous knowledge, it was, but for whom Julian wasn't quite sure yet.

"But your sister and her husbands, they—"

"Are quite the handful, are they not?" he asked, turning away from Violet. It was enough that she was blushing as she was, face flushed more like a dewy-eyed debutante than the cook she'd proclaimed herself to be.

The worry melted from her face as she sent another one of her heart-stopping smiles his way, though he only glimpsed it from his periphery, turned as he was under the guise of not paying attention.

What a farce that was. If Julian could preserve these happy looks, these unguarded moments with this woman, he would never want for anything again.

It had been so very long since anyone but his family had treated him like this. Hadn't wanted anything from him. Gazed at him as soft-eyed as Violet was now, even when she didn't think he saw.

"They are," she confessed before turning to continue down the hallway. "I want to make sure you're comfortable here while you visit your sister. You don't know what a boon it's been to the town for your sister to come teach here."

"And I will be, Miss Shield. Of that I promise you. Consider me the same as any other boarder, please."

She nodded, falling into step beside him. "Then please, call me Violet."

Julian nearly stumbled over his own feet at the invitation, and when he turned a surprised look on her she shrugged. "No one calls me Miss Shield. I don't—well." She paused and looked down at her feet. "That's for a lady."

"And what are you if not a lady?" Julian asked before he could stop himself. He was elated at her allowing him to speak to her on friendly terms, but the slight frown, the pinch in her brow, that little slump to her shoulders that reminded him of a wounded bird wouldn't allow him to enjoy the pleasure of saying her given name.

Violet's eyes moved away from his. "I just...I'm not a lady," she replied, her voice quiet in a way that Julian hated for the way she seemed to shrink in front of his very eyes. "What I mean to say is that I'm a working woman," she added with a laugh that sounded hollow.

"Working or not, it has no bearing on whether you are a lady. Believe me when I tell you I can spot a lady at a hundred paces. And you, Violet, are a lady of the first degree."

She laughed then, a real laugh that had his heart singing as loudly as the bells that rang in the New Year at Trinity Church.

"You say the strangest things, sir," she said when they came to stop in front of a door that Julian supposed was meant to be his for the duration of his stay.

He held a finger aloft and gave it a wag. "We can't have that."

"Have what?"

"If I am to call you by Violet, then you can't address me as sir or Mr. Baptiste. That's my father. You must," he said, then gave her his best beseeching look, "call me Julian."

"But I-I'm just the cook. I'm not, I mean, I'm no one."

Julian felt her words as surely as if he'd been caught unawares at the weekend boxing club he frequented. It was sharp, cutting, and left him shaking his head.

"That is quite wrong," he told her. This woman was someone—could be someone to him—but he batted away that errant thought and continued speaking as if it hadn't come unbidden to him as easily as it had. "Jobs do not determine who a person is. What you are on the inside does. Everything else is just details, Violet. Please call me by my given name. I beg you."

Her eyes widened at the word *beg* and Julian wished he could rip it back from the air as soon as it fell from his lips, but he supposed what was done was done, so he forced himself to look unbothered by that little slip of the tongue.

"All right, si—er, Julian," Violet said, her voice soft and unsure as if she were testing the word out for herself.

He quite liked the sound of his name on her mouth but knew better than to reveal it.

He smiled at her then. "Thank you."

"Of course." She leaned closer as if she wanted to say more, but then leaned away again and held his keys out to him. "These are for your rooms. Breakfast is served between the hours of seven and eight and lunch is at noon, but I am happy to make you a bite whenever the mood strikes you. If you need anything at all just, well, please ask."

He took the keys from her and ignored the way her fingertips brushed his or the fact that the metal was still warm from her hand. Shoving it into the lock, he inclined his head.

"Thank you."

"You're very welcome..." She paused, as if not trusting herself to say his name without incident. "Julian." She took a step back and again smiled a smile that made him feel light and alive in a way that he hadn't known in years. At that Julian said the only thing he trusted himself to say.

"Goodnight, Violet."

ABOUT REBEL CARTER

Rebel Carter *loves* love. So much in fact that she decided to write the love stories she desperately wanted to read. A book by Rebel means diverse characters, sexy banter, a real big helping of steamy scenes, and, of course, a whole lotta heart.

Rebel lives in Colorado, makes a mean espresso, and is hell-bent on filling your bookcase with as many romance stories as humanly possible!

instagram.com/rebelwrites
twitter.com/twitter.com
facebook.com/rebelwrites

Made in the USA
San Bernardino, CA
18 August 2019